HOW TO HEAL

a Heartbreak

New York Times & USA Today Bestselling Author

CYNTHIA EDEN

PROLOGUE

"He's not here."

Claudia Fairmont shook her head, sending the gossamer wedding veil sliding over her shoulders. Her grip tightened on the blood-red roses in her hand. The bouquet shouldn't have felt so heavy, but suddenly, everything felt heavy.

Her brother's jaw locked. "We've got a church full of people, but no groom. The ceremony should have started an hour ago, and we can't keep the guests waiting forever."

"Something is wrong," she whispered.

"Damn straight something is wrong." His eyes, the same icy blue shade of her own, narrowed with fury. "The asshole has left you *standing at the altar*. I told you he was trouble. Told you he was no good from the very beginning, but you wouldn't listen to me. Because you thought you were in *love*."

She dropped the bouquet and reached for her phone yet again. She'd been trying to call Holden ever since she'd first received word that he wasn't at the church. She'd called. Texted. Even checked at the local hospitals. "He wouldn't do this to me."

Cooper surged forward. His hand closed around her wrist. "He would. He *has*."

No, no. She knew Holden. "We have to call the police—"

"We did that already. There's been no reported accidents. No news about anyone matching his description. I even called and had a neighbor check Holden's place." His grip tightened. "He's not there. He's gone."

She jerked free of his grip. Claudia took a quick step back and nearly tripped on her train. "Let me just try to call him again." Her trembling hand lifted the phone to her ear. Fear made her tremble. Not anger. *Holden wouldn't do this to me.* She knew him. Trusted him. Loved him. Holden wouldn't just stand her up. Something had to be terribly, terribly wrong and—

"Claudia." He'd answered. Holden finally answered her call.

Her breath expelled in a relieved rush. "Holden! Thank God! I was so worried about you!"

Silence.

"Holden?" Her stomach twisted. "Are you okay?"

"Not going to make it to the church today."

She almost fell. The shock was so great that her knees just gave way. Luckily, Cooper locked his hands around her shoulders, and her brother's strong grip held her upright. "You're...*what?*" Pain knifed through her. "Holden?" This could not be happening. No way.

"Sorry."

Just...sorry? That was all? That was—

Click. He'd hung up on her. Her breath shuddered in and out, and the pain spread through her whole body. In shock, Claudia stared at the phone in her hand. The loud drumming of her heartbeat echoed in her ears. Over and over and over.

And her thundering heartbeat seemed to be echoing Holden, saying over and over...*Sorry. Sorry. Sorry.*

"Claudia?" Her brother lightly shook her. "Look at me."

Her gaze swung to him.

"What's happening?" Cooper asked her.

Shock. Heartbreak. Consuming pain. That was what was happening. "He's...sorry."

"*What?*"

Her voice sounded strangled to her own ears as she added, "Holden is...not coming to the church."

Cooper swallowed. Rage burned in his eyes, and Claudia wished that she could be angry, too. But she wasn't. She hurt too much for fury.

"I'll take care of everything," Cooper told her with a firm jerk of his head. "Change out of the dress. Get the hell out of here. I'll handle it all." He pressed a hard kiss to her forehead. "And I will fucking destroy him, I promise you that."

She didn't want Holden destroyed. She didn't want...

I love him.

And he'd left her. Wearing the white dress. The veil. The train that made her feel claustrophobic because it pulled back on her with every step that she took.

"I told you he couldn't be trusted," Cooper bit out. "He just wanted to hurt our family. He always hated us."

But I love him.

Cooper's arms wrapped around her in a fierce hug. "It's okay. I swear, it will be okay."

She'd been left at the altar by the man she loved. There was no part of that situation that would qualify as okay. A waking nightmare? Absolutely. But okay? Not so much.

Cooper released her. "Change. I'll have the limo waiting out back for you. You can slip away, and you don't have to see a soul."

He hurried for the door. She noted the stiffness in his back, and she knew just how furious he was. Cooper had never liked Holden. Because of their pasts. Because of who Holden was.

A rough and dangerous fighter. Too violent. I don't want him near you.

Her brother had said those words when she'd announced her engagement. He'd warned her. She'd failed to listen. Now Cooper was off to clean up her latest disaster.

A public humiliation. Dumped at the altar. But... "No."

Cooper's hand froze above the doorknob. His head jerked as he glanced over his shoulder at her. "We can't leave them sitting in the church."

No, they couldn't. "I'll tell everyone." Her wedding. Or, her would-be wedding. So it was her job to face the crowd.

He shook his head. "Claudia, you don't have to do this."

Actually, she did. Her hands fisted in the skirt of her gown. A stupid expensive gown. She lifted up the skirt and marched forward even as the weight of the train tried once again to pull her back. At any moment, Claudia feared she might be physically sick. Her stomach wouldn't stop churning, and she just kept hearing Holden's voice in her head...

Sorry. Sorry. Sorry.

The echo chimed in tune with her steps. She entered the chapel. The harpist was playing, but everyone swung toward Claudia because she'd yanked open the sanctuary's doors with too much force. Her gaze swept over the crowd. She could see the shock in people's expressions. The gaping mouths. The pity in their eyes.

Her chin lifted. "I think you've been in here long enough." She wanted to offer them a smile but couldn't. The act was simply beyond her. "How about we all go to the reception hall? There is quite a feast waiting. And cake. Cake that is supposed to be sinfully good."

She felt a light hand at the base of her spine. Cooper had followed her. Her and Cooper—them against the world. That was the way it had been since her father had died and her mother had run off to start a new life far, far away.

No one moved from the pews. Everyone just kept watching Claudia. Their pity felt suffocating.

"There isn't going to be a wedding today. Change of plans." Her whole body shook. All the people just kept sitting there. Why wouldn't they move? "Sorry for the inconvenience."

Sorry.

Sorry.

Sorry.

Tears filled her eyes, but Claudia would not let them fall. This should have been the happiest day of her life. Wasn't that what everyone always said about your wedding day? *The happiest day of your life.*

Everyone was wrong. The day was shit. "I need some wine." If the guests weren't going to the reception on their own, then she'd just lead the way. Claudia spun on her heel, kicked at her train, and walked out of the chapel.

***

The knock sounded on her door around two a.m. Loud and pounding, she would have liked to say the knocking pulled her from a deep sleep. That would have been a lie, though, because she hadn't been sleeping. Instead, the events of the day had just been spinning through her head on automatic repeat.

She rose from her position on the stairs—she'd just been sitting halfway up the staircase—and slowly descended. Claudia had a fairly good idea who had decided to pound on her door so late. After all, she'd figured he would show up, sooner or later.

Later. Much too late.

When she reached the landing, her bare feet crept slowly across the wooden floor. No heavy train pulled her back any longer. She'd ditched the train long ago.

The pounding continued at the door.

Peering through the peephole, Claudia easily saw his grim features, and she thought about just ignoring him. But a problem didn't go away when you ignored it. Hadn't her mother taught her that? Her mother had run away because she'd thought that had been easier. It hadn't been. Her mother had simply traded one set of problems for another.

You had to face things head-on in this world.

Swallowing—three times—because it was hard to choke down the lump in her throat, Claudia opened the door.

Holden Blackwell's towering form filled her doorway. Too big. Too strong. Too painful to see.

"Hi, Holden," she heard herself say. "You're a little late."

"Let me in." Grim. Rasping. Desperate? Oh, surely not. Holden had never been desperate, at least not where she was concerned.

Her answer was simple and soft as she told him, "No."

His hands flew up and clamped around the doorframe. Her gaze slid to the left. The porch light fell on him, and she could see the bruising near his knuckles. Her stare shifted back to his face. Not classically handsome. More rugged. Fierce. Hard jaw. Glinting eyes. And...bruises? Yes, that was definitely a dark spot along the sharp edge of his square jaw. "You've been fighting."

That was what he did, though, wasn't it? Holden was one of the best MMA fighters in the world. She'd been to a few of his matches, and they absolutely terrified her. Too savage. Too brutal. Each punch had her flinching. She'd been covered in sweat by the time those bouts had ended.

He was out fighting...when he was supposed to be marrying me?

"We need to talk," Holden said. His voice was the deep, dark rumble that always sent shivers down her spine.

Correction, the voice that *had* sent shivers down her spine. Before he'd wrecked her. "Sorry." Her own voice was tight. The one word a very deliberate choice. *Sorry.*

"Claudia—"

"You missed the wedding. It was a lovely affair. The harpist performed beautifully. The food was top-notch. The bride got a little drunk, but, hey, sometimes stuff like that happens, am I right?"

He reached for her.

She flinched away, taking a quick step back. "Don't."

His hand hung in the air.

"You left me at the altar." Her voice cracked. "I was afraid you were hurt. In a car accident. Bleeding on the side of the road."

His fingers slowly fisted, then his hand dropped.

"I went into the church and told all of those people that the wedding wasn't going to happen. You weren't there." She shook her head, still having trouble with that concept for some reason. "You weren't there." Dazed, she squinted at him. "I thought you would always be there for me. I loved you."

Loved. Past tense. But that was a lie. You didn't just turn off emotions like a faucet. Pain knifed through her, yet the love was still there.

Eventually, it would fade. Die. She knew it would. But seeing him right then just made everything hurt so much worse.

And he wasn't speaking.

"Tell me that you were kidnapped." Dammit, why was she still talking? "Tell me that someone held a gun to your head and made you leave me. Tell me that you were forced to stay away from the church. That you would never, ever have willingly done that to me." She darted a glance down at his fisted hand. At the bruises she could see. Dark spots that would have come from fighting. "Tell me that this wasn't all some long con just so you could get some kind of twisted vengeance on my family."

Bitter blood. She'd been warned to stay away from him. Warned over and over and yet...

"Tell me that this is all a bad dream and that I should wake up now," she whispered, the words far too close to pleading. But...

He isn't speaking. Holden wasn't telling her anything. He just stood in the doorway. All big and strong and grim.

She grabbed at the ring on her left hand. Claudia yanked off the engagement ring, and she slammed it against his chest. "Take it."

He didn't. He just stood there. Watching her with green eyes that swirled with unnamed emotion.

Her hand jerked back. The ring fell.

He didn't even glance down at it. His gaze remained on her.

He'd come to her door, pounding. He'd told her they needed to talk, and now he said nothing?

He'd never been the strong, silent type. Not Holden. Holden talked all the time. He was bold and exciting. He was charming and seductive. Cocky. Confident. Larger than life.

A liar. "Did you ever love me?" Why, why did she even ask that question?

"I should never have touched you."

She flinched. Just the apologetic words she'd longed to hear. *Not.* This was clearly not going to be some epic grovel scene where he begged for her forgiveness and said it was all a terrible mistake. That he loved her. Would love her forever...

"You never said you loved me." The red flag she'd ignored because she wanted him so much. "I convinced myself you did, but you never said those words. You told me you needed me. That you wanted me. You asked me to marry you, but you never said you loved me."

"Claudia..."

She waited. He still didn't say those words. *I love you.* Three little words. He just stared at her with a gaze that seemed to burn.

"You could have called off the wedding before I had a church full of people waiting." She could feel tears coming again, and Claudia refused to let them fall in front of him. "Having me in the wedding dress waiting for you—that was just cruel. I know you hate my family, but I didn't realize you hated me, not until I was ready to walk down the aisle." *And you weren't there.*

"Hate isn't what I feel for you." Grated.

"Then what do you feel?"

Before he could answer, she heard the growl of an engine on the road. Starting low, then getting louder the closer it came. Louder and angrier until it sounded like a snarling animal. The dark car whipped past them, shattering the silence on her quiet street.

"Fucking fuck," Holden swore, voice vicious.

And, again, she flinched. "Well, that's certainly a lovely sentiment. Fucking fuck to you, too, Holden."

"I have to go."

Of course. With no explanation as to why he'd hurt her. "You broke my heart, damn you."

"Claudia—look, I'll be back, I swear, but I have to go, *now*." He spun and bounded toward the edge of her porch.

"Don't come back. I don't want to see you again." Because it would just hurt too much.

He froze. "You don't mean it. You don't—"

"I don't want to see you again. I don't want you coming after me, and I will not be coming after you." She wanted to run inside and slam the door. She *would* be doing that, but first, he had to understand that they were done. "To be clear, I would not come to you again unless my world was on fire."

He spun toward her. "Look, Claudia, I have to leave, but I'll be back. I will—"

"*On. Fire.* The flames would have to be scorchingly intense, and you'd need to be the only man in possession of a fire extinguisher." She backed into her home. "Goodbye, Holden."

Claudia slammed the door.

And the tears started falling.

CHAPTER ONE

Five years later...

Step One: Find a way to get back into her life. Proximity is key. She can't fall for you if you can't get close to her. So...get your ass close. Close enough to touch. To kiss. Close enough that she stops being a ghost and becomes a reality for you once again.

Holden Blackwell hesitated in front of his office door at Wilde, the elite security and protection firm that had become a refuge for him. When he'd first been recruited by Eric Wilde, the owner of the place, Holden had thought for sure he'd crash and burn as an agent.

Instead, he'd become a VP. His office was on the top floor. Swanky as hell. He could have stopped taking field cases long ago, but Holden enjoyed the adrenaline rush far too much to give up the day-to-day operations that sent him out on cases.

His latest client was waiting for him on the other side of that door. Eric had sent her to wait, and, moments before, he'd just calmly told Holden that Claudia Fairmont was inside. Calmly dropped that bombshell, and Holden had hauled ass to get there and greet her. Only now...

Now he was standing in front of his own door like some kind of scared kid. Screw that. He grabbed the knob. Twisted it. And shoved the door open. He marched across the threshold and ventured inside, making sure to keep his face expressionless as he asked, "So...where's the fire?"

Claudia had been sitting with her back to the door. She'd taken a position in one of the two waiting chairs that faced his desk. At his words, she stiffened, then slowly rose. His gaze drank in the thick curtain of her hair—brown but shot with streaks of gold—and he held his breath as he waited for her to slowly turn and face him.

I have missed her. Too damn much. Too—

She turned toward him. Makeup carefully applied. Soft red lipstick on plump, kissable lips. The faintest dark eyeshadow to frame her killer blue eyes. A dusting of blush on her high cheekbones. "Holden." Soft. Sensual. She always sounded sensual when she spoke. "As charming as ever, I see."

He bounded toward her. Two quick steps. But he caught himself before he actually reached out and did something crazy like, oh, haul her close. Kiss her as if his life depended on it. Never, fucking ever, let her go.

Instead, he sucked in a breath, but could have sworn he tasted her sweetness, even as his gaze trekked down her body. She wore a body-hugging gray dress, sleeveless, and her delicate feet were encased in red high heels that had probably been designed to make a man beg. They looked helluva sexy on her, but truth be told, he thought pretty much everything was helluva sexy on Claudia. She could be wearing jogging shorts and a trash bag, and he'd still think she was perfection. Runway ready.

Not that he could tell her that. Not that he could do much except drink her in like a man dying of thirst. *I should say something else. Speak again. Not screw up this big reunion.* He dragged his hungry stare back up to her face. "I have a fire extinguisher."

A little furrow appeared between her elegant brows. "Good for you?" The words were a definite question.

He cleared his throat. "You said you'd only come to me if your world was on fire."

Her eyes—a light blue with gold buried in the depths, a gold that matched the highlights in her dark hair—widened. "Of course, you'd remember that part." She tucked a lock of hair behind her left ear. "I suppose it thrills you that I had to come to you for help."

I am thrilled to see you, hell, yes.

She turned her back on him and paced toward the windows on the right. She stared out at the busy city of Atlanta. "I didn't want to come here." Her shoulders were stiff. Her spine ramrod straight. "I didn't exactly have a choice."

"Wilde is the best protection and security firm in the country." And the fact that she was there—yeah, okay, sure, after he got past the happy-to-see-her part—hell, he was worried. "What's wrong?" Because you didn't come to Wilde unless you had a problem. A very dangerous and deadly sort of problem.

Her arms wrapped around her stomach as she continued to peer out at the city. "I'm not looking for some sort of favor. I mentioned your name at the front desk, but I can certainly be assigned to someone else."

Uh, no. Never in a million years. He had her, and there was no way he'd pass her off to another agent.

"I don't normally name drop, but I wanted to be seen today. I wanted to be taken seriously."

"I take you very, very seriously." He crept toward her. Inhaled her scent. Same lush strawberries and cream scent that used to drive him to madness. "Tell me what's happening, and I'll eliminate the problem for you."

She glanced over her shoulder at him.

"Fire extinguisher, remember? I can stop whatever is bothering you." Whatever or whoever.

Her throat moved delicately as she swallowed. "How much is your rate?"

Like he'd have her pay a dime. No way. He'd square things with Eric. "It's negotiable."

"That's not an actual number."

Holden shrugged. "We can get to the rate after you tell me about your problem." Why was she hesitating? "Look, you're at Wilde because you need protection. That's the reason most people step through the shiny doors downstairs. You got a clinging ex? Someone who is harassing you? Someone who—"

"Wants to kill me?" Again, soft. Husky. But her words rocked through him as if she'd shouted.

His mouth hung open in surprise. He finally managed to snap it closed so he could snarl, "Who the fuck would want to kill you?"

"I have no idea." Her hands fell back to her sides as she swung to fully face him once more. "I was hoping you could help me figure it out."

Rage built inside of him. The idea of someone physically hurting Claudia...of someone actually trying to *kill* her... "You've gone to the cops?"

Her gaze cut away from his.

"Claudia." Rough. Demanding.

Her stare darted back toward him.

"You've gone to the cops." A statement this time, not a question.

But her head moved in the smallest of negative shakes as her tongue swiped across her lower lip.

"Why the hell not?" Holden exploded as he surged toward her.

She immediately backed up a step. Then another.

He froze.

They stared at each other.

Thick tension suddenly hung in the air between them. A stark awareness as the past and present tangled together. The last time he'd seen her, he'd surged toward her then, too. She'd retreated, when normally, she never retreated from him. Claudia came running to him. She smiled at him and her eyes lit up, and she stared at him like he was some kind of conquering hero. She didn't retreat as if he was the bad guy.

Yet she's definitely retreating from me.

Right. Because in her eyes, he was a bastard. Hell, not just her eyes. Most of the world saw him that way. Truth be told, he was a bastard, and he'd never had a problem being one. Until now.

"The cops were at the scenes," she said, clearing her throat. "Each time, they took my statement, so I guess you could say I *have* talked to them. But everything—it all seems so random that not even Cooper believes me."

Cooper. Another blast from the past that Holden would deal with, later.

"There's bad luck," Claudia continued with a twist of her full lips, "and then there's what has been happening in my life."

"Tell me everything."

But her gaze drifted around his office. "I...ah, maybe I should talk to another agent. I'm sure the last thing you want is to be working on a case with your ex."

Not true.

"Having to be close to me again is probably a nightmare for you, and, like I said, I just used your name to get inside. I needed to be seen today. I-I've had friends who worked with Wilde, but I didn't exactly want to tell them about my situation. Bad enough that my brother thinks I'm imagining things, but if word spreads, well..." A shrug of her shoulders. "I've had more than enough gossip circulated about me over the years. I'd rather stay below the radar as much as possible."

Because the heiress who'd been left at the altar had gotten a ton of press after the wedding-that-wasn't. Her face had been splashed everywhere. At the time, he'd been an MMA star. Scandal and fighting and money? Hell, yes, that was a mega story. She'd been dragged through the mud because of him, and every time he'd seen her face on social media or on some gossipy news site, he'd wanted to go to her.

Fuck it. The sad, twisted truth? He'd become a stalker for a while. Shit that he wasn't proud to admit. But, yeah, he'd secretly dodged her steps for a time. Because he'd needed to know she was safe.

I still need to know it. Some habits were very, very hard to break. "You could never be a nightmare for me."

Her long, thick lashes flickered, but her gaze didn't return to him.

He wanted to look into her eyes. The eyes were supposed to be windows to the soul, wasn't that how the saying went? And when he looked into Claudia's eyes, he'd always been able to read her emotions so easily. She'd never held back from him. Hadn't played games. In a world where everyone seemed to be working an agenda, Claudia had been different. A true lamb surrounded by wolves.

Then she'd had the misfortune of becoming engaged to the baddest wolf in the pack.

"It has to be bad," Holden said, voice gruff as he fought the urge to touch her. To run his fingers over her silken cheek. To catch her hand and enfold it in his. To wrap her into his arms. "Very bad," he continued, "if you're so desperate you came to me."

Because five long years had passed, and she'd made a point of staying away from him.

"I don't want to die," she told him simply. "Seeing you is certainly the better alternative when compared to death."

Well, fuck. "Don't pull any punches. Tell me how you really feel."

Now her eyes did meet his. "You're a fighter. You'd hate it if someone pulled punches with you."

Her stare was...different than it had been before. Same blue eyes with the sparks of gold inside, but her emotions were shielded. A careful mask. She'd never worn a mask before.

But five years was a very long time. People changed in five years. *I sure as hell have changed.*

"Take a seat," he advised her with a wave of a hand toward one of the waiting chairs. "Brief me. I have to know what I'm up against so we can get a plan of attack going."

Her delicate brows arched. "That's it? You're taking the case? Just like that?"

He needed to put some space between them because his control was not going to last. If he stayed so close to her for even another minute, he would be touching her. Neither of them would be ready for that. In the past, when he'd touched her, savage need had immediately blasted through him. His response to Claudia had never been normal. More like off-the-charts ballistic. Primitive and basic, he'd hungered for her as he had never needed another.

"Just like that." He turned away. Exhaled heavily when she couldn't see his face and strode for his desk chair. He sat down and the chair rolled with him back into position. At least with the desk in front of him, she wouldn't notice the very physical and very obvious reaction he had to her presence.

His eager dick had taken one look at her and immediately stood to full attention in a salute.

She nibbled on her lower lip, because, clearly, she liked to torture him, then Claudia edged back toward the seat she'd been in before. With her usual grace, she slid into the chair, crossed her sensual, killer legs, and lightly swung one high-heeled foot. "Do you always take cases so quickly? Is that a Wilde thing?"

"No. It's a me-and-you thing."

She blinked.

"You need me, I'm there. No questions asked. Done."

"It's...it's been a while."

Five years. Three months. Six days. Not like a guy could forget what could have been his wedding day. Not like a man could forget her.

"I wasn't sure you'd even want to talk to me," she added.

He flattened his hands on the desk and leaned forward. Was she serious? "You were the one who wouldn't talk to me." He'd tried. Several times. He'd been frozen out. Then she'd been gone. Flown to Paris.

And stories had started circulating about her and some prick who owned a vineyard.

His jaw clenched. Now was not the time to walk down jealousy road and yet..."Does your boyfriend know what's happening?"

"I don't have a boyfriend. I'm not involved with anyone right now."

Hell, yes. Hell, the fuck yes. But his expression didn't change. "So who does know what's happening?"

"Cooper. Me." A pause. "You." Her foot swung a little more. "Cooper thinks I'm exaggerating things. That I am blowing stuff out of proportion."

"You're not the type to do that."

Her foot stopped swinging. Her gaze collided with his.

"Start at the beginning," Holden urged her. "Tell me everything."

"Then you'll decide if I'm exaggerating?"

No, he'd already told her she wasn't the type to do that. "Then we'll come up with our plan of attack," he reminded her gently. He'd already told her that before, too.

Her fingers tapped against the arm of the chair. "This is a really nice office. I didn't expect—"

"For an asshole fighter to work his way to the top?"

Her eyes widened. "No, ahem, I was going to say that I didn't expect for you to get out of fighting. You loved it so much that I couldn't imagine you giving it up for anything." A pause. "By the way, you're the one who just called yourself an asshole, not me."

"Ah, come now, we both know what you think I am."

She didn't deny the charge. What would have been the point in that? He knew she hated him. *But she's here.* Desperate, scared, but there. And the twisted, sad part of it all? *I will take her any way I can get her.* Finally, he had Claudia back in his life, and Holden was so thrilled he could hardly stand it.

He was fucked up.

Then Claudia began explaining... "It started with a flat tire. Not a big deal, right? Happens all the time. Except the tires were brand new. And it was like something had been done to the tire to make the air slowly leak out so that when the car stopped, I was on a long, dark, and empty stretch of road." Her breath shuddered out. "There was no cell service in that area. I got out, and when I checked my spare, it was flat, too."

His muscles tightened.

"I was standing at the back of my car when I saw the headlights coming toward me. At first, I was grateful, thinking maybe I could wave down the driver and get help."

No way did he like this setup. A beautiful woman, on an empty stretch of road. No means of calling for help. "What time was it?"

"Eleven p.m." She inhaled. "The car stopped about twenty feet away from me, and the headlights were on bright. I couldn't see the driver, but I started walking toward the car."

He didn't move.

"The driver side door opened. A man got out. He had on a thick coat with a hood. And—and I could see something in his hand."

"What was it?"

"It looked like a knife. The hood was pulled low over his head, and the headlights were so bright...and then he started walking toward me, and the light hit the blade."

Fuck. Fuck. Fuck.

"I ran. I just turned and ran into the woods, and he chased after me. He never said a word, didn't yell, didn't call out at all, but I could hear his footsteps thundering after me." Her words came faster. "The bushes and the twigs pulled at me, and I didn't even know where I was going. I just knew I couldn't let him get to me. Then—then I burst out of the woods and into the road...and a semi nearly ran right over me."

His back teeth had clenched. Rage and fear gnawed in Holden's stomach.

"I jumped out of the way, and the driver pulled over. She radioed for help when I told her what was going on and..." Once more, Claudia's stare cut away from his as she peered toward the floor. "The police arrived, but the other vehicle was long gone by the time they got there. The cops thought I had gotten confused in the dark. They thought maybe he'd come out with a screwdriver or a small jack—something to help with changing my tire. They basically told me that I'd overreacted. Said it was natural to be afraid when you were alone in the dark like that."

"I don't remember you being afraid of the dark."

Her lashes lifted as she looked at him once more. "Back then, I wasn't." Her delicate nostrils flared. "I am now."

He didn't want her afraid of anything or anyone. "What else happened?"

"A string of what Cooper calls 'exceedingly bad luck' happened. The locks jammed on the front and rear doors at the Fairmont Winery one night after closing, and I got locked inside. The security system went down at the same time, and all of the electricity turned off. I was trapped in total darkness." Flat. Emotionless. "I was supposed to be there alone, but I could have sworn I heard footsteps in the dark with me."

Sonofabitch.

"I broke a window and climbed out to escape."

His hands curled into fists. "What else?"

"A fire broke out at my place. I was sleeping at the time. The fire inspector believes candles were left burning in the den, and they caused the fire." She pressed her lips together, then said, "I did *not* burn those candles. The last time I saw them, they were in my closet. I don't even know how they got into the den."

He had an idea. "Someone came into your home. Took out the candles and lit them." *So fucking bad.*

"The candles caught fire to the curtains in the den. I have smoke detectors that should have gone off, they didn't. The downstairs detectors never went off, only the ones upstairs. When the fire inspector examined one of the scorched detectors from the den, he found out that there were no batteries inside." It was her turn to lean forward. "I put fresh batteries in all of my smoke detectors every six months. Someone else took the batteries out. Someone *had* to take them out."

A flat tire that had left her as vulnerable prey in the dark. An attempt to trap her at the family winery. And a fire in her home. Bad luck? Hell, no. *Someone is after her*. It was clear as glass. Why wouldn't her brother believe her? Why hadn't Cooper already surrounded her with a security army?

"There have been other things," she said in her hushed, sensual voice. "Mostly nuisance stuff that began long before the flat tire."

"What kind of things?"

"A broken windshield on my car. When I was at a crosswalk, someone accidentally shoved me forward when a bus was coming."

"Fuck."

With a hand that slightly trembled, she once more tucked a lock of hair behind her ear. "Maybe it wasn't so accidental. I can tell you that it's quite terrifying when you look up and see a bus barreling straight for you."

Yeah, he was certain it had been terrifying. "How the hell long has this been happening?"

"Six months."

He surged out of his chair. "And you're only coming to me now? You should have come to me on day one!" He rushed around the desk. Loomed over her. *Some bastard is trying to kill Claudia.* And he hadn't known. She'd been in danger, and he hadn't been there.

A little furrow appeared between her brows as she looked up at him. "Not like we're close. I can't just run to you with my problems." A weak, nervous laugh slid from her.

Screw that. He put his hands on the arm rests of her chair and leaned in toward her, pinning

Claudia in place. "You should have come to me sooner."

"We haven't spoken in years—I didn't even realize you worked with Wilde until I read that story about the long lost princess recently and saw mention of your name." She shook her head. "Bet that was some case. You made international headlines with it."

Fuck that case. He loomed closer. Yes, dammit, he was all up in her space. He should back away. He had *zero* intention of doing so. "You get scared, you come to me. Some jerk tries to hurt you, *you come to me*. You know the rules. We've always had them in place."

Her head tilted back. "That was then," she murmured, the words barely seeming to be a breath. "The rules changed for us long ago."

He wanted her mouth. He wanted *her*. Seeing her had brought his past crashing back on him. Every single one of his hopes and dreams and fantasies? They were all tied up in *her*. "The hell they did. I will protect you, always. I will protect you from any pain—"

"Except the pain you cause me?"

Her words were like ice water pouring over him. Yes, dammit, yes, he was the one who'd hurt her.

Jaw locking, Holden let go of the chair arms and straightened. "I won't cause you any more pain. That's a promise."

She peered up at him with her bring-a-man-to-his-knees eyes. "You shouldn't make promises you can't keep."

He'd keep this one. "I need a list of everyone close to you. Friends, lovers—"

"I told you, I don't have a—"

"*Ex*-lovers," Holden cut in to say. "Anyone with a grudge against you. Any business competitor you've angered. We'll get the names, and Wilde can start running checks on everyone while I make sure that you're protected, twenty-four, seven." He spun away and reached for the phone on his desk.

"I lied." Soft. Low.

His hand hung in the air. Slowly, his hand lowered. He eased back toward her. "Say again?"

Claudia huffed out a breath. "I lied. Or, I just told part of the truth. When I said that I name dropped you in order to get inside today...I-I actually came because I wanted to see you, specifically."

He eased a hip onto the edge of his desk as Holden angled to watch her. Euphoria spread through him. *I wanted to see you.* Fucking finally. She'd come back to him. They were going to pick up where they'd left off. Well, fine, not *exactly* where they'd left off because he had no intention of leaving her at the altar. Claiming her? Keeping her? Definitely part of the plan. He would—

She bent down and started fishing in the very large, black bag that sat on the floor near her chair. Then her hand lifted, and she pushed a big, brown envelope toward him.

Curious, he took the envelope. "What's this?"

"Open it and see."

He unhooked the top of the envelope. It had been secured by one of those little metal prongs.

His fingers eased inside, and he pulled out photo paper. Several large photos of...

"*Fuck me*." Stunned, he stared at the photos.

"Actually." A delicate clearing of her throat. "I think that is me, fucking you. Or you, fucking me. Both. Either." Another throat clearing.

Stunned, he thumbed through the photos. "This is us. Having sex." His gaze rose to collide with hers. "What in the hell is happening?"

"I was hoping you could tell me."

He looked back at the photos. Absolute savage lust had been stamped on his features in those pictures. "Where did you get these?"

"You didn't take them?"

What. The. Actual. Fuck? He shoved the photos back in the envelope. "No, I didn't take photos of you without your permission—"

"Or a video? You didn't make a video of us?"

Holden lurched off the edge of the desk. "I didn't make a sex video of us!" What he'd done with her had been private, for them alone. *Because she is only meant to be mine.*

"You didn't?" Claudia asked, biting her lower lip.

"I did not," he gritted.

Her shoulders fell. Wait, hold up, was she actually disappointed that he hadn't made a video or taken pics?

"If you didn't do it, then who did?" Her voice and her eyes seemed lost, as the mask finally fell away, and her emotions blazed through again.

"When did you find the first picture?" A snarl.

"The day after I had the flat tire."

Sonofabitch. There had been three pictures in the envelope. "And the others?"

"I found one in my office at the winery, the night I got locked inside. And the third—it had a note on the back, did you see it?"

He snatched the pictures back out of the envelope and flipped them all over. He read the note and swore viciously.

You were even better in person. Lucky thing I have the videos so I can relive those moments. And if you're not good to me, I'll let the whole world see just how dirty you are.

He wanted to rip those pictures into pieces. But they might contain evidence Wilde could use. Slowly, carefully, he put the photos back into the envelope once again. Turning his back to her, he lowered the envelope to the desk. Released one breath. A second. Deep breathing wasn't exactly helping to quell the fury coursing through his veins.

The message to her had been printed on the back of the photo, not handwritten. And the fact that the photos had arrived in conjunction with the dangerous incidents in her life? *So not good.* And, unfortunately, her visit to Wilde was making even more sense now. "You came to see me today because you thought I was the one tormenting you." That was why she'd gone to Wilde instead of a different protection firm. *Why she asked to see me.*

"You were in the pictures with me."

He whirled toward her. "I didn't take them. I didn't leave the photos for you to find. I didn't have some freaking camera hidden in my bedroom while I was making love to you."

She rose. Elegance and grace but with fear in her eyes. "If you didn't, then who did? Who was watching me way back then?" A shake of her head. "And who is trying to hurt me now?"

He didn't know, but Holden intended to find out. Then he'd destroy the bastard. "Say that you hire me."

"What?"

"Say that you hire me. We'll sign the paperwork soon. Right now, I just need the words to get the ball rolling." *So I can obliterate some deserving jackass out there.*

"I-I hire you?" A definite question. Then she nodded, more certain. "I want to hire you."

He extended his hand toward her. They'd shake on this deal.

Her gaze darted to his hand, then back up to his face. Her hand cautiously extended toward him. Her soft palm brushed against his.

His fingers closed around hers, the grip tight but careful. Because with her, he would be very, very careful. "Sweetheart, you just got yourself a bodyguard."

CHAPTER TWO

Step Two: Don't screw up. If you make the same mistakes, you're done. This is your second chance. No way in hell will you get a third time.

Heat shot from her hand, up her arm, and spread through her body.

Some things just didn't change. She could still touch Holden and experience instant, burning attraction. After all the time that had passed, Claudia had rather hoped that particular side effect had vanished. But, alas, no such luck. It would seem she was still as susceptible to him sexually as she'd always been.

Super problematic.

She could feel the calluses on his fingers and palm. He might have this big, shiny office now, but he was still a fighter at his core. She'd be willing to bet he maintained the same brutal workout routine that he'd followed years ago. Waking up every day at five a.m. Hitting the gym. Then, of course, if any fools thought to challenge him for a fight...a vicious battle until his opponent surrendered.

Holden didn't lose his fights. He never quit. Not until his enemy cried for mercy. There was a reason his nickname had been "No Holding Back"

Holden when he battled. He gave one hundred and twenty percent. And never, ever stopped.

Rather frightening characteristics, but considering the current drama in her life, Holden might be exactly what she needed.

And he was still holding her hand. *Swallowing* her hand in his bear-like grip.

She tugged her hand, trying to pull it back. He didn't let go.

"Had to be hard for you to come see me today," Holden rumbled in his deep, dark, and, dang it, sexy voice.

Hard would be an understatement. Seeking out the man who'd ripped her heart into a million tiny, brittle pieces? Who the hell would want to do that? She'd carefully avoided him all of these years because Holden was walking pain for her.

Then the photos had arrived.

"I will protect you," he vowed, and he was still holding her hand. Not tightly, though. Carefully. An unbreakable hold that didn't bruise. He'd always been incredibly conscious of his strength and size with her.

Her gaze swept over him. Still ruggedly handsome. Rough around the edges, even in his expensive suit. She was used to seeing him in jeans. T-shirts that stretched across his powerful chest and the sleeves that were nearly ripped by his biceps. Uncontrolled, devil-may-care, that had been the Holden she knew.

Honestly, his wildness had attracted her. He'd been so unlike anyone she'd ever met before. Primitive. Powerful. And the sex...

The sex between them had been so—

Incredible.

"Why are you blushing?" Holden asked.

Her mind scrambled for a plausible reason—one that didn't involve her having a flashback of phenomenal sex with him. "Because my new bodyguard is holding my hand and not letting me go, and that is *not* the way to start a business relationship." Wow. Her voice had come out all crisp and annoyed. Claudia was impressed with herself because acting was definitely not her forte.

Her brother had warned her for years that she wore her emotions on her sleeve. The world always knew what she felt. Being an open book was dangerous. It left you vulnerable to too much pain.

Holden's green gaze lowered to their joined hands. His much bigger hand enveloped hers.

She tugged again.

"My bad." A growl from him as he let her go.

Claudia's hand whipped back. She immediately rubbed her palm against her dress, not to wipe away his touch, but to try and cool the heat she still seemed to feel against her skin.

But his eyes narrowed at the movement, and his jaw clenched. "Not good enough to touch you?"

"What?" Truly confused, she shook her head. "You've fucked me, Holden. I'm pretty sure that means you were more than good enough to touch me."

His stare rose. Pinned hers. The air between them seemed to thicken.

Okay. Claudia blew out a breath even as she took a quick step back. "You know, maybe I should have another bodyguard lead the case. You're a VP, so I doubt you get out in the field much—"

"I get out plenty. You know me and adrenaline. Just can't get enough." He crossed his arms over his chest. "There won't be another bodyguard. You're mine."

Her lips parted. "Ah—"

"My client," he continued smoothly. "And sure, I'll have someone working backup for me, but I'll be the agent who takes primary lead on your case. After all, I'll be the one who can slide seamlessly into your life."

Her lashes fluttered. "What do you mean?" Wary suspicion cloaked her.

"There's a target on you. Maybe your dumbass brother thinks you're just the unluckiest woman alive—"

"He's *not* a dumbass—"

"But I don't believe in random coincidences. I don't believe you've randomly had all these terrifying experiences just as you also get photos that someone should *not* have taken of us. I didn't send the pictures, and since I wasn't the one who wrote that damn message on the back of the last one..." He paused, his forehead furrowing. "When did you get that last photo? You didn't say."

"It...I found it upstairs in my bedroom. When the fire was over, and I was allowed back inside to see if anything was salvageable." Unfortunately, nothing had been. Smoke and water had drenched the place. So even the things that hadn't been burned? *A loss.* Except...except for the pristine photo she'd found waiting at the foot of her bed. "Someone put it there, after the fire. I grabbed it as soon as I saw it."

"Did you show it to the authorities?"

"No. Not like I wanted to flash my bare breasts and my orgasm face at the fire inspector who was there with me."

His jaw hardened. "No. Wouldn't want that."

"I grabbed the picture, and I shoved it into my bag."

"That could have destroyed evidence."

Yes, she knew that. "I panicked, okay? It's not as if I've been in this situation before." Wasn't that why she was at Wilde? "I want to find this guy. I want to stop him. And if there are really s-sex videos," she stumbled over that part, "I don't want them getting out. My life has already been dragged through the mud before. I don't want that spotlight on me again." Things had just gotten back to normal for her.

A jerky nod. "If there are any recordings, I'll do everything in my power to destroy them."

"Right." An exhale. "Not like you want it to get out, either. I'm sure your girlfriend would not want to see you with an ex—"

"There is no girlfriend."

"Oh." *Move on. Move on. Do not linger on that discovery. It doesn't matter. You and Holden are old news. Ancient history. Dead and buried.* "The video probably would just help your rep, though, wouldn't it? Guys look like studs in those videos while women—"

He took a lurching step toward her. "I don't want any sex video about us getting out into the public. The last thing I would want is for it to be viewed by anyone but me."

That was good to know. It would help with his motivation to track down the thing. "Because you value your privacy, too. Understood." Perhaps they could be professional about this, after all. They were mature adults. This *could* work out.

"It's because the moments with you are fucking *mine*." Savage. Raw. Not professional. At all. "Because I didn't share you then. I won't share you now."

All of the moisture seemed to dry from her mouth. "I don't..." *Know what to say. Didn't expect you to ever tell me those words*. He still seemed possessive, as possessive as he'd been when they were involved before. And the undercurrents between them were about to drag her down deep. "This was a mistake." She'd been too desperate. Running on too little sleep and not thinking straight. "I'll go to another agency. I'll find someone else." Abruptly, she turned on her heel and marched for the door.

"Too late. You already hired me, remember? That's why we just shook on the deal."

Claudia grabbed for the door handle. "Consider the deal off. Sanity is back. I'll just take a moment to—"

"Magically find someone else who can slip seamlessly into your life? Find a guy who already has the perfect cover in place so that he can move into your home and keep a perfect watch on you? Draw some man out of thin air who won't raise suspicion and tip off the world about what is really happening to you?"

Her fingers tightened around the doorknob.

"I was getting into the role when I said I wouldn't share," he said, voice easy. Casual. "I probably should have warned you about it, but the idea just came to me, and I went with it."

Claudia glanced over her shoulder at him. "What are you talking about?"

"I have to act possessive and protective." His arms were still crossed over his chest as he once again leaned a hip against his desk. His pose was as causal as his tone. "It will fit the character."

She spun fully toward him. "Excuse me?"

"The character I'm going to play on your case. I'll be the boyfriend who just couldn't stay away any longer." His eyes gleamed. "The man who never got over you and is determined to fight for his second chance."

"What is happening right now?" Claudia almost wanted to pinch herself because this scene felt way too surreal.

"I'm telling you about the cover I'll be using to explain my sudden presence in your life. You don't want the world to know we're searching for a sex vid and a crazy stalker."

Crazy stalker. Yes, yes, that was what Claudia feared she had. Someone who wanted to hurt her very badly. She swallowed, not speaking.

Holden plowed ahead, saying, "You don't want to warn off the jerk who has been terrorizing you, so we just need to act like two reunited lovers. It's the perfect plan."

"I don't mean to pop your bubble." Truly, she didn't. Yet the job had to be done. "But I don't see how that is perfect in any shape or form."

"No?" His dark brows rose, as if in confusion. "But it's genius."

"No," she said. "It's not." It was the opposite of that. "Everyone knows that you're a Wilde agent. The story about you doing royalty protection work has been everywhere. If people suddenly see us together—"

"They don't need to jump to the conclusion that you hired a bodyguard. Yes, I work for Wilde, but it's pretty common knowledge among the gossip sites that I also used to be engaged to you. We want people to think we're back together romantically and not because you've hired me? It can be done. Easy. People will believe whatever we want them to believe." He tipped his head toward her. "I can be very convincing, I assure you."

Convincing in his role as her reunited lover? She had a feeling that role would involve a whole lot of...intimacy. "Is it hot in here? It feels hot." Claudia fanned herself. What was up with the air conditioning in that place? She expected more from a fancy high rise.

"Hear me out." Holden flashed her his signature smile. The one he'd always tossed to reporters when he used to do his pre-fight press conferences. The one that was cocky, confident, and designed to disarm.

She stiffened her knees. Lifted her chin. That smile of his was still way too charming. It was the reason the man had become a media darling. Tough as nails, fierce in a fight, but with a smile that made you swoon.

I am not swooning. Not ever again. "I'm listening," she snapped back. "I just haven't heard anything particularly earth-shattering yet. And I'm rather in the middle of a personal crisis, so if you could speed things along, it would be appreciated."

"Absolutely." He straightened from the desk. His hands slid to his sides. "You need someone who can slip right into the fabric of your life. You just said you didn't have a boyfriend."

She had mentioned that fact, yes.

"So if you suddenly pull a mystery man out of the woodwork—if you go to another agency and get a bodyguard to drag into your life—people will wonder about him. Even if you lie and say he's your new lover, it won't make sense to those close to you if he's immediately living in your home and spending every night with you."

"Why wouldn't that make sense? I could be in the middle of a sudden, hot affair." She *could*. Stranger things had happened.

He shook his head. "That's not you."

Fabulous. Her sexy ex had just said she wasn't the type for a hot affair. And to think, she still wondered why he left her at the altar. *Because Cooper was right. Holden was never into me. It was all a game.* She needed to get the hell out of there before she humiliated herself even more. Claudia spun away so he wouldn't see the tears that filled her eyes.

But Holden clearly wasn't done. He told her, "You're commitment. You're exclusivity. You're the kind of woman who wants forever and who doesn't let some random jerk put his hands on her the first time they meet. The man has to earn the privilege of touching you. And getting into your bed? No way would some bastard get to do that on the first date."

"You have no idea what I do on my first dates." She swiped at her eyes. She'd never let Holden see her cry, and she wasn't about to start now. It was just—she hadn't been sleeping well, and she was constantly looking over her shoulder for threats. "This is ridiculous—"

"Those close to you wouldn't believe you'd let a stranger hop into your bed, but people would buy that you'd let me back into your life."

Her head shook. "Those *close to me* would never buy that. They know how I feel about you."

"Don't be so sure, sweetheart."

He needed to stop that sweetheart business. The word seemed to rake along her skin.

"Love and hate are intimately twined," Holden added. "Your friends and close associates would believe that we came into contact again, and the desire we've always felt for each other overwhelmed everything else. Trust me, I can sell overwhelming desire for you. I can do it in my sleep."

Surprised, she whirled back toward him. She'd barely heard the last words he'd spoken because she'd gotten hung up on the first bit. "You think I hate you?"

He wasn't flashing his charming smile. In fact, his expression had turned grim. "A strong emotion either way will work to seal the deal for us. The tension between us will be real, even if it's motivated by hate on your part."

She crept a little closer to him. "I don't hate you, Holden."

His lips—sensual, but with a slightly cruel edge—tightened. "This partnership isn't going to work if you lie to me. I'll need to know every secret you possess. Holding out won't get you safety. It will just put you in jeopardy."

"I'm not holding out. I just don't hate you."

He didn't so much as blink.

"Hate eats you up on the inside. It makes you hurt yourself. Those close to you." She paused. "You had a whole lot of hate when we met. I knew you hated my father because of his affair with your mother." There, yes, she'd just dropped the big elephant right into the middle of the room. "They died in that car crash together, and it ruined your life. I get you wanted vengeance. But that hate was your path, not mine."

His eyes widened. "You think I hated you?"

"Uh, you left me standing at the altar wearing a wedding dress. It's more than obvious that you weren't motivated by overwhelming love."

"Claudia—"

"Hate hurts innocent people. I don't have time for it in my life." She pulled in a deep breath, then let it go. "I don't hate you."

He was the one to advance. With silent steps, he eliminated the remaining distance between them. "Then what do you feel?"

Every part of her wanted to say...*Nothing. I feel nothing at all when I look at you.* But hadn't he just said she shouldn't lie? "You really think that us pretending to be reunited lovers will help to catch this guy?"

"I think the ruse will let me into your life so I can protect you *and* investigate easier. Doesn't have to be the choice we make. You could always just tell everyone you've hired me as a bodyguard, but—"

"But that might scare off the bad guy." She understood that risk without him saying a word.

His head inclined toward her. "It would certainly make him more cautious. It would also get plenty of people prying to try and figure out *why* you need a bodyguard."

Yes. "I'm staying at the guest house at my family's estate. I had to move there after the fire at my house. It has two bedrooms. I suppose there would be no harm in you using the spare." Not like they'd be sharing one bed or anything. Separate rooms. Separate beds.

"You're overwhelming me. Truly."

"And it would *just* be an act. Not like we're actually getting back together. It's really not a big deal, I guess, if we go with this cover story." The words were more to convince herself than anything else.

"No big deal at all. Check. Just us hunting some psycho who is trying to hurt you and who may have been obsessed with you for quite some time."

Her mouth opened. Closed. Opened once more. Only no words actually emerged. *Okay, fine this sounds like one incredibly big, terrifying deal.*

"You get that, don't you?" His head tilted to the right. "If I didn't take the pics, then that means someone else was watching you way back then.

Someone who may have been nursing an obsession with you for quite a while. Only now he is accelerating. Not just watching, but actually trying to hurt you. I've seen cases of obsession. Some of them have brutal endings."

Chill bumps rose on her arms. "I can definitely get on board with pretending to be reunited with you. Genius plan, just like you said. Consider me all in." She licked her lower lip. "When do we start pretending?"

"We start right now."

She glanced around the empty office. "Why pretend here?" Where no one could see them?

"We're going to pretend *everywhere* because we never know when the perp might be watching."

How utterly chilling. Now they were talking about a *perp*.

"We make our plan, and step one is that we need to have a reunion scene that is very public and very, very believable."

He sounded so confident. "Do you come up with covers like this all the time? Is this part of your job?"

"Working undercover is, yes. To be successful, you need to slip easily into your client's life. But my covers aren't *exactly* like this. I've never pretended to be the besotted ex who can't stay away from the woman he loves for even a moment longer. A guy who would do *anything* to get her back."

She squinted at him. "Did you just say 'besotted' right then?" Not a word she expected to hear from Holden.

He rolled one shoulder. "Besotted. Lovesick. Madly obsessed...we'll let the bastard out there think he's not the only one addicted to you. Something tells me he'll believe that cover very, very easily."

Her head was spinning. "Okay?" Yes, her response was more of a question than anything else. "So how do we set the scene? How do we bring you back into my life in an ever-so-public way?"

His charming grin spread slowly across his face. "Easy, sweetheart. I fight for you."

CHAPTER THREE

Step Three: Fight dirty. Fight hard. Use every trick that you know and even those you don't.

"So, hi." The man with the sandy blond hair slid onto the bar seat next to Claudia. "You come here often?"

She turned her head toward him even as she kept her fingers wrapped around her glass—and her untouched apple martini. The music was blaring, so he'd leaned in a bit to talk to her. This was not her scene, not typically, but it was hardly a typical night.

They were in a ritzy club, one packed with too many people pretending to be trendy. There had been a long red carpet rolled out in front of the place. Claudia had already eyed two celebrities being escorted up to the VIP area. She wore a body-hugging black dress, one of the sexiest pieces of clothing she'd ever seen. Way more daring than her normal clothing options. The dress had been purchased that day. The back was non-existent, and the plunging V in the front darted way below her breasts. Hope and a prayer were keeping the clingy material in place.

The man smiled at her. Slow. Bold. He expected her to fall right into his hands. That was, after all, the plan. Because she'd met the man in front of her earlier, when she'd still been at Wilde. Elias Rook. He was another agent, but his job tonight wasn't to keep her safe. Instead, it was to seduce her.

Or, fine, to *pretend* to be seducing her. All part of Holden's scene setting for her case.

He'd picked the location. A place where people went to see others and to *be* seen. Holden was sure their encounter would be recorded and broadcast far and wide on social media. He'd picked the guy to hit on her, and Claudia was supposed to accept Elias's offer to dance.

Then Holden would enter the picture...

"I don't come here often at all," she said, pitching her voice a little higher than normal so he could hear her. "My first time."

"Then I guess it's my lucky night." He extended his hand toward her. "Want to dance?"

The last thing she wanted to do was enter the throng of gyrating bodies, but she nodded and released her drink so that she could put her fingers in his.

Unlike Holden, his skin was smooth. No calluses. According to Holden, Elias Rook was normally busy working behind the scenes in the tech department. But the man had been itching to get out and stretch his wings in the field.

So Holden had given him this opportunity.

An inch or two shorter than Holden, Elias led her onto the crowded dance floor. He pulled her against him and curled his fingers around her hips. His head came toward her left ear. "Breathe," he urged her. "And try to look a little less like an inmate on death row who is being led to your execution."

Surprised, she gave a little jerk. Her gaze flew around. No sign of Holden, not yet.

"It would probably help," Elias whispered as his mouth came near her ear again, "if you smiled. Maybe if you laughed, like I just said something insanely hilarious to you."

She forced a laugh. Did it sound as fake as it felt?

"Better." His head lifted. His gaze—a dark, deep brown—dipped over her face. "You're completely safe," he murmured. "Don't forget that."

She didn't feel safe. With all of these strangers around her, she felt scared. Anyone could be watching. There were too many bodies, and the crowded dance floor had her feeling overheated and on edge.

The music kept blaring. Lights rolled overhead, concealing, then spotlighting the crowd, and her nerves got the best of her. She pulled from Elias. "I'm sorry, I just need a minute—" She turned away from him, wanting to get some fresh air. But she'd only taken one step when...

"Claudia."

She'd taken one step and nearly slammed straight into Holden. Where the heck had he come from? She'd just looked around that club, and he hadn't been there.

He stared at her—wow. He stared at her as if he could eat her alive. His eyes glittered, his whole face turned hard and intent, and he reached out to curl his fingers around her shoulder.

At his touch, heat lanced through her body.

"I have missed you," Holden told her, and his words sounded so incredibly believable. For a moment, she simply stood there, caught by the burning need in his gaze.

Dammit. This is way too much like one of my fantasies. Except, he wasn't on his knees begging her forgiveness. That usually happened in her fantasies, not—

"Hey, buddy," Elias snapped from behind her. "Get your hand off her. She's with me."

Holden's gaze never left her. "The fuck she is. She's mine and always has been." He used his hold to pull her closer.

And then—

Then his head bent toward her. *As if he would kiss her.*

Her hands came up automatically and pressed to his chest. "Stop!"

He froze. Pain flashed across his face. "I need another chance. I am dying without you."

Words that were music to her ears.

She shook her head. No. They were *not* music. They were lies. This was a staged scene. She knew what was supposed to be happening so she needed to get a grip.

"Yeah, buddy," Elias drawled. "How about you go die somewhere else? She's going home with me tonight." Then *his* fingers curled around her other shoulder, and he pulled her back from Holden.

Her heels clattered, and she tripped. Elias truly had not grabbed her hard, but she was in way over her head, and she'd stumbled because of nerves, and, with mounting horror, Claudia started to go down hard.

Holden caught her. He snagged her wrist and yanked her up against him. His breath heaved as he stared into her eyes. "I've got you."

"Asshole," Elias seethed. Someone was certainly getting into his part. "I am tired of your shit. Get the hell out of here before I *make* you leave."

Holden's head turned toward the other man. "Try," he dared.

Other people were watching. She saw phones being aimed at them. Her nightmare—being the focus of so much attention. *The past is coming back.* But it was necessary...

All part of the plan, check. The big master plan that Holden had concocted.

Holden pushed her behind him. "Take your best shot," he challenged Elias. "Let's see what you've—"

Elias swung. She'd peeked around Holden, so she saw the blow coming, and she expected Holden to dodge. This was, after all, a staged fight. Not the real deal, but Holden *didn't* dodge. The blow landed.

She heard a gasp from nearby.

Her head turned.

"Oh, shit," the guy with his phone in the air gaped. "That dumbass just took a swing at 'No Holding Back' Holden Blackwell. Dude is dead."

She heard thuds. Grunts. Her head whipped back to discover Elias curled on the floor, with his hands around his stomach.

"That wasn't a very good 'best shot' from you," Holden said as he stood over Elias's prone form. "I think my hit was much better."

Because she'd been looking away, she'd missed his attack. But she'd seen him fight in the past and knew just how skilled he was. He had a reputation for executing his opponents. Few ever lasted long against him. His attacks were too powerful. His big fists like hammers.

Elias groaned again and rose shakily. "My...mistake..."

"Yeah, it was." But Holden turned away from him. Focused on Claudia.

All of those stupid phones were still recording. She knew this was what he wanted, but she hated being the focus of so much attention. *The circus is starting again.* Only Holden said the circus was a necessary part of her staying alive.

Because he thinks I have a stalker who may want me dead. She feared the same thing. Wasn't that why she'd agreed to the show?

Holden extended his hand toward her. "Come with me?"

Ah, the big reunion. Elias slinked away. She knew the next part, but she still hesitated. Maybe that hesitation made the whole thing look all the more believable. Holden just waited for her, with his gaze steady and hungry, his face tense, and his hand extended.

Slowly, she took his offered hand. His fingers closed around hers.

***

"You did well." Holden used his body to shield Claudia from prying eyes. They were outside of the club—a club that had been a deliberate choice for him because he'd known he would be recognized there. The place tended to pull in people who followed the fight scene. Sure, Vegas held the main action when it came to the battles, but Atlanta had its fair share, too. Especially for those trying to move up the ranks.

"Did you hurt him?" Claudia asked, voice sharp.

His brows rose. "I spar with Elias all the time. I know how to hit without doing permanent damage."

"That's not exactly a yes or no answer."

No, it wasn't. "The hits were real, but they didn't have my full force behind them. Neither did the punch he threw at me." Elias's upper cut was getting better and better. When the guy had first announced he wanted to start field work, Holden had taken it upon himself to make sure the man could handle himself in hand-to-hand situations. Elias had proven himself to be a fast learner and someone who didn't mind fighting dirty. Two traits Holden adored.

"You're actually telling me," she muttered, "that 'No Holding Back' Holden actually—"

"Held back? Yep, I did. I'm not the same guy I was back then." That guy seemed like a stranger to him some days. But, back to the matter at hand because they needed to get things moving. After glancing quickly at his watch, he said, "Next bit of business. After you pick up a change of clothes from your hotel, you come home with me. We spend the night together. And we go from there."

The club's door opened. Noise and music drifted in the air.

A limo cruised to a stop near them.

He smiled at her. "Your carriage awaits."

Huffing, she brushed past him and climbed into the rear of the limo. He followed her, nodding to the driver who'd gotten out to hold the door. Another Wilde agent, the driver would make sure they got safely to their destination. Stop one would be her hotel. And while the driver was watching the road, Holden could focus on other issues...

Her.

"Thanks, Francis," Holden said to the agent.

Francis inclined his head.

The door shut behind Holden, and he and Claudia were enclosed in the intimate confines of the limo. Soft lighting illuminated the scene, and classical music poured through the speakers. Chilled champagne waited for them.

"Someone knows how to set a romantic scene," Claudia noted as she crossed her legs and perched on the seat across from him. "Did the driver think someone was going to follow us inside?"

He cleared his throat. Yeah, the scene setting had been his idea, and it didn't have a thing to do with anyone following them. It was part of a whole different strategy. "Guessing that means you don't want a drink?"

"I want to go back to my hotel. I'm not staying the night at your place." Her voice was cool, but a little brittle around the edges. "I get that you had a whole elaborate plan ready to roll, but I need some space tonight. We can pick up the full-on fake relationship bit tomorrow when we go to my home in North Carolina."

"I can't just drop you off tonight and walk away." Not going to happen. "I'll come inside your hotel room." Holden would have preferred his place because he had top-notch security, but he wasn't going to push her. She wanted to stay at the hotel, fine by him, but he'd be with her.

"You're not *staying* in my hotel room."

The limo had pulled away from the curb. He picked up his phone and scanned through his app. A quick search showed...*Yep. Videos are already loaded.* That was the thing with social media these days. Anything could be shared, instantly. "I can sleep in the spare bed."

"There *is* no spare bed in my hotel room. I got a king bed because I wanted to spread out."

So that means there will be room for two. Wisely, Holden refrained from saying those words.

"You can see me to my room, but that's it. I'm sleeping alone tonight."

He put down his phone. "You seem to be having trouble with the concept of a twenty-four, seven bodyguard. You should have read that contract you signed a little more carefully." Because she *had* signed the contract. They were bound together now.

"I'm pretty sure the client gets to dictate the rules, Holden."

Wrong. "I'm pretty sure that when your safety is on the line, I get to make the rules." He smiled at her, but knew the grin would look far too much like a shark's smile.

She sniffed. "You're not getting into my bed."

A guy can dream.

"It's awkward enough doing this whole fake reconciliation bit, and I'm warning you now, I still don't think those closest to me will buy it. I think I should just tell my friends and my brother the truth—"

"Big problem with that, sweetheart."

"I am not your sweetheart." A pause. "And why is it such a problem?"

Because I need everyone to believe we're lovers again. But he tried to be a bit more tactful than just baldly making that announcement. "Because one of your friends could be the one after you. The perp could very well be someone in your inner circle, so how about we don't warn them of our plans and give them any additional power?"

Her fingers drummed against her thigh. "My brother is certainly not the one doing this to me. I should be able to tell Cooper, at least, that you're working as my bodyguard."

Holden stretched out his legs. "Ah, yes, the dear brother. The brother who didn't believe you when you tried to tell him what was happening."

She looked away. "Maybe if I'd told him about the photos, Cooper would have believed me. But I just...They were so intimate. I couldn't show them to my brother."

Right now, Holden thought the less Cooper knew, the better. After a moment of contemplation, Holden said, "It could be someone close to Cooper. He says the wrong word, and our plan goes up in smoke."

"He's not going to like you being back in my life. If we tell him that you're not really my-my lover, then he might go along easier."

He hadn't missed the slight stutter when she'd called him her lover. "Not too concerned about what's easy with him. Cooper never liked me, and the feeling was mutual." Dislike wasn't what they felt for each other. Hate? Way closer to the truth, but Holden shrugged. "We'll both deal."

"Cooper loves me, and you...hurt me. So there is bound to be some tension between the two of you."

He leaned toward her. Wanted to touch her and barely held back the strong impulse. "He hated me before the end of our relationship."

"He didn't trust you. I shouldn't have, either." She kept staring out of the window, seemingly focused on the lights they passed along the street.

Holden wanted her focused on him. So he gave in to his impulse. Holden reached out, and his fingers touched the top of her knee. Claudia flinched. Her gaze jumped to his.

"If this is going to work, you'll have to trust me." He was trying his best to handle her with kid gloves. He wanted to grab her. Hold tight. Run the hell away with her and never look back.

But that wasn't what she wanted. So he was *trying* to fight his baser urges.

"After what happened," Claudia licked her lower lip, "how can you ever expect me to trust you again?"

Holden's jaw locked as he ground his teeth together. "You came to me."

"Because you were prominently featured in those not-so-lovely photos."

Granted. But... "It was also because you thought I could help you to track down whoever is after you."

Once more, she looked away.

"Nope." He moved to the seat right beside her. Caught her chin and gently turned her face toward him. "You don't get to pretend I'm not here."

"That's not what I was doing."

Liar, liar. "Fine. You don't get to pretend I'm just an employee you can ignore when I piss you off."

She jerked her chin away. "First, I never ignore any of my employees because I am not an asshole."

He could still feel the softness of her skin beneath his fingers.

"And, second, yes, fine, I *am* pissed at you. You left me at the altar. You vanished when I counted on you, and all I got was that incredibly lame *sorry*. Do you know what it is like to stand in front of two hundred people and tell them a wedding isn't going to happen? That you've been stood up?"

He opened his mouth.

She blazed on, saying, "No, you don't know because you were the one who left *me*. I was there. I was ready to vow before everyone that I would love you forever."

His heart iced.

"You weren't there. You were *sorry*, but you weren't there." Each word held a savage, brittle edge. So odd for Claudia because her voice was usually warm and almost musical. Seductive. He loved listening to her talk. He loved—

"So excuse me for holding a grudge, but it's there," she snapped. "Do I trust you? Don't make me laugh. There is no way in hell I would ever trust you with my heart again."

The chill spread through Holden's body. He'd expected this news, but it didn't mean he liked it one bit. "Good thing it's not your heart I'm after." Now who was lying? "It's your life. Can you trust me with that?"

She sucked in a sharp breath.

"I think we both already know the answer to that or else you wouldn't be in this car with me right now," he said quietly. "Despite what happened between us, you know that if danger is coming, if your life is threatened, I would do *anything* to keep you safe. I'm not like the other bastards in your life who never get their hands dirty. I fight hard, and I obliterate my opponents. You *can* count on that. You hired me because you wanted a wolf guarding you, and that's exactly what you have." He needed her to understand this. "You're mine, and I will do whatever it takes to protect you."

"I'm not yours."

Fuck, fuck, fuck. He had to dial things back. "My client," Holden clarified. Why was he having so much trouble? He could usually be fairly charming, but with her, he was practically reduced to primitive growls. "You're my client, and if you've researched my history at Wilde, then you know I take my responsibility to my clients very seriously."

And he *knew* she'd researched him. After all, Claudia was far, far more than just a pretty face. *Pretty? She's stunning.* A beauty that was seductive and electrifying. Not a perfect face, but something that was somehow a million times better. When her features all came together, they were captivating. You saw her, and you never forgot her.

Just one of the reasons she haunts me still.

Another reason? She was wicked smart. People underestimated her because Claudia tended to be on the quiet side while Cooper was bold and outgoing. But after being around them for just a few days, Holden had quickly come to the realization that Claudia was the brains of the operation. Cooper might be the face of the winery, but it was meticulous Claudia who made the business so successful. He had no doubt that she'd thoroughly investigated his work at Wilde.

She knew what he'd done. What he could do.

"Trust me with the case," he said, working hard to make the words less growly and more moderated. "Trust me to protect your life."

The privacy shield lowered before she could speak, and the driver turned toward them. "Valet is backed up and the front of the hotel is jammed with traffic," Francis informed him. "Gonna pull up to the side so you can get out there."

"Thanks." He cleared his throat. Holden hadn't even realized that they'd made it to their destination.

"You don't have to follow me in," Claudia rushed to say. "I can just jump out and go inside. We can talk tomorrow."

That was cute. But, no. "We need to talk about a few more things." No way was he done with her.

"What can't wait until tomorrow?"

The limo had stopped. Or at least, slowed to a near stop. Without waiting any longer, Claudia reached for the door handle and shoved it open.

She bounded out, but he was right on her heels. And those high heels of hers did slow her down so he was able to reach out and curl his hand around her elbow. "Something that has already waited damn long enough," he rasped in response. "I need to explain what happened all those years ago." *And, no, I can't wait until tomorrow. I can't wait any longer.*

She spun, fast and impressively in the two-inch stilettos. "No. I am not doing this tonight." Claudia pulled away from him.

They were about thirty feet from the front of the hotel and the line of cars waiting to drop off guests and their luggage. As he watched her, Claudia hurried from him. She skirted around a very large and elaborately hedged bush—

And some sonofabitch jumped out from behind the bush and grabbed her arm.

What the fuck?

As he hurtled for her, Holden saw the flash of a blade coming toward Claudia. The attacker had a knife. Not even aware that the thunderous roar echoing was his own, Holden bounded forward. He grabbed for Claudia and yanked her back even as he lifted his forearm to block the blow—and the knife—that barreled toward him.

CHAPTER FOUR

Step Four: Be patient. Play the long game. Don't expect to see success instantly. You have to go the distance and—dammit. She's right there. Everything I want. How the hell am I supposed to keep my hands off her?

He'd tossed her into a bush. A very large, somewhat prickly bush. But a prickly bush was far better than facing a knife-wielding attacker any day of the week. Claudia pushed herself upright even as some of those prickly bush leaves clung stubbornly to her dress. She'd lost a shoe somewhere in that bush, but she'd deal with finding it later.

At the moment, she had to help Holden.

Or, as she saw once she succeeded in freeing herself from the bush, she had to stop Holden from killing someone. Because he had her attacker on the ground. The knife was a few feet away. Holden had the guy pinned to the cement. His fist was drawn back to strike, and he'd clearly already hit the other man more than a few times.

"Holden!" She grabbed for his arm.

He turned his head toward her. "He came at you with a *knife!*"

Holden's expression was just...savage. Twisted with rage and fury. She'd never seen him look quite that way before. Never witnessed this primitive tension fueling his body. Sure, she'd seen him all intense and focused during a bout, but this was completely different.

Uncontrolled. Primal.

Claudia heard the pounding of footsteps and looked up to see several hotel staff members—and just some random people from the hotel—rushing toward them.

Their driver lurched from behind the limo, hurrying forward, too. He stopped near the knife, peered down at it a moment, and when he looked up again, his face appeared nearly as savage as Holden's. She knew he wasn't just a driver. Francis was also a Wilde agent. Holden had introduced her to him earlier in the night.

"What is happening here?" a man demanded. He wore the familiar dark red hotel uniform and had a radio strapped to his hip. "Get off that man! Let him go immediately!"

"This *man* just attacked my girlfriend with a knife!" Holden snarled back. "Call the cops. I want him arrested!"

Claudia nodded, still feeling dazed. "He did." Her voice came out shaken. "He jumped from the side of the bush and swiped out with the knife. I- I think he was aiming for..." Her voice trailed off. She'd just slid her hand over her left arm and realized two things. One, her purse wasn't hanging off her shoulder. Two...*I think I'm bleeding.* "He cut my purse strap," she said, even as she lightly touched her arm once more. "And I think he cut me."

"He did *what?*" Holden thundered. "You sonofabitch!"

Francis grabbed Holden and hauled him back before Holden could do more damage to the attacker. "Let the hotel security handle him," Francis advised, voice gruff.

With Holden restrained, the attacker immediately tried to jump up and run. He slammed his shoulder into the uniformed hotel employee who'd spoken earlier.

"Screw this," her attacker snarled as he tried to make his getaway.

Breaking from Francis, Holden leapt after the jerk. Grabbed him and hauled him right back. "You're going *nowhere.*"

The man cried out, "I was paid to do it! Given one hundred dollars! Told to wait for the limo and then to swipe the lady in the black dress's bag! I'm sorry, I'm so freaking *sorry!*"

She wrapped her hand around the wound on her arm. Blood seeped through her fingers. Oh, no. Claudia had watched Holden's brutal matches—watched them as her stomach churned because the truth of the matter was that she'd always had issues with blood. She'd been able to watch his fights because someone *else* had been doing the bleeding. But when she had to deal with her own blood...*The worst.* She always got dizzy. Sometimes, she even fainted. There was just enough light from the hotel that when she lifted her hand and peered at the cut on her arm...

Oh, no. No. "Holden?" High. Sharp. "That's a lot of blood." Way more than had been there a moment before.

His head swung toward her. His eyes widened. "Fuck." He shoved the still-apologizing attacker at Francis and shot toward Claudia. "Look at me, baby," he urged, his voice suddenly low and crooning and tender. "I've got you. You're fine. You are *not* going to pass out."

She had fainted once before with him. When they'd been in his kitchen and they'd been cooking dinner together and a knife had slipped and she'd wound up slicing her palm open. She'd taken one look at the gaping wound and the next thing Claudia knew, she'd woken up cradled in Holden's arms.

Her breath heaved in and out.

"Let me see it," he urged her.

Voices rose and fell around them. Someone was calling the cops.

Her frantic gaze darted over the crowd. Wait, was that a guy filming the scene? It seemed like—

"Lift up your fingers," Holden ordered quietly.

Trembling, she did. Her gaze snapped to his face.

His jaw locked. "Not bad at all," Holden said as he surveyed her wound. He blinked and sent her a smile. "Easy fix."

Automatically, she started to glance at the wound—

"Nope." He caught her chin with his hand. Tipped her head back. Ignored the chaos around them. "No point in you looking at it. Just look at me."

"Found her purse!" Francis called out. "It was in the bush, right next to one of her shoes."

"I was just paid for the job!" A wild cry from the attacker. "I didn't mean to hurt her. I was just trying to cut her purse strap!"

Her gaze remained on Holden.

"I've got you," he told her. "Everything is going to be fine."

She could feel the blood dripping down her arm. "This is what I was talking about," she mumbled. "I have really, really bad luck." Bad luck just kept plaguing her.

"Baby, it's not bad luck. It's some sonofabitch targeting you. And I promise, I'm stopping him."

***

"Eyes on me," Holden said.

Her breath caught, but her gaze whipped toward him.

They were in the ER. And, oh, God, she was being stitched up. Her arm had been numbed moments before, and the very cheery ER doc had assured her that the process would be pretty painless.

A young nurse was actually doing the stitching job. Or, preparing to do it. The place smelled of antiseptic, there was a bustle of noise from just beyond the white curtain that separated Claudia from the other patients, and nerves had her left foot doing a little shake.

Meanwhile, Holden seemed completely unruffled. This was, after all, probably a super small injury to him, especially considering all the brutal hits he'd taken back in his fighting days. She hated to make such a big production of things, and Claudia was trying her best to woman up and put a brave face on things. "I'm all right." *Except for the nausea and the spinning of the room.* "You don't have to stay with me. You can wait outside." As long as she could avoid looking at the actual wound and the stitching process, she'd be great.

Holden smiled at her. His warm, charming smile. "Fuck that," he told her. He reached for her right hand. The one not attached to her injured arm. His fingers curled with hers. "I'm not going anywhere."

The nurse touched her arm and got to work.

"Eyes on me," Holden said once more, only this time, the words held a curious tenderness.

***

She ended up staying at his place. Very much *not* her original intention, but after her mugging and the hospital visit, Claudia was truly not in the mood for any other unfortunate surprises. Going back to Holden's place where he'd assured her he had a top-notch security system? Sure, yes. Why not? *Let's go with that plan.*

He secured the doors and dropped her bag near his couch. The helpful Francis had picked up her belongings and checked Claudia out of her hotel room. She knew Holden had spoken with the cops several times—both before they'd left the crime scene and then again on the phone after they'd left the hospital. He'd gotten briefed by a cop that he seemed to know, and she was dying to learn more info.

"You can take the bedroom." He pointed to the right. "I'd like to say I have a guest room, and, technically, I do, but it's currently filled with a pile of random boxes that I didn't unpack after moving in."

She didn't head toward the bedroom. "What did you learn about the attacker?"

"Name's Tom Willis. A guy with a history of snatch and grabs. Not-so-good Tom can't describe the person who paid him. He was just supposed to grab your bag and deliver it to a drop-off location. Once delivery was made, Tom was going to get paid through an app on his phone." Holden raked a hand through his hair. "That's how he was contacted originally. A different app. Someone seemed to know that our mugger specialized in jobs like this, and they used him. Only he didn't get the job done."

Her arm throbbed a bit. The numbing had already started to wear off. "Why would someone want my bag?"

"The person who hired Tom probably wanted your phone. Get your phone, you get access to your life. Or the guy pulling strings could have wanted your keys." A shrug. "Keys would make getting into your home and workplace easy."

Chill bumps rose onto her arms. "I would have changed the locks if my keys had been stolen."

"Yeah, but that takes time. Maybe our mystery puppet master thought he'd have the chance to use them first." A roll of one broad shoulder. "Didn't happen, though. He didn't get what he wanted." His jaw clenched even as his gaze slid over her. "I'm sorry."

Her back stiffened. "I should tell you, I don't particularly enjoy those words from you." Talk about words that haunted her. *Sorry*.

"Too bad. You're getting them again. I'm sorry that I screwed up tonight." He advanced toward her.

Maybe it was time for her to run into the bedroom. It was helluva late. She turned—

He caught her right wrist. "I should have protected you. I should have been in front of you. Standing between you and the world. I thought I had time to set the scene. To build a cover. I wasn't on my guard enough, and you got hurt because of me."

She shook her head and tried to ignore the spark of awareness that burned through her. "I got hurt because some jerk with a knife sliced at me." Claudia could vaguely remember feeling a quick sting on her arm before Holden had launched her away from the attacker. "Probably would have been a lot worse if you hadn't been there." Swallowing, she added, "And the bad guy would have gotten away *with* my bag. You did jump him and pin him, remember? I hardly think that qualifies as a fail of a night."

"Anytime you get hurt, it's a fail." His voice roughened. "I can assure you, I won't be making that mistake again. You can count on me to keep you safe."

His finger moved lightly along her inner wrist. She was pretty sure her pulse immediately skyrocketed, and to hide it, Claudia tugged her hand back. "You think the person who is stalking me hired the mugger."

"Don't you?"

Unfortunately... "Yes."

He nodded. "That means he's followed you to Atlanta. He's keeping very close watch on you, and that's a dangerous thing."

"He doesn't care if I get hurt," she whispered.

"No, he doesn't."

"Because hurting me is his goal?" An idea that would give her plenty of nightmares.

"Yes." Gritted.

"How wonderful. I've got a person I don't know out there who wants to torture me. Lovely." Weary, she turned away. "I will take your bedroom. Thanks." She needed to crash. Or, technically, she needed to go off and lick her wounds in peace. *Then* crash.

She took two steps.

"We're talking about it."

Claudia frowned, but didn't look back. "I thought we just talked about the attack."

"I mean us. We need to clear the air."

She waved her right hand. "Air is clear." So much easier to say these things without looking back at him. "You were pissed at my family. Wanted revenge. And lovesick me fell into your lap like a ripe plum."

"I *intended* to marry you."

Now that gave her pause. Shifted her memories. "Because that was a better revenge? You know, I hate to tell you, but I had nothing to do with what happened between our parents. Is that a spoiler for you?" Before he could answer, she turned and fired him a glare. "I'm tired. Big day. Big night. All the things were big. If you insist on doing a rehash of our past, let's do it in the morning, shall we? I'm so much more of a morning person."

"I know you had nothing to do with what happened between our parents. I didn't fall for you because I planned to use you or because of some crazy revenge idea. I fell for you in spite of all the other chaos out there. I knew I should stay away from you. Didn't take a genius to figure out we were playing some fucked-up version of Romeo and Juliet with the warring families."

Romeo and Juliet?

"I fell for you because there was no other option for me, and I didn't show up at the church for the same damn reason." His hands flexed and released at his sides. "I get you're over me. Understood. Message received. You were over me the minute you flew to France. But I need you to know what really happened. I wanted you to know for a long time, but it wasn't safe to tell you."

That was some very odd wording. *It wasn't safe.* Holden had always loved being mysterious. As for her trip to France, there was no mystery involved at all. "I had to do research for the company, so I took a trip across the Atlantic."

"And when you fucked the vineyard owner over there, was that research, too?"

That response floored her. Her brows shot up. "Excuse me?" Her chin notched up to match her eyebrows. "I'll go back to the 'it's late' situation and it being a crazy bad night for me, but I could have just sworn you said I fucked a vineyard owner."

"I saw the posts online about the two of you, Claudia. You moved on from me helluva fast."

"Someone sounds jealous." Impossible. "And you—of all people—should know not to believe everything you read. Wasn't that the whole point of our scene at the club?"

He took a lurching step toward her. "So you didn't fuck him?"

Wow. "That's none of your business. Hate to tell you, but you seem awfully jealous for an ex." Bed. That was what she needed. To escape him and go to bed. "My arm hurts." Mostly it was just throbbing and she could deal with that, but Claudia desperately wanted an excuse to end this painful conversation. "Good night." She did an abrupt about-face that would have done a soldier proud.

She didn't stop her walking until she was safely inside his bedroom. With the door shut. She'd flipped on the light, and her breath left her in a heavy, relieved rush. *Privacy. Solitude.* Claudia kicked off her shoes. She could actually take a minute and think about the madness of the night and how utterly and completely terrified she'd been when the attacker had come at her and—

Something on the nightstand caught her eye.

Blinking, sure she was mistaken, Claudia tip-toed closer to the nightstand.

A knock on the bedroom door had her jumping.

"Got your bag," Holden called. "I'll just bring it in and leave it near the bed."

She whirled toward him as he opened the door.

"Just putting down the bag," he muttered. "Not going to bother you at all."

He bothered her all the time. "Why do you have a picture of us on your nightstand?"

He dropped the bag. Glanced at the nightstand. His features tightened before he looked back at her. And he *shrugged*. "Why wouldn't I have a picture of us?"

"*Why?*" Her voice was entirely too loud. Too sharp. But, she asked again, even sharper, "*Why?*"

He crossed his arms over his chest. "It was a good picture. We got it when we went to Gatlinburg, remember? We were on the lift and you were laughing your sweet ass off and—"

"I *know* where the picture is from," she cut in. "I don't know why you have it on display when we've been over for—*oh*." Embarrassment had heat flooding her cheeks because Claudia suddenly realized what was happening. *My bad*. "You were doing more scene setting, weren't you? Putting out little pieces of evidence to suggest that we're really a couple again." Made sense, and she shouldn't have jumped to conclusions. By putting out the pics, he'd make people believe that he'd always had a soft spot for her. "You probably even put up a pic of us at your office, didn't you? I have to say, when you set a cover, you really, really set a cover." Someone took his craft very seriously.

"Yep." Emotionless. "That's what I do. Go all in. 'No Holding Back' Holden, am I right? Not just a name for fighting. Covers everything I do."

Her cheeks had to be bloodred. "Thanks for bringing in my bag."

"I have a pic of you in my desk drawer at Wilde. Should anyone go plundering, that's what they'll find."

"Great cover. I will, uh, make sure I get some pics of us and put around places when I go home, too."

"You do that." He didn't move.

The room was really quite massive, so why did it feel so overwhelmingly small to her? Probably because she was standing next to his king bed and he was blocking the door, and a traitorous part of her was suddenly thinking about them in that bed. Wrecking it. She cleared her throat. "Thanks, again."

Holden started to nod, but stopped. Instead, he shook his head. "Fuck thanks."

"Excuse me?" Claudia rocked back on her heels.

He stalked toward her.

Oh, no. There was no place to run. The nightstand—with their picture—was right behind her. He was suddenly looming in front of her, and her heart raced hard enough to shake her chest. "Holden—"

"I'm a liar."

Her breath shuddered out. "You never intended to—"

"I've had that picture of us up forever, just like I've had the one in my desk there for ages. No one is gonna get inside Wilde and rifle through my shit. The photo is not there as some cover."

She could not speak.

"It's *you*," he added grimly. "You've haunted me. You've obsessed me. You've driven me crazy...and I had to keep you close. I had to see your picture because sometimes, the sight of your smile was what got me through the day."

Now she was the one to shake her head because no way was that right. He couldn't actually mean those words.

His hand rose and curled around the nape of her neck. "I never got over you."

This wasn't happening.

"I missed you, baby."

Before she could think of something—anything—to say, his mouth claimed hers.

CHAPTER FIVE

Step Five: Play it cool. You're obsessed? Fine. She doesn't have to know. No sense scaring her off when you finally have her close again. So, I repeat. Play. It. Cool.

You're gonna screw up, aren't you?

He should not be kissing her. Holden knew he should be walking out of the bedroom. Going to find the coldest shower in the world. Getting *away* from Claudia.

But he wasn't.

He was kissing her. Tasting her like a man who'd been starving for some sweetness. Her body pressed against his, and she was the softest heaven he'd felt in years. He hadn't been bullshitting. He'd longed for her. Craved her.

Obsessed much? With her? Yeah, he was.

That was why he was holding so tightly to her when he should be playing the gentleman.

She just tasted so good. And her body felt so good. And she was making that sexy little moan in the back of her throat that had always driven him extra crazy.

Her hands rose to curl around his upper arms. He felt the light bite of her nails against his skin. His dick shoved eagerly against her. She still wore that incredible, body-hugging dress, and it would be so easy to lift her up. To put her on the bed. To yank that dress up to her hips and rip away her panties and plunge back where he *most* wanted to be.

For so long, he'd ached for her. Woken up at night with her name on his lips. He'd had to pretend he'd moved on. But there were some things you just didn't move past. Some *people*. For him, she was it.

And she was—

Pushing against his chest. Not pulling him close, not any longer. Because he'd screwed up. Gone in too hard and fast and desperately.

Shit. And she's got stitches. She was attacked tonight. I'm supposed to be her protector, and I'm doing this.

He backed away, immediately. Put about three feet between them and locked his eyes on her. Claudia's lips were plump and red from his mouth. Her eyes wide. Faint spots of color stained her cheeks.

Damage control, that was what he needed to do, stat. He should reassure her that this kind of thing would not happen again. But, instead of doing that, Holden opened his mouth and heard his own fool-ass say, "Wanting you is as natural as breathing for me."

Her eyes widened even more. Right. He should have dialed things back. He'd try again. In a rush, Holden added, "I should have kept my hands off you." So much better. Clearly, he was on the right, reassuring track, and he needed to keep reassuring her so she didn't run off and do anything hasty like, oh, say, hire another bodyguard. "But I can't." Wait, he was screwing up again. "I want to put my hands all over you."

Yeah, he was being blunt.

She was not speaking.

But she *was* listening, so he might as well get all of his revelations out now. "I intended to marry you five years ago. Didn't give a shit about your family. Didn't care that your brother thought I would never be good enough for you or that my old man warned that he'd disown me the minute I said 'I do' to you." So there had been...obstacles. Screw them. Obstacles didn't matter when there had also been Claudia waiting. "But I lied to you back then."

She wet her lips. "You seem to lie a lot."

He winced. "Occupational hazard."

"I don't buy that."

Had her voice trembled a little bit?

He sucked in a deep breath and thought about what she'd said to him that long ago day...and all the things he'd wanted to tell her over the years. "I was kidnapped."

Claudia sucked in a sharp breath. "Do *not* make fun of me right now."

"I would never dream of it." Not in a million years. "Someone held a gun to my head and made me leave you."

Her blue gaze flashed fire at him. Not ice. *Fire.* "That's not funny."

"Good. I didn't intend it to be a joke." She just didn't realize how very on the nose she'd been all of those years ago when he'd stood on her doorstep. Her words blasted through his mind because they'd been *burned* there. *Tell me that you were kidnapped. Tell me that someone held a gun to your head and made you leave me. Tell me that you were forced to stay away from the church. That you would never, ever have willingly done that to me. Tell me that this wasn't all some long con just so you can get some kind of twisted vengeance on my family.*

"Get out," Claudia ordered as her breath sawed in and out. "Right now. I don't care if it is your room, *go*."

Not yet. "I was forced to stay away from the church," he added, voice wooden. There would be no stopping now. "Despite what you may believe, I would never, ever willingly have done that to you. It was not some long con for revenge. I intended for you to be mine, forever."

She swiped at her cheeks. "Just when I thought this night could not get any worse."

"I lied to you. I kept parts of myself hidden. When I was a fighter, I made some...unusual connections."

Once more, she swiped at her cheeks, but his words seemed to slowly register, and her hand froze, with her fingers near her left eye.

She was listening. That was good, wasn't it? So he went all in. "Sometimes, it could be one hell of a lot more dangerous *outside* the fight than in it. I was approached by certain...entities to use my connections. To get in close to certain people. To gain intel."

"I..." Her voice trailed away. "What are you trying to tell me right now? That you were some kind of—of what? Undercover agent? Spy?"

"Sweetheart, I'm hardly what you'd call CIA." Though he had crossed paths with plenty of those pricks. Even on his last case, he'd come into close contact with the CIA yet again. They always seemed to be lurking around. "But let's just say I did show an early penchant for undercover work." He inclined his head toward her even as he tried to ignore his giant, aching dick.

Now is not the time to focus on your hard-on. Now is the time to clear the air. She'd either believe him or she wouldn't. And if she didn't, he fully expected Claudia to tell him to kiss her ass.

"That penchant is why Eric Wilde brought me into the fold at Wilde. He'd seen a bit of what I could do. When my life imploded..." Otherwise known as when he'd lost Claudia... "Eric gave me a fresh start." Because Holden had made a whole hell of a lot of enemies, and he'd needed serious help burying some bodies.

A little furrow appeared between her brows. "You were working undercover back then? Seriously? That's what you're telling me?"

Seriously. As crazy as it might be for her to believe. "I was infiltrating a criminal organization." Saying "organization" felt better than just blurting out "mob" to her. Exhaling slowly, he explained, "I was trying to get intel to take them down." Fuck, fuck, fuck. This next part was gonna hurt her a whole lot. "Because that wreck that killed my mom and your dad? Despite what you've been led to believe, it wasn't an accident."

She backed up. Her hip bumped the nightstand. "*What?*" Their picture wobbled.

He should be handling this business with more care. But after finally getting a chance to reveal all, he was just shoving everything out as fast as he could. "It was a hit."

"No, no, it wasn't." An instant denial. "I don't know why you are saying this to me! Our parents were having an affair. They betrayed their families, and they were going to run away together, but instead, my dad drove too fast on a mountain road in North Carolina. He missed a curve, and they *died*. He killed them both." A ragged exhale.

That was one version of the story. The version he'd come to believe was dead wrong. "My mom was a prosecutor, and she was working on a case that got her killed. I don't know if she was sleeping with your dad or not—that was the story everyone was supposed to believe, but some digging I did later put some holes in that theory." *This is gonna hurt so much, and I'm sorry but...* "I think your dad had ties to the mob, baby."

Shock flashed on her face, followed instantly by denial. "My father owned a winery! He did not participate in—"

"Money laundering. And, yes, he *did* have ties. Or at least, all signs pointed to them. When I was initially approached for the undercover work, I saw the file that the Feds had on your father. I also saw that my mother—your dad had gone to a few meetings with her before their fiery crash."

"Because they were having an affair."

No. "Because I think he wanted a deal." But his mother had been on the low rungs of the ladder at her office and she hadn't been able to get

Caldwell Fairmont what he wanted. At least, not in time. "To stop them both, they were eliminated."

"That's bullshit."

He got that the story sounded crazy. But sounding crazy didn't mean it was wrong.

She surged toward him. Jabbed him in the chest with her index finger. "If this is true, why didn't you tell me? I mean, tell me right from the start. Before the engagement, before—"

"Because I wasn't supposed to be falling for you. Because I wasn't supposed to be sleeping with you. Because I was a fighter in over my head and trying to work with Feds who wanted to take down some very bad people, and if I could have gotten real proof—the kind of proof that holds up in court—I would have told you. I would have brought it straight to you and given it to you as a damn wedding present."

"This is insane." She jabbed him again. "I can't believe you are saying—"

"The bad guys found out what I was doing. I walked out of my bachelor party, and they jumped me. Normally, I'm pretty good in a fight."

Her blue eyes narrowed.

"But there was at least seven of them and one of me. They got me in the back of their SUV. Knocked me out. When I woke up, my ass was tied to a chair in some godforsaken cabin. A gun was put in front of my head, and a phone was pushed to my ear. You see, they thought a runaway groom would be easier to explain away. A guy who got cold feet and vanished because he didn't want to give up his playboy lifestyle." Such BS. From the moment he'd met Claudia, there had been no one else for him. "They thought it would take people longer to look for me. *If* anyone looked. You sure as hell wouldn't send out a search party to find a would-be groom who'd ditched you." It had been the perfect setup to eliminate him.

Her lashes flickered. "On the phone...y-you said you weren't making it to the church."

"Yep, I wasn't. I had no idea where the cabin was located, but a gun was jabbing into my forehead, and I was tied up. Definitely not making it to church." He paused. "And I was sorry about that."

She yanked her hand back. "What? I—" Her eyes squeezed shut. "You had bruises when you finally showed up at my place." The words seemed a little dazed.

"Yeah. See...I had to fight my way out. Took a hell of a long time to do the job. First, I had to get out of the ropes. Then, second, I had to knock out the bastards left to guard me. Their boss was coming in. Going to take care of me personally. Apparently, I really pissed him off."

Claudia just stared at him.

"I was in the middle of fighting the assholes who'd been guarding me when the Feds came storming in. They got there before the big boss arrived. Rushing to my rescue. Better late than never, am I right?"

She didn't speak.

He plowed on by saying, "They rushed in, but they must have tipped off the target. He didn't show at the cabin, and the men he'd left? They either died in the shoot-out that happened—"

"A shoot-out?" She paled.

"Or they suddenly got very extended amnesia. They wouldn't turn on him. All I knew was that the man who'd orchestrated everything was still out there, and I'd never been able to ID him." Holden had also been helluva pissed at the Feds for their timing. He remembered the words he'd said to the team right after they'd broken down the door. *What the fuck took you so long? I missed my wedding.* Then he'd spat blood on the floor.

Claudia's hair slid over her shoulder as she shook her head. *"Why* didn't you come to me if this was all true? As soon as you were free, why didn't you find me?"

"I did come to you." He'd been desperate to get to Claudia. "But then I realized I needed to stay the hell away." He'd been tipped off as he stood on her doorstep. Holden remembered the snarling engine that had ripped through the night as the dark car raced down her street. When he'd seen that car, he'd feared that he'd led his enemies straight to her.

And he'd known he needed to back away from Claudia. "There wasn't a choice. I wanted you, but being close to me put a target on your back."

She blinked. "What?"

"He was still out there. If he wanted to hurt me, all he had to do was make you vanish. Let you have an accident like your dad and my mom. I had a vulnerable spot. He knew it. So when you told me to stay away, I realized that was the best thing I could do for you."

Her body trembled. "You're saying that you stayed away...to keep me safe?"

"Didn't think I was that noble, did you?" Not like nobility was a trait most associated with him. But she'd understand now that—

"I didn't think you were that much of a dumbass!" she snapped. "That's what I didn't think—that you were such a giant dumbass."

His mouth hung open. After about ten seconds, Holden realized he should really snap it closed. He did. With an effort.

"Dumbass," she hissed. "That's what that move was. I *loved* you back then. Don't you think I deserved to know that your life had been put in jeopardy? That someone might be hunting you? And if that *someone* had killed my father, didn't you think I had a right to know the truth?"

It wasn't that simple. "The Feds made it clear I couldn't talk to you about the investigation. Talking would jeopardize their case."

"Screw their case!"

She didn't understand. "They had agents who were working undercover. Lives were on the line." He forced his back teeth to unclench so he could speak normally and not just grit words. "It was bigger than me."

Her breath sucked inward. "Bigger than us, you mean."

Nothing is bigger than us. You don't get it. You were in danger. By staying away, I made it look like you didn't matter. If you didn't matter, my enemies wouldn't go after you. Because he just hadn't been sure who he could trust.

He also hadn't missed the way she'd just used the past tense. *I loved you back then.* Another reason he hadn't brought his danger to her door. He'd killed what she felt for him. "You moved on fast."

Her lashes fluttered. "Excuse me?"

"Paris, remember? The vineyard? You flew away and didn't look back so I thought you realized what a mistake we would have been—"

"I never slept with Louis. He and I were friends. Nothing more. So this jealousy bit? Get over yourself already."

It's getting over you that I can't do.

Claudia dragged a shaking hand through her hair. "I don't understand why you are telling me this *now*."

He was making his way to that part, and it wasn't a matter of it being better late than never. It was a matter of her safety. "Got word about six months ago that the Feds thought they'd officially broken the case."

"It took that long?"

Justice could move very slowly, especially when you were dealing with the mob. "The mysterious leader was identified but before he could be arrested and brought to trial, he committed suicide." Holden swallowed. Another tricky part. "You actually went to his funeral."

"Who are you talking about?"

"Eddie Wells. Suspected of drug trafficking, murder, witness tampering, and about fifty other charges that I won't bother to name right now. Of course, you knew him better as Edward

Wellington, the father of your brother's best friend, Seth."

A choked laugh escaped her. "You can't be serious right now. Edward had nothing to do with any murder! No charges have ever been brought against him. I would have heard about something like that."

"The Feds didn't officially charge him. They were working up to that. Just when they were making headway, Eddie took his own life. What was the point in charging a dead man? Especially when the Feds could use what they knew to bring down the others in his circle. Didn't want to alert them, so they moved on to other fish in the sea."

"No. No, I don't believe you. Edward Wellington was my godfather. My dad's best friend. There is no way he'd do anything like this. I *knew* him my entire life."

Yeah, he'd realized that would be a problem. Wellington held all of her trust, even in death. "You asked why I was telling you all of this now. Well, I'm doing it because I can't be sure that the stalker after you isn't somehow tied to me."

Her lips parted.

"It's a possibility I can't overlook." Thus the big reveal of all the dirty parts in his life. "Like I told you before, you're my vulnerable spot. If this is about me, about what I did in the past, then I wanted you aware of just how serious the threat could be."

Her brow crinkled. "You just said yourself that the man behind all of that is dead! Not that I believe Edward did any of those things, but...he's *dead*."

Precious. His lips twisted. "You think Eddie was my only enemy? Try again. I did a lot of work for the Feds. My enemies stretch for miles."

"This is unbelievable."

Yep, she kept going back to that. "The true things usually are." He swung away from her. But before he could advance to the door, she'd grabbed his arm.

"You just said my father was murdered."

He looked down at her hand. So small. Delicate. Fragile. "That's my suspicion. Sorry to say I never found one hundred percent conclusive evidence to prove it."

"That's one hell of a bombshell to drop on me, don't you think?"

"Yes, it is. Here's another one." Holden lifted his stare so that he could chain her with his gaze. "I loved you with all my soul five years ago. If a gun hadn't been pressed to my head, I would have been at the church."

She swallowed.

"If my past is what is threatening you now, I am fucking sorry." There. All revealed. No more secrets. He could finally take a breath and not taste regret. "And, either way—my enemies or yours—I will keep you safe. I won't screw up again." He thought of the stitches in her arm. "You will not be hurt again on my watch. That's a promise. I will not ever break a promise to you again."

"What am I supposed to do with all of this?" Soft. Husky. But with a thread of desperation.

"You're supposed to use it. See if it makes anything click in your mind. Anything about that jackass Eddie or any associates he had. Anything that might have happened with your dad before his death."

"I was a kid when my dad died. I barely remember anything."

Yes, it was only years later that Holden had come into her life. Her mother had cut out and left the country after her dad's death, and her older brother had raised her. Then one day, Holden had gone into her orbit, and his whole world had changed. "Use the info I've given you to make sure that you stay on guard. You need to realize the threats coming at you can be from those already in your inner circle. *They can be coming from people you trust.*" Wasn't that the reason he'd wanted the charade of being a reunited lover with her? Because, sure, plenty of people would know he worked for Wilde. No way would Cooper not have that intel.

But there was a difference between being a bodyguard who'd been hired and being a besotted man who was obsessed with the love of his life. By being her boyfriend, he'd get a pass into her life—and into the lives of her acquaintances—that a mere hired guard would never possess. Being seen as her boyfriend was key to getting into her inner circle—the one that might just be populated by a killer. "You're vulnerable, and we have to eliminate that vulnerability."

Her fingers bit into him. "And we're just going to keep up the ruse of being together again? Keep pretending that we're these desperate, reunited lovers who can't keep our hands off each other?"

"Yes." He was already drinking in her touch. "Unless, of course, you decide you want the real deal."

Shock flashed on her face as she snatched her hand back. Dammit, not like he'd burned her. She didn't have to jerk back so fast. Sighing, he noted, "Guess that's a no."

"Stop toying with me!"

Oh, was that what she thought he was doing? "Never," he vowed.

Her expression tightened.

Holden leaned in closer so he could be very, very clear. "I would never toy with you. I was one hundred percent serious. When it comes to you, that's what I've always been."

"Not anymore," she whispered. "I-I've moved on. You've moved on."

"That what I've done?"

Her gaze searched his. "Haven't you? It's been five years."

And he was an obsessed man. *Not* just playing a role.

But she shook her head. "I'm a case to you now. A job. And maybe some sort of loose end that you want to tie up."

Laughter erupted from him. She'd just gone from being precious to hilarious.

"I don't think anything is particularly funny." Claudia's hands went to her hips.

Right. He should probably stop laughing. But it took him a few moments to regain control. After the fear and rage he'd experienced during her attack, the laughter felt good.

"Holden."

"Ahem. Sorry, but...sweetheart, you are many things to me, but a loose end is not one of them." He should walk out of the bedroom. Remove himself from temptation because he'd already dropped enough bombshells for one night. But... "Have you?" Holden heard himself ask.

"Have I what?"

"Moved on?"

Her lips pressed together even as her thick lashes lowered to veil her eyes.

He wasn't going to hold back from her ever again. "Because I haven't. Probably should have considering that you hate me and you kicked me out of your life."

"Holden—"

"But I think about you all the time. Dream about you. Fantasize about the most fantastic sex I ever had. We sure wrecked some beds, didn't we?"

Pink stained her cheeks. She didn't reply. But, yes, the answer was obvious. They'd wrecked some beds. A lot of them.

"No one else is you," he said because this wasn't just about sex.

Her lashes lifted. Her stark, confused gaze met his.

"No one else could be." He didn't love easily and he didn't love often. She'd marked him, and he'd no doubt carry that mark to his grave. Probably not the best time to share that part. She seemed on edge enough. "Good night, Claudia. If you need me, I'll be the guy with his body halfway hanging off the couch." With a little salute, he turned and headed for the door. He reached for the knob, turned it, and strode slowly out.

He kept hoping she'd say something. Maybe make some passionate declaration about how she hadn't gotten over him, either. But she didn't.

And the door closed softly behind him.

***

Claudia didn't move. Her feet had rooted to the spot, and the rest of her body seemed to have turned to stone. Her mind was swirling as unease slithered through her core.

Her father...murdered?

Holden...kidnapped? Working to break up some kind of crime group?

This was—crazy. Absurd. And yet...

And yet...

Someone was after her. The series of *accidents* seemed far too sinister. And the mugging that night? Her aching arm reminded her it had certainly been no accident. She'd been the intended target.

Because someone was obsessed with her? A dark and dangerous obsession? Or because someone from Holden's past was trying to use her in order to hurt him?

No, no, there is a major problem with the last option. I've been out of Holden's life for years. Why would anyone come after me now? Because, surely, everyone would think Holden had long since moved on from her.

But he said he hasn't.

Her breath whispered out.

He said he hasn't.

And what in the hell was Claudia supposed to do with that knowledge?

CHAPTER SIX

Step Six: Don't bulldoze your way into her life. Use finesse. Charm. Come on too strong, and you'll scare her off and...hell, it's already too late for this step, isn't it? Sonofabitch.

"What in the hell is he doing here?" Cooper Fairmont bounded down the stone steps in front of the house that Holden had always thought more resembled some old school manor than a home. Giant, sweeping windows. Huge white columns along the porch and sides of the structure. At least four chimneys. The first time he'd gone with Claudia inside the place, Holden had been intimidated as hell. But she'd held his hand and smiled at him and everything had been fine.

She wasn't smiling today. A shiver slid over her body as she stared up at her brother. This time, she was the one feeling nerves, and that situation just wasn't going to stand. Holden took her hand. Twined his fingers with hers and, with her brother glaring at him, Holden lifted their joined hands and kissed her knuckles. "Guess what?"

Cooper's face mottled with angry color.

"We're back together," Holden added.

Cooper rushed at him.

"No!" Claudia jerked free of his grip and stepped in front of Holden.

Holden promptly locked his hands around her waist, lifted her up, and positioned her behind him. "Sweetheart, never put yourself in harm's way. Rule one."

"That's my brother! He would never harm me—"

"Not you, Claudia. I wouldn't hurt you," Cooper affirmed. "I'd just hurt this asshole who doesn't need to be anywhere *near* you." He locked his fingers around Holden's shoulder and spun him around. Cooper's fist flew toward Holden's face.

Not like he was just gonna let the guy hit him, so Holden dodged even as he made sure to keep Claudia shielded with his body. "Nice," he mocked. "So gentlemanly and refined. Having a fight on the front lawn. Whatever will the neighbors think?"

A snarl broke from Cooper as he swung again.

Easy to dodge that blow, too. "You have like, zero fighting experience, don't you? Sad. Very sad. I'm almost tempted to let you land a punch just so you can feel better about yourself." He pretended to consider the matter. "Nope. Temptation has passed. I'm just going to swing on my own and—"

Claudia was there. She'd jumped from behind him and put herself in front of Cooper.

Holden's eyes narrowed. "Sweetheart, what did I *just* tell you rule one was? Hmmm?"

"You wouldn't harm me." Her chin lifted.

"Uh, yes, he would!" Cooper snapped. "That's all he does to this family! He *left* you. The jerk doesn't need to be anywhere near you, and he should not be—"

Claudia glanced back at her brother. "I'm giving him a second chance."

Cooper flinched as if he *had* been punched. "The hell you are."

"Yes." A nod. "The hell I am."

Sometimes, the woman just took Holden's breath away.

"After what he did?" Cooper demanded. "No way. *No way.*"

Claudia turned her attention back to Holden. She crooked an eyebrow, and her expression seemed to say...*See, told you he'd have trouble buying it. We should just tell him the truth.*

"I mean, I saw that BS on social media," Cooper plowed on. "Couldn't believe it. Thought it had to be a deep fake or some PR bullshit that was just being cooked up."

Her second eyebrow joined the first before she peered at her brother. "Why would I pull a PR stunt?"

"Because we're getting ready to announce our new wine? You're the PR guru, not me. I mean, you *have* to be working an angle, right? Or else you've just lost your ever-loving mind. Only two options that fit this scene."

No, there was an option number three. *She's in danger, and she needs me.* Instead of saying that, Holden released a long sigh. "Cooper, Cooper, *Cooper.* How did I forget what a total asshat you are?" He took a step toward his target.

Claudia's hand rose, and her palm flattened against Holden's chest. "That's not helping."

He smiled at her. She had a point. "There is no way to help an asshat."

"*Get off the property*." A flat order from Cooper. "Get off or I will throw you off!"

It would be fun to see Cooper try, but Holden was gonna have to save that joy for another date.

"If he's leaving, so am I." Calm, but flat. Claudia's voice didn't waver at all.

Holden tugged her back to his side so they could face her brother together. "We're a package deal."

Cooper's mouth opened. Closed. Opened. "This is my worst nightmare."

Holden nodded. "I thought it might be in your top five. Didn't realize I'd make it all the way to the number one spot. I'm honored, man. Honored."

Cooper's gaze—the same icy blue shade as Claudia's—met his. "I hate you."

Mutual. Because this bastard had been in his way from day one. Always telling Claudia that she should stay away from Holden. But Holden smiled at his nemesis. "That hurts me. Down deep." No, it did not. "Maybe we should go to a couple's counseling session or something? Think that will improve things for us?"

"We are not a couple, so no, it won't improve jack shit."

"Right. Family counseling then." A nod. "That's what we need. Because we will be family, once I can convince Claudia to make things legal with me."

Claudia sucked in a sharp breath.

Whoops. He hadn't told her that he would be bringing up a potential wedding, but, oh well. Marrying Claudia had always been on his to-do list.

"Do not," Cooper warned. "Claudia, you *can't*." His eyes flashed.

"Relax, Coop, things have not progressed that far." Her head turned so she could toss a very firm look Holden's way. "They have *not*."

Not yet, no. But a man could dream. Sometimes, dreams were the only thing that could keep you going. The previous night had been one major pain in the ass for him. He'd hunkered down on his couch—mental note, he seriously needed to invest in a longer and far more comfortable couch—and he'd been highly conscious of Claudia's presence down the small hallway. Sleep had been an impossibility. Needing her? Wanting her? Having her so close?

Hello, torture.

"Thank Christ." A relieved exhale from Cooper. "Fuck him if you want. Get that shit out of your system."

Holden blinked.

"But don't marry him. Revenge fucks are fine. Do whatever." Cooper waved his hand. "Just don't get serious again."

Revenge fuck? Intriguing. He turned from Cooper to focus completely on Claudia. "You want to fuck me for revenge?"

"I—" She broke off.

She didn't deny the possibility.

"At your service," he told her and thought about giving her a little bow. "You name the time and the place, and I am there. Revenge fuck me all night long." He could not wait.

"Such a bastard," Cooper threw out at him. "You see this, right, Claudia? You have to see it. The guy is a total dick."

Her tongue slid over her lower lip. "I see him."

Holden saw her. He'd always seen her. All of her. Always had. Always would.

"I can't believe this!" Cooper was obviously not done raging. Holden had anticipated the reaction, but it was still a pain in his ass.

Holden's hand rose and curled under Claudia's delicate jaw. "Mind if I have a private word with your brother?"

"Oh, I have plenty of words for you!" Cooper huffed. "They don't have to be said in private. They can be said right here and now."

Claudia ignored her brother. After nibbling on her delectable lower lip, she asked, "You think that's a good idea, Holden?"

Talking with Cooper was never a good idea, but he needed to cement the cover and get the guy to stop buzzing around like an angry bee looking for the perfect moment to sting. "It's a genius one," he assured her.

She winced.

Fine. Maybe it wasn't genius, but he still had to take care of the chat. "Get settled in the guest house. I'll come behind you in a few moments so I can get moved in, too."

"*Moved in?*" Not a huff from Cooper. More of a roar. "Are you fucking kidding me right now? Claudia, no. *No.* Don't get taken in by him again!"

Holden leaned forward and brushed his lips over hers. "Trust me," he said. Maybe if he said it enough, she actually would. Had she believed the story he'd told her the night before? Because all of that twisted shit had been true. The FBI. The undercover work. The gun to his forehead on what should have been his wedding day.

She might not get it, but *everything* he'd done since that day had been designed to protect her. Her safety was the only thing that had mattered, so he'd stayed away. Watched from a distance. Been a freaking stalker in his own right. Then, six months ago, he'd got wind of Edward's upcoming arrest—and then heard about the suicide. Edward had taken his own life. The big, bad threat had seemingly been eliminated, and Holden had started strategizing on ways to get back in Claudia's world.

Before he'd been able to put those plans into action, she'd returned to him.

I won't lose her again.

Someone was coming after her. Staying in the shadows wouldn't cut it any longer.

"Get your lips off my sister!"

Deliberately, Holden kissed her again. "Why? She likes them on her."

Her hand brushed over Holden's chest. "You're just antagonizing him." A murmur.

He moved away from her plump lips and put his mouth near her ear. "It brings me joy." But he really did need to clear the air—and do a security analysis of the house. He had a partner due to arrive later that afternoon, and they'd be making sure that any security inadequacies were addressed, immediately. His head lifted, and Holden offered her a smile. "Give us five minutes alone?"

"Don't kill him."

Tempting as the idea was, he'd long since passed up that option. It would upset her, after all. "You have my word."

Shaking her head, she backed away. "I want a fresh shower. And I really need to change the bandage over my stitches."

"Stitches?" Cooper latched onto that word. "Why the hell do you have stitches?"

But Claudia didn't stop walking. Just waved and headed down the stone pathway that would take her to the guest house. Or, as Holden thought of it, mini-mansion number one.

Holden waited until she was inside the guest house—he had a clear view of the guest house's front door—then he turned back toward her brother. The siblings had a lot of similarities. Same hair color. Same eyes. Cooper's features were harder, one hell of a lot rougher. And while Claudia was charming and graceful and elegant—

"How much will it take to get you out of my sister's life for good?" Cooper demanded.

Claudia is charming and graceful and elegant, but her brother is a total jackass. "More money than you've got." He didn't want to have this conversation out in the open so he sauntered past Cooper, headed up the steps, and just let himself into the house as if he owned the place.

Holden heard growling and huffing behind him, so he figured Cooper was doing his best imitation of the big, bad wolf as he stomped inside.

The door slammed—one of the two front doors. Because, of course, massive, arched double-doors made up the entrance to the home. Not bothering to look back, Holden turned to the right and let himself in the library. The library was one of the things he actually liked about the place. Probably because he knew Claudia had spent most of her youth in that room. All the books that lined the shelves? Hers. Not just leather-bound classics. Though, sure, some of those were there. He'd be willing to bet those first editions were worth one hell of a lot, but plenty of current books filled the shelves, too. Thrillers. Romances. True crime novels. He moved toward one shelf and idly ran his index finger down the spine of a book.

"How much?" Cooper's voice deepened. "I know you can be bought. Hell, it didn't even take money to make you leave her before."

No, it had taken a gun to the forehead and the realization that he could get Claudia killed. "You don't have what it takes to make me leave her."

"Why are you toying with her?"

His shoulders stiffened. Claudia had asked him a similar question. Why did anyone think he'd toy with her? "Being with Claudia isn't a game to me. She's not some damn toy that I amuse myself with because I'm bored."

"No? Then what is she?"

He finally turned to face his foe. "Everything."

Cooper laughed.

Holden didn't. "You never thought I was good enough."

"Uh, you weren't. *You left her at the altar*."

"You hated me before that. I get it. Can't say that I ever liked you, either. You're a pompous ass, and you should spend a whole lot less time trying to control your sister's life. Maybe if you got your *own* life and stepped out of hers, you wouldn't be so much of a dick."

A muscle jerked along Cooper's jaw as he strode toward Holden. He stopped when they were about two feet away from each other. "You don't know me. You make assumptions about me, but you know nothing. *I* was the only one there for Claudia when our dad decided it would be a great time to just leave his family behind and die in a reckless accident with his mistress. Our mom basically turned away from the whole world after that. She was mortified by the embarrassment, you see. I don't think she actually cared that he was dead. She found a doc who would give her any pills that she wanted, and she faded away. Even before she flew out of the country, she was *gone* from our lives. And the only time she *did* talk was to rage at us. To focus her fury on me and Claudia because—guess what? Lucky us, we have our father's eyes."

Yes, he knew they did.

"I raised Claudia. I was there when she had no one. I swore to protect her, and I saw trouble coming her way the minute you closed in on her. You were too violent, too hard, and you were going to hurt her. The twisted past you shared was bad enough, getting beyond that would have taken a freaking miracle, and you were no miracle."

"Thanks for noticing. I've often personally felt like I was more hell-sent than a gift from God."

A muscle twitched along Cooper's jaw. "I knew that you had to be working an agenda from day one with Claudia. Meanwhile, all I wanted was to protect her. That's all I have ever wanted."

Okay, so the guy had at least one redeeming quality. "Claudia was mugged last night. The attacker came at her with a knife and sliced her purse off her. His weapon cut her arm, and I took her to the hospital to get stitches."

Cooper's eyes widened. "Mugged?"

"Shouldn't have happened. I should have been closer to her. Should have assessed the danger better."

The furrow between Cooper's brows deepened. "I saw the video of you fighting some guy in a bar—when the hell did the mugging take place? Or—wait, was he the one who mugged her?"

Nope, he would be another Wilde agent. "The mugging occurred shortly after that incident. I was seeing Claudia back to her hotel. As I said, I should have been closer to her. I intend to be very, very close from now on."

"Oh, I see." Understanding flashed in his gaze. "You're using the attack as a way to worm your way back in her life. Playing hero, huh? That really a role you think you can handle?"

"I can try it. Who knows? Maybe it will be fun."

Cooper's jaw tightened.

Okay. Perhaps he should just cut to the chase. "She told me about the accidents."

Cooper didn't change expression. Just kept right on glaring.

So Holden pushed more. "The flat tire in the middle of nowhere, the lock-in at the winery, the fire at her place..."

"You sonofabitch. You *are* playing hero. You're trying to make her think something sinister has been happening and that—what? That she needs big, strong you to keep her safe?"

He flexed a few muscles. "Glad you noticed the strength. I do like to work out."

"You don't take *anything* fucking seriously."

Not true. "I take Claudia seriously. There is nothing in this world I take more seriously than her."

Cooper studied him—glared at him—and studied Holden more.

"You can't use money to get me out of her life, Coop." Deliberately, he used Claudia's nickname for her brother. "You can't use your connections. Can't dig up shit from my past that you try to use as blackmail to get me away from her." All techniques that Cooper had used in the past. They'd failed then. They'd fail now. "She's mine, and I will fight for her."

"You'll disappear again." Cooper crossed his arms over his chest. "Might take a little while, but one day, Claudia will look up, and you won't be there."

Only if I'm dead in a grave. "You didn't believe her when she came to you about all the dangerous incidents that have been happening?"

"The accidents? Sure, I believe they happened. I don't get what you mean—"

"The fact that you call them accidents is precisely what I mean."

"Oh. Right." Mocking laughter. "You're a Wilde agent, now, aren't you? Not some guy who just randomly beats the shit out of someone else for profit and entertainment value any longer."

"Try stepping into a bout and see if you really think it's just about entertainment," he dared.

But Cooper shook his head. "I get what you're doing. Nice try, by the way. I'll give you points for creativity. Playing hero by acting like you're some super agent who can swoop in and save her? Certainly an interesting technique. Only she doesn't need saving. What happened to her was a series of *accidents*. You think I didn't have things investigated? You think I didn't talk to the fire inspector at her house? A candle was left burning. Claudia always loves her candles. She lights them while she reads, and she just forgot to put the candle out before she went to bed. She had some old boxes downstairs—shit of yours that she'd packed up—and the fire spread fast because it hit them."

Shit of mine? Claudia hadn't told him that his belongings had burned. He hadn't even realized she still had things that belonged to him.

Except for his fucking heart, of course. She had that.

Moving on. Because he couldn't be sidetracked at the moment. "I want to read the report from the fire inspector."

"Good for you. Go find the fire inspector and ask him about it." Cooper's head shook. "I don't buy that you seriously think something sinister is happening—"

"She was mugged last night. Didn't you hear me when I told you that?"

"Yes, I heard you, and, okay, that's bad but—"

"The attacker was told to target her, specifically."

Cooper took a surprised step back.

Oh, good. Now do I have your attention? "You should be more concerned about everything that's been happening in her life, but you're not, and that's weird to me. In fact, it's the whole reason I wanted us to have this little one-on-one chat without Claudia present. Because, see, I know she loves you."

Cooper's hands fell to his sides.

"As much as you are a dick, it's not like you to ignore danger threatening her. So the fact that you're not worried makes me wonder...*just what the hell secrets are you keeping?*"

Cooper's expression turned hard and unyielding. "I'm not keeping any secrets. Claudia knows everything about me."

"Does she? Because I'm not so sure, and this is your warning that I *will* be finding out all your dark and dirty truths. Like you so astutely noted before, I'm working with Wilde now. Got plenty of people there who love digging up intel. I suspect that you might have some big enemies out there. And if one of those enemies is coming after Claudia—"

"No, that is *not* what is happening! She's had some bad luck. She's not being targeted. The idea is preposterous!"

Tell that line to someone who wasn't kidnapped on his wedding day. "I am giving you the option to do things the easy way. Cooperate with me now."

"Or what?"

"Or I won't be so *nice* to you anymore."

More mocking laughter rang from Cooper. "I am shaking in my shoes."

Holden stepped toward him. "You should be because I don't give a damn about you. I would have destroyed you years ago, had your whole precious world tumbling around your ears, but I held back for Claudia's sake. *I* know where all the bodies are buried. I know how to destroy your house of cards."

Cooper's laughter faded. "You're threatening me."

"Now you get it." The whole reason he'd wanted to be alone with him. So Claudia wouldn't see...*hell, what? Who I really am?* "Fuck with me, keep getting in my way, and I will take away everything you value in this world. Cooperate with me, help me find out why some jackass is messing with *my* Claudia, and I'll leave you to your kingdom of lies."

Cooper swallowed. His Adam's apple bobbed. "You're bluffing."

"I don't bluff."

"She's not yours."

"Sure, she is. She's been mine from the first moment I saw her. You want to know why I'm back in her world? It's simple. Because no one hurts what's mine."

"Except you, huh? You get to hurt her."

Not ever again. He would make certain no one else hurt her, either. "I found out about the accidents. There aren't going to be more. No one will stand between the two of us." His gaze swept over Cooper. "If you try, I'll just run your ass over."

Cooper's lips thinned.

"Are we clear?" Holden asked with a smile. Probably the kind of smile a shark sent to his prey right before he took a big bite.

Cooper's head moved in a jerky nod.

"Fantastic." Holden slapped his hand on Cooper's shoulder. "I think we're on the way to being best friends."

"No, we're not."

"Right. We're not." *But I am on the way to finding out what the hell is happening in Claudia's life.*

***

She'd showered. Applied a fresh bandage. Changed. And realized that Holden's little chat with her brother had gone far, far longer than five minutes.

A pissing match. One she had not cared to witness. If Holden and Cooper wanted to be assholes, they could have that fun without her.

But as she strode past her bed, her phone jingled. Claudia paused at the sound of the text, then craned her head to look over at the phone.

She didn't recognize the number, but she could just see the first few words of the text...

He can't protect...

Frowning, she moved closer to the bed. Her hand reached out and picked up the phone. She tapped the screen so she could read everything, and she realized a photo had accompanied the text. A photo of her and Holden. She was clutching her arm as it bled, and Holden loomed over her.

A shiver slid over Claudia's body. The photo had been taken at her mugging scene. Vaguely, she remembered someone holding up a phone, but she hadn't seen the person's face. As dread twisted into a heavy ball in her stomach, Claudia read the message one more time...

He can't protect you from me. No one can. See you soon.

CHAPTER SEVEN

Step Seven: Undercover cases require a top-notch acting ability. You can play a dozen different roles depending on the situation. With Claudia? I'll be the love-obsessed fool. I can nail that role in my sleep.

"He can't take his eyes off you," Mercedes Shay said as she lifted her wine glass and took a light sip. "I swear, I think he's undressing you with his gaze right now. And that is just...*hot*."

The building was too hot, that was the problem. Too many people were inside the winery's large lobby as they milled and gossiped and celebrated. It was launch day for the family's new wine, the one for which she had painstakingly crafted an advertising and promotional plan. The night was supposed to be a perfect success. No mistakes at all. She'd invested way too much money for mistakes.

The Fairmont brand was respected in the industry, yes. The family business had been operating for a very long time. But she'd wanted to come out with something fun and trendy, and Fairmont's Folly had been born. The full-bodied chardonnay had flavors that hinted at apple and teased a delicious note of vanilla. Innocent at first, designed to fool, but with a kick that would leave you wanting more.

"He's coming this way," her friend added in a rushed whisper. "Look at that intent. That heat. That focus. That...oh, damn, just have sex with him right now, why don't you? Right *now*."

Mercedes always tended to say exactly what she thought, and she clearly thought Holden was hotness personified. Granted, he looked extremely attractive in his elegantly cut suit. He should have appeared polished and perfect in the attire, but his power couldn't be contained. The man kind of oozed a raw sensuality.

One Claudia had been doing her best to ignore for the last week and a half. *A week and a half.* He'd been living in her guest house—in the second bedroom—for ten excruciating days. Each day had just seemed to amplify the fierce tension between them.

In public, he played the devoted lover.

In private, he didn't touch her.

And she was going out of her mind because her desire for him? *Growing and growing.*

"I get why you took him back." Mercedes enjoyed another delicate sip. "I would have, too. Absolutely. A woman has to do what a woman has to do."

Mercedes hadn't been around for the infamous breakup—one of the reasons why Claudia loved spending time with the other woman. Mercedes had never pitied her. Never asked awkward questions. She just accepted Claudia as she was. She let the past die.

It's not dead. It's stalking toward us and, yes, Mercedes is right. Holden does look like he's undressing me with his gaze.

But all of that heat? All of that passionate promise? Just for show. As soon as they were alone behind closed doors, it was hands-off time with Holden.

Annoying.

People moved out of Holden's way when he approached Claudia. Not that he had to ask them to move. They just did. When you saw a train barreling toward you, you got off the track.

The train came for her, and he flashed his warm, sexy smile. "Your wine is a hit, sweetheart." He leaned toward her. His lips brushed over her cheek. A simple caress, but it still sent fire pouring through her veins.

Temptation. Longing. She'd been on a tight rope for days. Every pretend caress, every fake and tender touch just drove her closer to the edge. Tension sizzled between them. She knew exactly what he was doing.

Seducing me?

Okay, fine, Claudia might hope that was what he was doing.

He eased back and turned toward Mercedes. "I don't think we've met." He held out his hand to her. "Holden Blackwell."

"Mercedes Shay." Her hand extended, her long, red nails carefully polished. Her fingers curled with his. "Didn't think you'd live up to the hype."

"The hype?" Holden repeated with a questioning lift of his dark brows.

"Um, yes. The hype about the gorgeous, brooding ex. The one who came back for a second chance." Her grip tightened on him as she leaned forward. "The one who had *better* not hurt my friend again or else I will kick you in the dick so hard, you'll see stars for a week."

He blinked.

Mercedes pulled her hand away. "Pleasure to meet you. But I think I need to go mix and mingle with some of our distributors." With a dip of her head, she sashayed away.

Holden had a bemused expression on his face. That happened a lot when people met Mercedes. She was tiny, but she could pack a powerful punch. "She wasn't lying about the kick," Claudia felt duty-bound to admit. "Mercedes has a second-degree black belt in Tae Kwon Do."

"Of course, she does." He turned his attention to Claudia. "I'm glad you have a loyal friend, and I will endeavor not to give her cause to kick me in the dick."

"She's my friend *and* our VP of sales. We hit it off from the minute she joined the company." They'd been lucky to get Mercedes. *I've been lucky to have her in my life.*

"A lot of people are here tonight." His gaze swept the crowd. No doubt, searching for some threat. He always seemed to be on his guard.

Unlike many of the people at the winery, Holden did not have a glass of wine in his hand. Neither did she. They stood in silence a moment, and even that moment felt too uncomfortable because she was highly aware of everything about him. His masculine scent, the power of his body, the way the suit made him look strikingly, dangerously handsome.

"How's the arm?" Holden asked, all casual-like.

"Fine." Her voice emerged sounding far too much like a croak. After taking in a deep, fortifying breath, Claudia tried again. "The stitches were removed earlier today. Got a small scar, it's red now, but the doctor said it would fade with time."

"So he gave you the all clear?"

Confused, her head swung toward him. "The all clear for what?"

A shrug of one shoulder. "To resume normal activities?"

What did he mean by—laughter. It slid out of her on a warm wave. "I was hardly told *not* to pursue normal activities. And by normal activities, I'm thinking you mean sex."

He didn't smile. "I do mean sex."

Her laughter trailed off in a rather awkward manner because there was so much intensity in his green stare. "I-I wasn't ever told not to have sex." Was that why he'd been holding back? No, couldn't be. When they'd been at his place in Atlanta, he'd—

"I get rough with you. Uncontrolled. Fucking frenzied."

Her gaze darted around the sprawling lobby. Was anyone close enough to have overheard him? She edged nearer to Holden. "We don't need to talk about this now."

"I was afraid that I might hurt you. I wanted you to heal."

Fantastic. Obviously, they should address an important point. Because someone was getting way ahead of himself. "I don't remember inviting you to my bed, and I am sure I would recall that act."

His gaze cut over her shoulder, and his eyes narrowed. Then his hand dipped under her chin as his stare returned to her. His head lowered to hers, and his mouth pressed lightly to her lips.

For show. Someone must be behind me. He's kissing me for the cover we still have in place.

His mouth lifted.

Such a teasing, brief kiss. That was the way most of his public kisses were. A press of the lips. Not even a little hint of his tongue.

I want his tongue. I want him tasting me. I want him kissing me like nothing else in the world matters. A little loss of control wouldn't be such a bad thing.

And what was wrong with her? This was a launch party. People were everywhere. Not like she was going to run off with Holden into the nearest tasting room and...

Have a revenge fuck?

She blew out a long, slow breath. Then she turned her head to look over her shoulder. Who had captured his attention before?

No one was there. The door to the nearby VIP tasting room remained closed. Confused, she glanced back at Holden. "Why did you kiss me?"

"Because I'm supposed to be completely obsessed with you. I need to kiss you. I need to stay close to you." His head cocked to the right.

"Honestly, I think we've been playing things a bit too restrained."

Oh, he thought that, did he? Since when?

"We need to kick things up a notch." His hand lowered and caught her wrist. "Come with me."

"But—"

He tugged her toward the VIP tasting room. The other tasting rooms were open to the public tonight, but this one—this one remained closed, the door locked. But Holden surprised her when he pulled out a key from his pocket to unlock the door. When had he lifted that key? She didn't get a chance to ask because he was already swinging her inside and pulling her into his arms.

The door slammed shut right before his mouth came down to hers and—

Her hands pushed into his chest before he could kiss her. "The door is closed. No one can see anything. You can stop the charade."

He froze. His mouth hovered over hers. Probably just an inch or so away. Close enough that she swore she could taste him.

Nope. You can't. Trying to keep her voice crisp, Claudia added, "Everyone is going to think we came in here to have sex."

He shrugged, utterly unconcerned. "Maybe."

"You mean probably." The image of them having sex in this room popped into her head. She could imagine him lifting her up onto the nearby table, moving between her legs as he shoved the skirt of her dress higher and higher—*Stop*. She slammed the mental door shut on those images. "What's happening with the investigation?"

Claudia sidled away from him. Some nice, safe space was clearly needed.

He watched her.

Still looks like he is undressing me with his gaze.

She fanned herself because it just felt hot in the tasting room. "Did the mugger ever talk to the cops?"

"Yeah, about him..." His hand shoved through his hair, making the already mussed style seem even—damn it all—sexier. "He vanished."

Her mouth wanted to hit the floor. "What?"

"Got out on bail and vanished in the wind. I found out this morning that he'd pulled a Houdini."

That was hardly the news she wanted to hear. "What about the intimate photos that you turned over to your team at Wilde?" The photos that made her skin flush with embarrassment because she hated the idea of anyone else seeing those images. "Did they learn anything about them?"

The faint lines near his mouth deepened. "Not much to share so far."

Wonderful. "And the text I got when we arrived back here?"

His expression told her there had been no news on that score, either.

"I see." She put her hands behind her back. "So we don't know anything else, and it's been ten days." Ten days when there had been no other accidents, so that was something. Wasn't it? "I can't...I can't keep using your services endlessly." That wasn't an option. She technically hadn't gotten a bill from Wilde, but with so much time passing, the fees were going to be insane. "I think we have to stop this."

"Stop?" He took a step toward her.

"I don't know what I expected." She'd been panicked. Scared. *And I ran to him.* Even after everything that had happened, Claudia had gone to Holden for protection. "I didn't realize you'd have to just give up your life to play undercover operative with me." She shook her head. "That's asking too much."

"I take undercover cases all the time. I knew exactly what I was getting myself into." A pause. "But did *you*?"

She licked her lips. "I've been keeping up my end of the deal. Letting people think we're reunited lovers and not that this-this relationship is about the attacks."

"You don't want me close." He took another step toward her. Moving in *closer*.

The tasting room felt even smaller.

Hotter.

And it wasn't a little room. There were two levels in the VIP space. Granted, the second level was smaller, lined with wine bottles, but the first floor had plenty of seating. A bar. A giant table in the middle of the cavernous space. And above that table? A high, sweeping chandelier, the glittering centerpiece of the tasting room.

"You don't want me close," he said again, "but close is where I have to be in order to protect you."

"There haven't been any other incidents." Maybe her stalker had moved on. Given up.

"You mean other than the mugging and the threatening text? The text that promised the bastard was coming for you."

Fine. He had a point. "Ten days have passed. How long are you supposed to keep acting like my lover?"

He was right in front of her again. "As long as it takes."

"That is not a real answer."

"I'm not leaving while you're in danger." His gaze dropped to her mouth. Lingered.

Her heart raced a little faster. "Did you find out if this was...about your past?"

"I've reached out to my contacts at the FBI. No red flags are waving."

She felt like there were some red flags waving between them right then.

"I want you."

His low, rumbling words had her whole body stiffening. "No one is here. You don't have to pretend."

His head moved in a slow, negative shake. "We both know I'm not pretending. I've been holding back because I didn't want to hurt your arm."

"Just a few stitches. Not a big deal." She swallowed. Her throat felt terribly dry.

"I see when you watch me, Claudia."

Oh, no.

"I've caught your eyes on me. You think I don't see the need in your gaze? I do. The desire is always there between us. The attraction that simmers just below the surface. When things get hot enough, it's going to explode."

She knew he was right. She'd been getting hotter and hotter with every day that passed. "It's not my fault you walk around in your boxers at night." Showing off his mouth-watering abs.

A slow smile spread over his face. "Like what you see?"

Too much.

"Because the revenge fuck is on the table," he murmured. "Anytime you want. Just say the word." His gaze cut to the side. To where a large, square table waited. "Literally, it can be on the table."

Her breath stuttered out. "There are a hundred people on the other side of that door." She pointed to the door they'd just entered.

He nodded. "And there are two people right here. Come on, Claudia. I know you. I see you. You don't want to be proper and controlled. You want me giving you an orgasm that makes you scream *while* they are all out there. You want to forget them and fuck hard."

When they'd been together in the past, she had thrown caution to the wind. Over and over, she'd just let go. Given in to a need that had just grown more and more powerful. And if she did it again, if she gave in, what would happen this time?

Revenge fuck. "I don't want a revenge fuck."

His chin lifted. "Fair enough." He turned for the closed door.

"Because I don't want revenge," Claudia added quietly. "That's not what I've ever wanted." Wanting revenge didn't do anything but twist you up on the inside. Why waste time and energy on all that hate and fury? After a while, it just left you exhausted. Or as twisted as your enemy.

Holden is not my enemy. He was the one man who had always made her feel safe. Wasn't *that* the real reason she'd gone to him without hesitation when the accidents had plagued her? Because something about him had always made her feel safe. Regardless of their feelings for each other, regardless of what went on between them, he'd had the ability to make her feel like he would move heaven and hell to keep threats away from her. "When it comes to you, I've never wanted revenge."

His shoulders stiffened. His body swung back around toward her.

"I'm not going to punish you forever. What's the point in that? And if what you've told me is true...about the things that happened to you—"

"They *are* true."

That was what she feared. Nightmares had slipped into her mind. Holden, with a gun to his head. Calling her on the phone. Being held captive. *And I never knew.* "Then I'm the one who is sorry."

His head whipped in a hard, negative shake. "The hell you are. *Never* say that to me."

"I didn't know. Maybe I missed something in your voice, a clue that would have told me what was happening. Maybe I missed danger around us and—"

"No!" He bounded toward her. Scooped her into his arms. Carried her to the table and put her down on the hard, wooden surface. The chandelier gleamed overhead, and the light hit the tear drop crystals that hung from its edges. Gleaming wood filled the walls of the tasting room and slid up to the ceiling.

There were plenty of other tasting rooms at the winery. But this was a private room. VIP access. No one else should be coming in there. They were alone. And she liked it that way.

Her hands curled over Holden's shoulders.

He gazed into her eyes with a blazing green stare. "Nothing that happened is on you. Nothing. Don't feel guilty for even a single second, understand?"

Kind of hard to do. The man she'd loved had been tortured and nearly killed, and she'd never suspected a thing. "I wish I had helped you."

"You helped me more than you will ever know." He leaned over her. Took her mouth. This time, it wasn't some pretend kiss. Not a careful peck for anyone watching. Not one that lasted only a moment and was gone, leaving her aching for the real thing.

No, this was so much different. His mouth was open. So was hers. His tongue slid inside her mouth, and Claudia couldn't stop the moan that rumbled from her. His taste intoxicated her better than any wine could. He stroked her. He seduced her. He kissed her with a slow, deliberate need and desire that had her whole body tensing even as her nails bit into him.

Holden had always been an incredible kisser. He could seduce just with his lips and tongue. Could make her want everything.

With him, she *always* wanted everything.

"I've missed you," he admitted against her mouth.

She could have told him the same thing, but he was kissing her again. Not so tender this time. Deeper. Harder. With a possessive edge that she couldn't deny. His hand slid to her thigh. Shoved her dress up even higher. Higher. His callused fingertips trailed along the sensitive skin of her inner thigh, and then he was teasing her with a caress right over her panties.

"Silk." He kissed a path down her neck.

Her head tipped back to give him better access, and the chandelier shone brightly as she locked her eyes on it. The tear drops seemed to dance and sway above her.

His fingers edged under her panties.

"You are so hot." Another kiss on her neck. A light, sensual lick. "And getting wet for me."

Her breath shuddered out. They should *not* be doing this here. Had he locked the door when they came inside? She didn't remember him locking it but...oh, jeez, his fingers felt *good*. Her body trembled. She should tell him to stop, but nothing had felt this good in a very, very long time.

His fingers stroked her clit.

"Easy," he soothed. "Are my hands too rough? You feel so soft, and I should be far, far more careful."

No, his hands hadn't been rough. Well, maybe the calluses on his fingers were a little hard, but she liked that slight roughness. She'd jerked because of the surge of pure lust that had lanced her. Before she could explain, he'd moved back. "Holden!"

"I'll use something other than my hands."

He snagged the panties. Pulled them. She heard the faint tear of the fabric, and her eyes widened.

"I swear, I'll get you another pair." He pushed her back more on the table. Spread her out. She was flat on the table, with her legs dangling over the edge, and this should *not* be happening.

"Tasting room, right?" he said. "Then I just have to get a taste."

He put his mouth on her. She would have surged right off that table if he hadn't been holding down her hips with his strong grip. His tongue and lips didn't hesitantly stroke her. He came at her like a man starving, and it was amazing. He licked and licked and her whole body fought his grip as she tried to surge toward his mouth even more.

Her gaze flew from the chandelier to him. His dark head was bent over her, and his mouth—his mouth—

Her hands reached out to touch him just as the climax slammed through her. A climax so intense and sudden that it seemed to blast through her whole body on a sharp explosion of pleasure. Every nerve and cell electrified. Her body tensed and shuddered even as her eyes squeezed closed. He kept licking her. Drawing out the pleasure and making her *crazy* because it was too good. Too powerful. She was getting swept away by him, and that was dangerous. The way he made her feel was so, so good, but too dangerous. Addictive and consuming.

Her eyes slowly opened. She stared straight up at the tear drops on the chandelier and they swirled and rolled and...

Wait. *Were* they actually swirling? Why the hell would they be swirling? Her heart thundered in her ears. "Holden?" Her breath stuttered. Those drops were definitely moving above her. Not her imagination at all. "*Holden!*" Her gaze flew to him.

His head lifted. His expression was rock hard. Brutal with lust. Need. But... "What?" he demanded. "Did I hurt you? What happened?"

"The chandelier!" She struggled to sit up because she was directly under the chandelier. "It's—"

Claudia didn't get to say the rest. His stare whipped toward the chandelier. She saw alarm flash on his face, then he grabbed her. He hauled her against him, and she automatically locked her arms and legs around him. Holden spun with her cradled against him, and as he whipped her around, she looked over his shoulder, back at the table she'd *just* been on, and the chandelier rushed toward it in a sickening blur.

A scream broke from her even as Holden leapt away from the table. The chandelier crashed into the wood, shattering the tear drops and sending chunks of the crystals flying.

CHAPTER EIGHT

Step Eight: Keep your control. Threats are everywhere, and you have to be on guard. Her safety comes first. Got it? So keep your dick in your pants and do the job.

The door to the VIP tasting room burst open. "What in the hell is happening in here?" Cooper roared.

Holden didn't spare him a glance. He'd hit the floor when the chandelier shattered, doing his best to cover Claudia with his body. She was trapped beneath him, and he lifted up slowly, worry and fear knotting inside of him. "Baby?"

She blinked dazedly. "That chandelier almost landed on us."

That chandelier could have killed you.

"I saw it swaying. I-I didn't even realize—"

"Are you hurt?" Holden cut through her stunned words to ask.

"No. I don't think I am."

That wasn't a good enough answer. He needed to check her whole body.

"Why did the chandelier fall?" Cooper demanded. Glass crunched—probably those broken chunks from the chandelier—as Cooper made his way inside the tasting room. "The thing is brand new! Cost a fortune. I had a crew install it not two weeks ago!"

Then they'd done a piss-poor job on the installation. Or...

Someone made it fall. Holden would be finding out exactly what had happened. First, though...

He was crouched between Claudia's legs, a position he normally would adore, but the situation was too volatile. He eased back a little more and swept his gaze over her.

"You're bleeding," she told him, paling a little, but she still reached up to touch his neck.

She wasn't bleeding, thank Christ, and he didn't care if he had a few cuts. Her safety was what mattered. He took her hands and lifted Claudia so that she was on her feet. Her dress slid down, covering her sensual legs. Slowly, they turned to look at the wreckage together.

Sonofabitch. The chandelier had been huge, and its twisted base had slammed into the middle of the table. The chandelier had to weigh at least fifty pounds, maybe more, and if that thing had careened into Claudia while she'd been on that table...

It could have killed her. That thought kept rushing through his mind.

If it hadn't killed her, at the very least, her delicate skin would have been ripped to shreds by all the glass.

There was a loud rumble of voices from the doorway. His head whipped to the side, and he saw the fancy-dressed guests crowding close. Their eyes were huge as they strained to take in the scene. "You need to keep them out of here," he snapped to Cooper. "This is a crime scene."

"What?" More glass—or crystal, whatever the hell it was—crunched beneath Cooper's shoes as he hurried for Claudia. "Since when?"

Holden kept one hand curled around Claudia's wrist. No way was she getting away from him. Pulling his gaze away from the crowd, he glanced upward. The second floor was small, stocked with bottles of wine. Shelves full of wine, probably designed specifically for some expensive, esthetic look. The second floor seemed completely deserted, just as it had appeared when Holden and Claudia first entered the tasting room. But appearances could be deceiving. Jaw locking, he brought his attention back to Cooper. The guy wanted to know when the place had become a crime scene? Easy. "Since that chandelier almost killed your sister. She was right beneath it when the thing came plunging down."

"Fuck," Cooper breathed. He ran a shaking hand through his hair.

"Exactly," Holden said. "So get those people *back*." He caught sight of black silk on the floor. Claudia's panties. Holden scooped them up and shoved them into his pocket, but he was aware of Cooper watching every movement.

"Fuck," Cooper said again. "Fuck *you*."

***

"Looks like an accident." The cop on scene surveyed the destruction with a critical eye. "Glad no one was hurt, and I'd sure recommend that you have an immediate talk with your installation crew. Can't play around with things like this."

Holden squeezed the bridge of his nose and counted to ten. "Officer Gains," he began.

"Yep?"

"A woman could have *died* tonight, and all you're doing is looking at the scene and just instantly calling it an accident."

"What else would it be?" Officer Zachary Gains appeared to be in his mid-thirties. Fit, average height, with a slightly receding hairline. When he'd arrived, his manner had been no-nonsense, and Holden had experienced a vague hope that he might get an actual investigation.

But that didn't seem to be happening.

"Why would you think it *wasn't* an accident?" Gains wanted to know.

"Uh, because the victim was the same woman who was hunted inside this very winery not too long ago? You were called out then, too, remember?" Holden had seen the man's name in the files Wilde had compiled.

Gains looked back over his shoulder. Claudia was giving a statement to his partner, a woman with short, black hair, and a trim, athletic build. "I remember her getting locked in," he allowed. "Sure, something like that would give plenty of people a scare, but there was no foul play with that situation." He scratched his chin. "Don't see why you think it's happening now, either. An accident is an accident."

A dull throbbing started behind Holden's left temple. *Accident, my ass.*

"You got some blood on your neck," Gains pointed out. "Did anyone tell you that?"

The blood had long since dried, and it was the least of his concerns. "She's had a series of *incidents* in her life lately. Dangerous incidents. How many have to happen before the cops start investigating?" Shit. No wonder Claudia had come to him. Everyone else just took the attacks on her life as pure random chance.

It's not random. They are not accidents. And he wasn't just going to overlook anything.

"Uh, excuse me, officer." A man in a dark gray suit stepped forward. His eyes darted between Holden and Gains. "I'm Reese Rawlins, and I'm in charge of day-to-day operations here at the winery. I don't know exactly what happened, but you can rest assured I will be having my maintenance team get to the bottom of this situation." His gaze rose to the ceiling. His eyes narrowed. "Fixture looks broken up there. Thing must have detached from the ceiling mount. Dammit, that *should* have been secured."

"So why wasn't it?" Holden asked flatly.

Reese's dark gaze slid to him. "Like I said, I'll be finding out. Sometimes, screw collars that attach the chandelier to the mount can break, but you don't usually see that on a new model. Hell, you don't usually see a chandelier falling like this at all. This kind of thing happens in movies, but, thankfully, not a whole lot in real life." Exhaling, he looked over at Claudia as she continued speaking with the female officer. "Just glad she's all right," he said, voice soft.

His stare lingered on Claudia. Lingered a bit too long and with too much intent.

So Holden moved to stand between the man and Claudia. "Hi."

Reese blinked. "What were you and Claudia even doing in here? The VIP room isn't open to the public tonight."

"Claudia isn't the public." He was conscious of Gains silently watching them. "She's the co-owner. She wanted a moment away from the crowd, so we stepped in here. The next thing I knew, the chandelier is coming right at us."

"Glad she wasn't hurt," Reese said, focusing on that point once more.

I'm damn glad, too.

"You've got some blood on you," Reese noted, motioning with his hand. "Better not let Claudia see that. She gets light-headed when someone is bleeding around her." He sidestepped away from Holden and made his way over to Claudia. His hand reached out and curled around her shoulder. Claudia turned to him, with a smile spreading over her face.

"Ahem."

Holden realized he was glaring. He turned his head back to the cop.

"Seems like we might be dealing with a faulty setup here." Gains put his hands on his hips. "But I'll still ask some questions. Poke around. Because I really don't like the fact that your girlfriend has been the target of two incidents here recently."

It's a whole lot more than two.

"I get the feeling you'll be digging, too."

Hell, yes, he would be.

"And if you learn something, you'll let me know, yes?" Gains prompted.

"Yes."

Gains started to walk away. He stopped. "Saw you fight once. You and Breakaway Brock James. You were vicious. Never seen a fighter like you before."

Holden inclined his head. "Thanks." He considered the term "vicious" to be a high compliment.

"What made you leave the fight scene? Why'd you walk away?"

Once more, his gaze darted to Claudia. That prick Reese still had his hand on her shoulder. Just how long was the comforting touch supposed to last? "Some things were more important than the fights. Figured it was time for a life change."

"Too bad. Really thought you were the best out there. Unbeatable, you know? No one ever took you down."

Not true. He'd been taken down hard, by a woman who stood at five-foot-four inches tall and seemed to be built of delicacy and grace. Her head turned, and her eyes met his. There were shadows beneath her eyes, shadows that hadn't been there before. *Before* a chandelier came barreling toward her.

"Can you tell me exactly where you were standing when you realized the chandelier was falling?" Gains asked. "Did it make any noise to alert you? How did you know it was coming down?"

I was between Claudia's legs with my mouth on the sweetest paradise. She called my name, and I heard fear when there should have only been pleasure. Squaring his shoulders, Holden directed his attention on the cop. "We were standing right beside the table. She happened to look up, and Claudia yelled. When I followed her gaze, I saw the thing swaying and shaking, and I jerked her into my arms and out of the way. The chandelier slammed into the table a few seconds later."

"Weird." Gains rocked back on his heels. "Of all the times for the chandelier to fall, it had to be when you were right there."

When Claudia had been right beneath it. *I think the timing was deliberate.* But if the timing was deliberate, that meant one thing...

Someone was watching us.

"Gonna poke around a bit." Gains twisted his lips. "And I do take my job seriously, just so you know. I looked around last time. I examined everything. I'll do that this time, too. But if evidence isn't here, it's just not here." He marched away.

While Holden wanted to take that opportunity to march *to* Claudia, he instead made his way up the stairs and to the second level of the VIP tasting room. His hand trailed over the wooden banister. Most of the guests had left. The big PR night had certainly ended with a bang.

When he reached the second level, he saw Cooper standing near the top of a glass guardrail. Cooper's gaze was on the activity below him. He acted as if he was not even aware of Holden.

Nice try.

"Where was my sister when the chandelier fell?" Cooper quietly asked him.

Holden moved to stand at his side. A clear glass guardrail formed a big square on the second level. The glass gave the area an elegant look. But the glass would have made hiding difficult for anyone who might have been up there, watching.

Difficult, but not impossible. Because Holden had certainly been distracted, and he *could* have missed the bastard.

"Where was my sister?" Cooper's voice was still quiet, but with a definite edge underscoring each word.

He'd lied to the cop. Holden decided to give Cooper the truth. The man needed to wake up to the threat facing Claudia. "She was on the table."

Cooper's jaw hardened. "You were fucking her?"

"Not really your business. And you should watch the tone." He put his hands on the top of the guardrail. The very top wasn't made of glass. It was wood. Painted dark. "No one came out of this room after the chandelier fell." He looked across the area, saw the walls full of wine. "There another exit up here that I don't know about?"

"Do you see an exit?"

"I see you being a dick and not actually answering my question." Which bothered him. "*Is* there another way for someone to get out from this level?"

Cooper retreated from the railing. His head moved in a jerky nod as he spun and took a few, quick steps toward yet another rack of wine. As

Holden watched, Cooper reached out and slid his hand beneath one of the bottles of wine.

Holden heard a faint snick.

The whole section opened about two inches—because it was a door. A door that led to a staircase.

"Goes back downstairs," Cooper said.

Holden's teeth snapped together. "I asked for full schematics of the winery." Only he hadn't gotten those schematics yet.

"Yeah, okay, you did, and Reese is in the process of getting that stuff for you—you asked like three days ago and he's been working to—wait!"

Holden didn't wait. He bounded down the stairs. He could hear Cooper cursing behind him. A door waited below, and as soon as Holden reached the door, he threw it open and stepped inside...an office.

A familiar office. One he'd damn well been in before.

"My office," Cooper groused from behind him. "And my office was locked during the event tonight. No one got inside, and I certainly didn't rush upstairs in order to send a chandelier swinging down on my sister."

Enough of this shit.

Holden whirled toward him. He grabbed Cooper and shoved him back against the nearest wall. In seconds, he had the asshole trapped as Holden's forearm slammed into Cooper's throat.

"What..." A strangled gasp. "You...doing?"

"I'm losing my patience, that's what I'm doing. I asked for schematics. I should've had them immediately. You stonewalled me."

Cooper tried to pry away Holden's arm. A pathetic try.

Holden leaned in even closer to him. "You had better not be involved."

Cooper's eyes widened.

"Because if you've been trying to hurt her, I will kill you."

"Holden!" Claudia's shocked cry came from the open doorway—the doorway that led to the hidden staircase. From inside Cooper's office, the staircase had been cloaked behind a bookcase.

Hell, Claudia had followed them down.

And she'd just heard him threaten to kill her brother. An absolute perfect ending to his night.

CHAPTER NINE

Step Nine: Get her to choose you. Right. Like that will happen. You're the devil. She's the angel. The only place you'll meet? The road to hell.

"Holden! Did you just threaten to kill my brother?"

He kept glaring at his prey. "Yeah, I did."

Her heels clattered across the floor as Claudia hurried toward him. Her fingers curled around his shoulder. "Let him go."

Dammit. He didn't want to, but...Holden's head turned so he could stare into Claudia's eyes. "For you." And he let go.

Cooper made a dramatic show of gasping and sucking in air. Rolling his eyes, Holden gave the prick a minute to wrap up his acting routine and then... "I meant what I said. If you're behind these attacks, Cooper, I will be destroying you."

Cooper put one hand on the wall, like he needed support or some shit. "You're crazy." His stare jumped to Claudia. "He's *crazy*. You see that, don't you? Why the hell you let him back into your life is beyond me. The guy can't be that fucking good in bed."

"Oh, actually, I am. Amazing in bed. But that's not why she let me back into her life." He reached for Claudia's hand.

But she snatched her hand from him.

And his attention was suddenly one hundred percent focused on her. "Sweetheart?" He ignored the brother, for now.

"Why would you threaten him?" Her stark gaze held his. "Cooper is my family. He was the only one there for me after my father died. He was there for me when I was alone at the church in a wedding dress. He has always been there for me."

And he could read between the lines. *Cooper will be the one she always chooses. If it comes down to me or him, she'll take her brother's side.* But Claudia didn't know all of her brother's secrets. Holden did.

"Kick him out of your life," Cooper urged her. "Now. We don't need him."

Holden didn't move. "You don't need me." He nodded. "Because you just have a run of bad luck happening in your life, right, baby?"

"What does her bad luck have to do with—" Cooper began.

"Bad luck that could have killed you tonight," Holden plowed over her brother's words. "But I was there. I saved you. Just like I was there for the mugging. I will continue to be there. I will be between you and danger because nothing matters to me more than you do."

"Oh, jeez. Not this bullshit again." Cooper stalked toward his desk. "Trying to convince you that he loves you again, huh? Don't fall for that routine, sis."

Claudia stared at Holden. "Why would you think my brother is involved in any of this?"

"Because the stairs lead to his office. Because he's just not fucking concerned enough. Because I do think he could have made the chandelier fall, then rushed back down the stairs and gotten to the VIP door in time to act like the worried brother. It would have been tight, but he could do it."

"Bastard," Cooper snarled. "Get *out* of her life."

Holden sent a glare Cooper's way. "Where were you when the chandelier fell?"

Silence.

Claudia's head angled toward her brother. "Cooper?"

"You know I would never hurt you."

"*I* know you didn't answer my question." Holden kept his hands loose at his sides. "Where were you?"

"In here. I needed a minute of privacy, so I was in my office, okay? Then I went to the lobby just in time to hear the chandelier fall."

Claudia's lashes flickered. "You were in here, alone?"

"Yes." A hiss. Then he hurried forward and grabbed Claudia's arms.

Holden stiffened.

"I would *never* hurt you. I didn't go up those stairs. I was in my office for a bit, going over some numbers, then I went to the lobby, and I heard the crash. I'm sure plenty of people saw me out there when the crash occurred."

"Yeah, maybe they did." Holden thrust back his shoulders. "But *maybe* you put the pieces in motion, huh?" He'd seen the chandelier's control panel on the wall of the second floor. Had the panel been sabotaged? Because he didn't buy that some loose screws or shady mounting was at fault. "Maybe it took a few minutes for the chandelier to actually fall so you had time to get out and set the stage so you could be seen—"

"I didn't do it!" An explosion from Cooper. "Look, I only realized you were fucking my sister when I saw her panties."

"Oh, no." Claudia's eyes squeezed closed.

"And a few minutes ago, I had to ask you where she was when the chandelier fell. Why ask if I knew, huh? Why—"

"Because you were trying to throw me off the scent. Didn't work. Now get your hands off her because you're squeezing Claudia too tightly and she just got those stitches out, so her arm is already sore."

Cooper immediately let her go. "Claudia?"

"I'm fine." But her hand trembled as she lifted it to push back her hair. "It's been a long night, and I really just want to go home." Her gaze found Holden. "Take me home?"

He'd take her anywhere she wanted to go. He offered her his arm. Occasionally, he could be gallant. Gentleman-like. When the need arose.

"Claudia." Frustration seethed in Cooper's voice. "He's the enemy."

Claudia's hand curled around Holden's arm. "No." Definite. "He's the man keeping me safe."

A furrow appeared between Cooper's brow. "Wait, hold on—"

"Holden is not my enemy." Her gaze caught Holden's. "And my brother is not my enemy. Why would you think that he'd ever want to hurt me?"

He opened his mouth but couldn't do it. Holden could not stare at her and shatter her illusions about her brother. Like she'd said, it had already been a long night for her, and he kept thinking about how terribly close he'd come to losing her. "Let's go home."

A weak smile tipped her lips as she nodded. He tugged her closer, and when that wasn't good enough, he curled his arm over her shoulders. Gently, he brought her into the shelter of his body, and some of the tension he'd felt finally slipped away.

Safe. She was safe and his to protect. *His*.

Her brother wasn't going to come between them this time. No one would. There was no way he'd lose her again. No matter what he had to do, Claudia would *stay* his.

***

Cooper watched his sister walk away. Before she and Holden left his office, the big, bastard of a bruiser looked back at him. In that intent and fierce look, Cooper saw a dangerous promise. He could almost hear Holden's threat one more time.

If you've been trying to hurt her, I will kill you.

The door clicked shut behind them.

"Sonofabitch!" Cooper slammed his hand down onto his desk. He grabbed the folder there and started to—

The door opened. Whirling, he expected to see Claudia or Holden, but...Reese Rawlins filled the doorway. His director of operations eyed him warily. "Everything okay in here?"

No, nothing was okay. "Her luck can't be that freaking bad."

"Excuse me?" Reese stepped inside and shut the door behind him.

Cooper's breath heaved in and out. "I asked you to increase security here at the winery. After Claudia got trapped inside, I told you that I wanted extra men and extra cameras. I wanted the place to be *safe*."

"It is safe."

"Then how come my sister came within moments of either dying or being seriously hurt tonight?" Only she'd been saved by that jackass Holden. Now, she'd view him as even more of a hero.

He's the hero, and Holden wants her to view me as the villain.

"I think it was just a faulty installation, boss." Warily, Reese shuffled closer. "What else could it be?"

It could be someone coming after my sister. Wasn't that what he feared even though he kept trying to tell Claudia that everything was fine? Protecting her had always been his job. He hadn't wanted Claudia worrying needlessly, and the cops hadn't seemed concerned at first.

Just a flat tire.

But then...

She'd gotten trapped at the winery.

A fire roared through her place.

He exhaled. Slowly. "I want to see the security footage from tonight."

"Ah, about that..." Reese winced. "The cops just tried to access it. Turns out there was some kind of glitch, and the cameras all went offline for a bit."

"When." A demand.

Reese glanced down at the floor. A sure sign that he didn't want to deliver bad news.

"*When.*"

"They went offline right before Claudia and her date went into the tasting room. The cop—Gains—he wanted our security guys to pull things up for him. I-I got the team to cooperate because we certainly have nothing to hide from the authorities."

They went offline?

"But the footage ended just as they were reaching for the door. Went black. We'll get some techs in to see if they can recover anything usable, but right now..." His words trailed away.

"Right now, we have nothing." And there was no more denial. No more pretending. Claudia had been right all along. There was no way security had magically just gone down right before that attack in the tasting room.

Someone had sabotaged security. Someone had made the chandelier fall. Just as someone had been behind all of the other attacks on Claudia.

And his sister was alive...his sister was safe...because of Holden Blackwell.

Sonofabitch. Now I have to thank the bastard.

***

"I'd like my panties back." Claudia held out her hand as she stood in the den of the guest house.

Holden looked at her hand. Then back at her face. "I tore them. I'll get you a new pair, promise."

She kept holding out her hand even as a faint blush slid over her cheekbones. "I can buy myself a new pair, thanks so much. Just give me back the old ones. Not like I want you carrying around my underwear as if they are some kind of—some kind of—" Seemingly at a loss, Claudia floundered.

"Trophy?"

"I was going to say souvenir, but yes, that, too."

He pulled the panties from his pocket and put the silk in her hand. She immediately wadded them up in her fist and whirled away. "Thanks. I'll just let you get to bed."

They needed to be clear on one point. "I don't see you—or your panties—as any kind of trophy."

Her shoulders stiffened. "Excellent to know."

"You're trying to freeze me out."

She marched to the kitchen and ditched the panties in the garbage can. With silent steps, he followed her. Claudia turned and gave a little jolt of surprise when she saw him.

"Do you regret what happened?" he asked, voice low.

"Nearly getting slashed by a chandelier? Yes, I do very much regret that incident, and I hope it never, ever happens again."

He closed the distance between them. Towered over her. "I'm talking about what happened between us. Do you regret it?"

"Well, let's see." She ran her tongue across her lower lip.

His hot stare followed the movement. The things he wanted her to do with that sexy tongue...*Dammit, man, focus!*

Her chin angled up. "You threatened to kill my brother."

"I said that if I found out he was behind the attacks on you, I'd kill him."

"You aren't even mildly apologetic!"

Nope, he wasn't. Was he supposed to be? "I'd want to kill anyone who hurt you." Not like her brother was getting special treatment.

Her mouth hung open. It took her a moment to snap it closed and say, "You can't do things like that." And she marched past him, storming right back in her den.

Once more, he followed. "Sure I can. I did it, didn't I?"

She spun toward him. "Fine. Correction, you *shouldn't* do things like that. Going around and threatening to kill people seems—" But she stopped.

He didn't. "Uncivilized?"

"There's that."

"Dangerous?" His eyes narrowed.

"That, too." Claudia huffed out a breath. "It also makes you seem like a guy looking for a fight."

"I don't usually look for them. They look for me."

"Holden."

"Fine. I get it. You don't want me to threaten your asshole brother, but, sweetheart, you don't seem to get it. Right now, *you* are the only one who matters. I don't care if your brother hates me. He always has hated me. Not like that's gonna change. And it's not like I look for him to suddenly appear at the door telling me that we need to bury the hatchet because he's been wrong and suddenly realized what an idiot he truly is."

Someone knocked on her door. A loud, demanding knock.

"What. The. Fuck?" Considering that they were on *very* secure property and that any guest would need to get past the guards at the gate, that knock put Holden on immediate edge. "You expecting someone?"

"After midnight? No, I'm not." Worry bloomed in her eyes.

He hated her worry. And her fear. Without a hesitation, he stalked toward the door. Holden stopped at the table in the small foyer and took out his gun.

"What are you doing with that?" Claudia wanted to know.

"Whatever needs doing." He'd put the gun in there earlier, just in case. Gripping it easily, he peeked around the curtain that covered the front window. When he saw their uninvited guest, he cursed. Just what he didn't need. "Your brother. Fabulous."

"Hide the gun! Don't let him see it."

To please her, he quickly placed the gun back in the table drawer. Then he yanked open the door. By way of greeting, Holden announced, "I am not in the mood for your bullshit."

"Good. Because I'm not in the mood for your bullshit, either." Tight, grating words. "I'm here because you were right. Claudia was right. And I owe you a major thank you for protecting my sister."

Holden stared at him. Then he squinted. He *was* looking at Cooper Fairmont, wasn't he?

"And you're staring at me with even more suspicion than you normally do. Typical. I'm here for a truce, Holden. You know what that is?"

This wasn't happening.

"We both want the same thing," Cooper continued in that same tight and tense tone. "For my sister to be safe. So how about you stop glaring daggers at me and you let me come inside for a minute?"

Holden didn't move. "Why the sudden change of heart?"

Cooper craned to see over Holden's shoulder. "I'm sorry, Claudia. I didn't want to believe someone was targeting you. I didn't want...I didn't want you to be in danger."

"She *is* in danger." Holden maintained his position. "What happened after we left?"

A long sigh escaped Cooper. "I found out that someone cut the security feed right before you and Claudia went into the tasting room. Reese says it could be a glitch, but...two glitches? The security feed dying and the chandelier falling? No way. It's too much. Everything—all of the incidents—they've been too much." He ran his hand over his face.

Holden noticed the faint tremble in Cooper's fingers.

"After the lock-in at the winery, I asked for security to be increased," Cooper revealed.

"You never told me that." Claudia's heels tapped on the floor as she inched closer.

"I didn't want to worry you."

"Little late for that," she assured him, voice crisp. "I was plenty worried the whole time."

He grimaced. "I asked for extra security there—and for increased video surveillance. If someone was after you, I wanted to catch the bastard."

Holden absorbed all this, and he didn't like where the info led. "The bastard knew what you'd done, and he took steps to make sure he didn't get caught."

"Yes."

That means he is someone on the inside. Someone close to Cooper and Claudia. Dammit. After shooting another hard glare at Cooper, Holden backed up. He knew exactly where this talk was going.

Cooper walked inside and stood awkwardly near the couch. "I didn't want you hurt," he said to Claudia.

She'd wrapped her arms around her stomach. "Good. I didn't exactly want to be hurt." Her attention darted to Holden. Her stare seemed to soften. To warm. "Holden yanked me off the table. Protected me. Saved me."

"That's why I'm here." Cooper braced as if for battle. "I owe you my thanks," he told Holden, and it only sounded as if he strangled a little bit on the words. "I'm grateful to you for protecting Claudia."

"Not particularly interested in your gratitude." Or in becoming besties with the prick. "Look, you bastard, I'm pretty much choking on the words but...*thank you*."

Holden's brows climbed. "I don't need thanks for being there for Claudia. Protecting her is what I do because she's mine."

He heard Claudia's quick gasp.

"I don't repeat my mistakes," Holden continued. "So you can be sure that I won't let her get away again. And the *last* thing I intend to do is let some bastard hurt her." But he had a dark suspicion that just kept growing with every moment that passed, and he stalked straight for Cooper. "You were increasing her security without telling her."

"I was trying to *help*. There was no need for her to worry unnecessarily—"

"Trust me, Coop," Claudia cut in to say. "There were plenty of reasons for my very necessary worry."

And Holden *knew*. "You did this shit before," Holden accused. "Sonofabitch. *You did it before*."

Cooper backed up a step. "I have no idea what you're talking about."

"You've hired extra security for her before, didn't you?" He surged toward Cooper. "When you didn't think she was *safe*. Back when she was with me."

Cooper didn't deny the charge. "So I want to protect my baby sister, what's wrong with that?"

"You hired someone to tail her. To watch her. Five years ago, you did it, didn't you? You had someone tailing her." *Fuck, fuck, fuck.* "Do you have any idea what you've done?"

Claudia hurried to Holden's side.

"I haven't done anything." But Cooper wet his lips. "What are you raging about?"

"Holden?" Claudia's confused voice.

His head turned toward her. "The photos were from five years ago, sweetheart. Photos that were taken without your knowledge or without mine. They're the same kind of photos that I've seen shady PIs take when they are trying to get dirt on someone. Your brother hired someone to watch you, and the jerk he hired took those pics of us together."

Her lips parted.

"What pictures?" Cooper demanded. "What are you talking about?"

He faced off with her brother. "Pictures of me and Claudia having sex. Pics and video. Some asshole made them years ago, and when her accidents started, the jerk left those pics for her to find."

Shock flashed on Cooper's face even as he reached out for Claudia. "Is this true? Someone has videos of you?"

Holden stepped in front of Claudia before Cooper could touch her. "Who did you hire? I want his name. *Now*." So he could personally nail the bastard to the wall.

"I-I—" Cooper shook his head. "No, no, I didn't hire someone to *stalk* my sister. I hired a professional to keep watch on her back then. Someone who came highly recommended! I didn't exactly trust you and the type of people you were associating with in those days. Maybe you didn't realize it, but a lot of them were *criminals*. You were getting in bed with criminals, and I didn't want my sister at risk!"

The only person he'd been in bed with had been Claudia. But Cooper was right on one thing, there had been a whole criminal element circling in. Only Cooper didn't know that Holden had been working undercover. *So you tried to keep her safe? From the world I was in?* Hell, what a tangled web they'd all weaved.

"A name," Holden barked. Though, now that he'd hit paydirt with Cooper, Holden knew he could always get the Wilde forensic accounting team to dive deep in the man's financials. They'd find the PI he'd hired, just a matter of time. *Follow the money*. Wasn't that always the way things worked?

"He's dead! It doesn't matter any longer. I read a news story about the poor guy dying about six months ago. Home invasion—someone broke into his house and when Danny confronted him, the intruder shot him. Shot him with Danny's own weapon, can you believe that?"

He was finding plenty of things believable these days. "Who recommended this Danny to you? And by the way, I want Danny's full name."

He was worried about Claudia. She was far too quiet next to him.

"Danny Crenshaw. Like I said, he's dead. No way can he be sending Claudia old pics and—and sex tapes or whatever the hell they are." He edged around Holden so he could better see his sister. "I wanted to protect you."

"By hiring someone to stalk me?" Her voice was emotionless.

"He was supposed to be a professional! And it wasn't stalking. The guy was watching you and trying to make sure Holden wouldn't drag you down into the mud with him."

Such a dick. "Who recommended him?" Holden demanded.

"He's dead, too," Cooper told him. "Don't you see? They're both dead so it can't be them."

Aw, hell. Holden got a bad feeling in his gut. His eyes met Claudia's. He saw the same knowledge in her eyes right before she asked her brother, "Was it Edward? Edward Wellington? Did he recommend the PI to you?"

"Well, yes, but you have to understand...he knew I wanted discretion. The same kind of discretion that mom wanted years ago when she suspected dad was having an affair. She also hired Danny to start digging. She went to Edward, and he gave her Danny's info. Danny had done work for him—hell, for *years*."

This got worse and worse. "Let me get this all straight." Shit. He'd have to call his FBI contacts again. "Your mother went to Edward because she wanted someone to follow her husband?"

A jerk of Cooper's head. "She thought he was having an affair. And he was, so...guess she was right to worry."

"No, she wasn't." *Holy fuck.* If what Cooper was saying was true...

"Holden?" Claudia's voice. Not emotionless. Lost. Scared.

He immediately took her hand in his. "It's okay."

Cooper went right on running his mouth. "Dad kept disappearing on her. Missing appointments. Slipping away. Mom thought he was having an affair, so she went to Edward because he was someone she trusted."

Edward Wellington should have never been trusted.

Cooper's stare bored into his sister. "Look, I only found all this out years later, okay? Right when Holden started nosing around you."

Nosing around? Fucking seriously?

"Edward approached me and told me how he had helped the family before, and he offered to do it again."

Claudia's hand was icy in his.

"I thought his PI might be useful. I wanted my sister safe. How was that so wrong?"

It was wrong in a thousand ways. Because what Holden suspected...

Sonofabitch. Your mother thought your dad was having an affair. He wasn't. Your dad was just about to turn on his shady-ass partner. When your mom went to old Eddie, the guy got tipped off. The next thing the world knew...Caldwell Fairmont and his "mistress" were both dead.

Only Eddie hadn't stopped there. He'd stayed involved. Watching. And when Cooper had gotten suspicious of Holden...*Eddie got his guy Danny on the job again. Danny tailed us. Saw something that tipped him off about my work with the Feds. And boom...my ass was kidnapped and I got a gun pressed to my forehead.*

"You have no idea what you've done," Holden snarled.

Cooper's brows shot up. "What I've done? Looked after Claudia? That's what I've done. What I'll always do. Sorry if you don't like it, but I'm not going to stop now. As for these videos and pics, there is no way they came from the private investigator I hired."

Holden thought that was exactly where they'd originated. "Like it wouldn't have been easy to steal them from the bastard's home or office after he was dead?" Seriously?

Cooper's eyelids flickered. "I...why would Danny take those kinds of pics of Claudia? Why have them at all?"

"Because he was a bastard on the take working for some bad people, and he probably accumulated all the incriminating evidence he thought he could use against anyone." *He saw how crazy I was for her. Claudia was my weakness.*

She still was his weakness. And he needed to talk to her. Without her brother watching. "Gonna have to ask you to get the hell out, Coop. It's late, and you've just dropped a whole lot of bombshells on us."

"I want to *help!*"

"Trust me," Holden drawled. "You've helped plenty." *In the worst possible ways.*

Cooper lunged toward him.

"Stop it!" Claudia stepped between them. "You two both need to calm the hell down."

"I am calm," Holden assured her. *And I will be happy to calmly kick his ass.*

"You are not calm," Claudia fired right back. "Your voice is rumbling and intense and your eyes are shooting fire at my brother. I am *not* letting you two fight, so just stop." Her head swung from Holden to Cooper. "Both of you, take a breather."

Holden smiled at Cooper. "Let's pick up this conversation in the morning, shall we? When we have...cooler heads." *After I've had a chance to talk to my team at Wilde and find out just what they know about your dead PI buddy.*

"Fine," Cooper snapped back. "The morning." But he made no move to exit.

So Holden made a shooing motion toward the door.

Cooper's eyes narrowed.

"Go, Coop," Claudia urged him. "I'm exhausted, and I get that you want to help me, but there is nothing more that can be done tonight."

Instead of leaving, he stepped toward her. His hand curled around her shoulder. "I love you," Cooper told her. "You are the most important person in my life. Anything I've done, it was because I wanted to keep you safe."

Your attempt to keep her safe wrecked our wedding. And it sure as hell looked as if that attempt had led to Claudia's current stalker.

"You can trust me," Cooper continued as emotion beat in his voice. "Whatever secrets you've got, you can tell them to me."

But she wasn't telling her brother the full truth. She edged away from him and his touch. Her shoulder brushed against Holden. "Good night," she told her brother firmly.

Lips thinning, Cooper inclined his head toward her and finally made his way to the door. *About time.* Holden stalked after him, intent on closing that door and locking it. But before he crossed the threshold, Cooper turned back toward him.

"You'll protect her?" Cooper asked.

"Always."

A nod. "And we *will* talk in the morning."

Oh, they'd talk, all right. Cooper wouldn't like what Holden had to say, but that would just be too bad. It was time to drag all of the dirty secrets into the light. "Hell, yes."

Cooper exited. Holden shut the door. Secured the locks. And then he slowly turned to face his obsession.

Her head tilted down, making her hair slide forward as her shoulders slumped. She looked tired. Defeated. *Not* the way he ever wanted his Claudia to look. She was fire and sunshine. Smiles and warmth. Not pain. *Not* this sadness.

"You think it was the PI, don't you?" Claudia asked the question without looking up at him. "My mom hired him, or thought she did, but he was really working for Edward. And the PI realized that my dad was turning on his business partner."

The partner who'd been laundering money through the winery. *And then your dad was eliminated, along with my mother.*

"Where's the evidence?" Her head slowly lifted. "The actual proof? Because everything that's happening—it's just a story you're giving me. And I'm filling in pieces. Am I doing that because I want to believe you? Or because—"

"You're doing it because it's true." He wanted to go to her so badly. Instead, he held his ground. Maybe it was time for Claudia to come to him. "I have never lied to you." Not once. Not ever.

Her lashes flickered, and he saw the swell of pain in her stare.

What the hell?

"Right." Stilted. "You never did." She shoved back her hair. "How about you and I talk in the morning, too? I think I've reached my limit for this day." With that, she turned away, walking to her bedroom and leaving him staring after her in silence.

In silence. With need. With an aching desire that wouldn't ever end.

I never lied to you, sweetheart. But I did hold some things back from you. And when she found out...

What would she do?

Fuck. He could not lose her again. Could. Not. But...

Do I even have her?

He had, for a brief moment. His mouth had been tasting the sweetest heaven, and then hell had come crashing down on him.

This stalker was really pissing him off. Holden couldn't wait to obliterate the guy.

CHAPTER TEN

Step Ten: Wage an all-out war against her enemies. They think to hurt her? Hell, no. Burn them to the ground. Every single one of them. And roast fucking marshmallows over the flames.

Too much? Nah. Not enough.

"Danny Crenshaw." Holden's voice carried easily as he spoke into the phone. "Yeah, yeah, he's some private eye in North Carolina. Or he *was,* until Danny died in a home invasion. Apparently, shot by his own gun. Elias, I want you to dig up every bit of intel on the guy you can."

Claudia crept closer to her bedroom door. She'd left it ajar, and light spilled through the small opening. She should have been sleeping, but sleep kept eluding her. Every time she closed her eyes, she saw a chandelier hurtling toward her.

As she'd been tossing and turning in bed, she'd heard Holden's voice.

Her hand curled over the doorknob as she slid the door open a little bit more.

"I called my contacts at the FBI. They always wondered how the hell things blew up so spectacularly five years ago, and now we have a solid lead on the cause of that explosion."

She slid into the hallway. Her bare toes curled against the hardwood floor.

"I think the PI discovered I was working undercover. He gave the info to his boss, and I found my ass with a gun pressed to my forehead."

As if pulled by his voice, her feet shuffled forward.

His body whipped around at the soft slither of sound. His bold green eyes immediately locked on her.

He'd changed his clothes. So had she. While she wore a pair of silk pajamas—pants and a short-sleeved, light blue top, Holden wore a pair of old, faded jeans. They hung low on his waist. No shirt for him. Just powerful muscles that stretched and twisted with his movements.

She inched toward him.

His hold on the phone tightened. "I need the info as soon as your fantastic hacker self can get it for me." A pause. "Thanks. Yeah, of course, I'm watching my ass. And hers."

A chill skated over her body.

"No, I checked with Harley already. She didn't see anyone coming out of the tasting room—or coming from the brother's office. She's maintaining her cover, and if she turns up anything we can use, you can be sure I will be spreading the word." He exhaled on a long sigh. "Thanks, man. And sorry I woke you up at..." His eyes narrowed as he glanced toward the round clock that hung on the nearby wall. "Nearly two a.m. Just know that one day you can return the favor. Call me whenever you want, and I will be there to help you in a heartbeat." After hearing a response from Elias, he hung up the phone.

She waited for him to say something to her, but the silence just stretched. Her tongue swiped over her lower lip as she darted forward a little more. "Who's Harley?"

He dropped the phone onto the table near the couch. "She's my partner."

Surprise had her steps slowing. "I—I haven't met her." But he'd mentioned before that his partner would be coming to town. Only the partner had never materialized. Or so she'd thought.

"That's the point of having a partner who stays in the shadows. She doesn't draw attention to herself, but she watches our backs. Harley is a good agent, even if she's still pretty new to Wilde."

He wasn't looking at her. "Harley was at the gala tonight?"

"Yep, in the mix of one hundred people, so it would have been hard for you to spot her. She hung back after we left, trying to see if the cops turned up anything useful. Told me that she got some intel from Gains, but not much."

Her arms stayed loose at her sides. A casual pose when she felt anything but casual. "What's the intel?"

"He's suspicious. Extra so since the security footage magically disappeared. He's calling in a crime scene team tomorrow to take another look at the place."

So the "incidents" were being taken seriously. Finally. "You talked to Harley, the Feds, and your friend Elias."

He nodded. His gaze still remained anywhere but on her.

"You were busy," she added.

"Needed to get shit done. Especially with the big reveal from your brother about the PI."

Unable to help herself, she eliminated the last bit of distance between them. Her hand reached out to touch his arm.

"*Don't.*" The one word seemed bitten off.

She flinched.

He swore. "Look, I'm not exactly at my best right now. You don't want to be touching me. Hell, you don't want to be this close to me." He backed up a step. "You want to go back in your room. You want to shut the door and pull those covers up to your chin."

"I couldn't sleep."

"Didn't say you had to sleep. Said you should go back in there. Put some distance between us."

They'd had distance for five long years. "You regret what happened?"

Now his gaze flew to her. "Fuck, yes, I do."

She took that hit straight to the heart. "I see."

"It was a damn chain of dominos falling, and I didn't know it. Your brother got wind of my activities, but instead of coming to me, he suspected the worst. Hell, can't even say I blame him for that. Only when he pulled in the dirty PI, Cooper took things from bad to infinitely worse. Wound up costing me...everything." If possible, the green of his eyes burned even hotter. So hot she could have sworn that he singed her skin.

Claudia swallowed. "I wasn't talking about what happened five years ago."

"No? Because that shit is always between us. The pain I caused you will always be there."

She looked at the small space between them. "I don't see anything between us." You could either let the past suck you into the ground and bury you like it was your grave, or you could move on. "When I asked if you regretted what happened..." Her gaze shifted to his face. "I meant what happened between us in the tasting room."

A muscle flexed as he clenched his jaw. "You don't want to go there right now."

"Yes, I do." Claudia knew exactly where she'd like to go. To bed. With him. "If the chandelier hadn't fallen, what would have happened?"

Claudia. Go back to bed.

"Only if you come with me."

His hands clenched and released at his sides. "Why?"

"What an odd question." The answer should have been obvious to anyone.

"No, it's not odd. Because I don't want just one fast fuck in bed with you."

"I don't remember you ever being particularly fast."

He reached for her. Caught himself. The hand he'd extended fisted and dropped back to his side.

"What is it that you do want from me, Holden?" Claudia asked him, voice low and careful.

The smile he sent her seemed to pierce Claudia straight to her core. "I want everything."

"That's quite demanding."

He shrugged. "We both know I'm a demanding bastard."

True. He was.

"Your brother never thought I was good enough for you."

She waited, wondering where this was going.

His head tilted. "You ever think he might be right?"

Squaring her shoulders, Claudia stepped forward. Her hands reached up and curled around his broad shoulders. His warmth sent an electric charge surging through her. "I never asked you to be good." She'd always preferred it when he was bad. In the best way.

"I have about ten seconds of control left where you are concerned," he warned her. "It's been a bitch of a night. I tasted you and it was heaven, but then that chandelier came to try and take you from me. *Nothing* can take you away. Not again. You get that, don't you? *I can't lose you again.*"

Claudia considered the situation for a few moments, then said, "I'm sure ten seconds just passed."

His eyes widened.

She pushed up onto her tiptoes and used her grip on his shoulders to tug him toward her. "Kiss me," she urged him.

And that was it.

Those ten seconds *had* passed because when his mouth took hers, she knew his control was gone. Truth be told, Claudia had always loved it when his control shattered. When he became primitive and wild. Desperate and so fierce in his desire for her. When they were together, nothing else seemed to matter.

She wanted that feeling again. The pain and the worry and the fear that someone dangerous was closing in...she wanted to let that all go, if only for a little while.

She wanted to be with him again. To pretend that everything was okay. That they still had their shot at a happy ending.

He kissed her with stark need. Rough skill. Ravenous hunger. A moan slid from her as he pulled her closer to the heat of his body. He always seemed to feel like a furnace to her, and she loved that warmth. She slid against him, wanting to be even nearer, and he scooped her up. Held her with that effortless strength of his. Wrapping her legs around his hips seemed to be the most natural thing in the world. She could feel the long, hard press of his arousal against her core. Her hips rocked against him as she rode his dick even through their clothes.

"Baby..." Guttural as his mouth tore from hers. "I have missed you."

She pressed a kiss to his neck. Then nipped him. "I missed you, too," Claudia confessed in a rush.

His muscles seemed to turn to stone. Her breath caught and—

He carried her back to her bedroom. Fast, surging strides. His hands seemed to brand her ass as he held her against him. Her breath panted out, and she kissed his neck again. Licked him. He'd always liked that in the past, and his savage growl told her that he still did.

He lowered her onto the bed. Came down immediately on top of her. Went back to kissing her with a wild frenzy even as his fingers snaked between their bodies, and he hauled off her pajama pants and her panties. She lifted her hips, helping him to get rid of the clothes. *Off.* She wanted them gone. She wanted to feel him, skin to skin. Sex to sex.

It had been far too long.

He lifted his upper body from hers, and she squirmed beneath him, twisting so that she could yank off her own shirt. Did she look too eager? Claudia didn't care. She was past the point of doing anything but feeling.

He took the shirt from her, tossed it over his shoulder, and she was left completely naked. His jean-clad legs pushed between her spread thighs. The fabric was slightly rough, abrading against her sensitive skin. Bracing on his elbows, he stared down at her. Light spilled from the open doorway and illuminated the bed even while leaving most of the room in darkness.

"I dreamed about you." Rasped. One hand moved so that his callused fingertips trailed over her nipple.

She bit her lower lip to hold back a moan.

"Fantasized about you."

She'd done the same with him. How many nights had she woken up with his name on her lips? And she'd gotten so angry with herself. *Stop wanting someone who never wanted you.* But...he had wanted her.

Wanting had never been a problem for them. Sex had always been fantastic. *The* best she'd ever had.

His head lowered and his mouth replaced the fingers that had been over her nipple. His warm, wet mouth. Lips and tongue. Her head pushed back against the pillow as a surge of arousal pierced through her. Her hips surged upward, but she just hit his jeans. "The jeans have got to *go!*"

Rough laughter. "If the jeans go, I'm plunging right into you."

"Good. Fantastic. Wonderful." Her hands snaked down so she could stroke him through the fabric.

His laughter died away. "Baby..." A warning.

"I want you in me. It's been *too* long."

He eased back. Climbed from the bed. She surged upright to sit and watch him as he kicked away his jeans. His thick, heavy cock sprang toward her. He took a step back to the bed, then froze. "*Fuck.*"

"Holden?"

"Do not move. I've got condoms in my suitcase."

He—

Was gone. He'd rushed out of the room, and she was left naked on the bed. Aching for him. Desire and need twisted through her body. *Oh, screw this.* She wasn't just going to wait. Claudia bounded out of the bed and headed for the door—

Only to run straight into him. "You're supposed to be in bed." He lifted her up.

A glance down showed the condom was on. She reached for his dick and guided him toward her sex even as her legs locked around him. "You're supposed to be in me."

He surged forward. Into her. "*I am.*"

They stumbled toward the bed. Fell together. When they hit, he thrust even deeper inside of her. She gasped at the sensation. So much pleasure but almost pain because it had been a while for her. And every part of Holden had been built on a rather massive scale.

At her gasp, he stilled. "Claudia?"

She sucked in a breath. Then one more. "Give me one sec." Maybe two.

His head lifted. "I'm hurting you." Grim. "Fuck me, I'll stop—"

"No." She clamped her legs tighter around him. "Just been a while. I'm adjusting."

His hand eased between their bodies. His fingers stroked her clit. Gently. Tenderly. "How long?"

Damn him. "How long has it been for you?" she snapped back. "Don't think this is the time to get into specifics, do you? Because I don't really want to hear about—"

"Five years." He withdrew. Pressed his thumb to her clit. Rubbed. "Three months." He plunged inside of her.

She met him with an eager upward surge of her hips.

"And just about—"

"*Liar,*" she snarled at him.

He kissed her. Hard. Passionate. "Hell, no."

He withdrew. Then stroked her again with his wicked fingers. Holden thrust inside of her. The combination of his fingers on her clit and his giant dick surging into her...

OhGod, ohGod...

"You think I could fuck someone else?" He withdrew. Plunged in even deeper. So deep that her whole body heaved off the bed. "Only you. *Only you.* I jacked off to you more nights than I can count."

No, no, he had to be lying. He'd always been a hypersexual guy. They'd made love several times a day when they'd been together before. He'd always wanted more and more. So had she...

So had...

"No one else for me," she whispered. Her eyes locked on his. "And I came to your memory more times than I could count."

What did that say about them? That they were both twisted and locked on the past? Obsessed when they each should have moved on? That—

A savage growl tore from him. He caught her legs. Lifted them over his shoulders as a wild fury of need and possession overtook him. His hips slammed into her as he drove his dick into her over and over again. She was slick and eager, her inner muscles clamping greedily around him. The climax didn't build. It just exploded through her. Her breath choked out, and her eyes squeezed closed as pleasure consumed her. She heard the thunder of her heartbeat, the rasp of his breath, and all she could do was clutch his powerful shoulders as pleasure poured through every cell of her body.

He held her tighter. Pounded into her. Then roared her name when he came.

***

He withdrew. A slow glide of retreat that drew a protest from her lips.

"I'll be right back," Holden promised.

Her lashes fluttered open. She saw him pad to the bathroom and knew he was ditching the condom. She was spread out in the bed, completely naked, and Claudia knew she should probably at least reach down and tug some of the covers over herself. And she would, in a minute. When she stopped feeling like her world had been decimated.

The floor creaked near her. Holden had already returned. He stood there, staring down at her, with shadows all around him. "Did you tell me what I wanted to hear?"

"Now..." Her voice came out too husky. She cleared her throat and tried again. "Now you're calling me a liar?" The light fell on the bed so she was revealed even as the darkness clung to him. "Because I've never lied to you. And I certainly didn't decide to start tonight." Okay, she should definitely grab the covers. Claudia sat up and reached down for them.

But he stopped her. Holden caught her hand. "I thought you'd fucked that prick at the vineyard."

"I told you before, I didn't. I don't care what the media posted, that never happened." Her hand flexed in his hold. "Not that Louis didn't indicate he was interested. Because he did. And I was just pissed enough at you—and hurt enough—that I almost said yes."

"Claudia..."

"But I don't do revenge fucks. Not *with* you, and certainly not with guys I don't care about in order to get back at you. I wasn't ready for another lover. I needed time for me." He kept towering over her. "What's your story? Abstinence isn't exactly something I associate with you."

"I didn't want anyone but you." Gruff. Simple. "How the hell could I think about sex with someone else? It would never be as good as sex with you. No one else would be you. Wasn't going to close my eyes and pretend I was fucking you. I wanted the real deal. Not an imitation."

Her breath hitched. "What am I supposed to do with that?"

"Admit that I'm your best sex, too. Though I think I have the claw marks on me right now to prove it."

Oh, crap. She *might* have clawed him. Probably had. "Sex was never our problem." It wasn't their solution either, but it sure felt good. "We're pretending to be lovers. Why not just be the real deal?"

He stiffened. "Sex but no emotion, huh? That how you're playing it?"

She had no idea how to play anything. Mostly because she didn't play. "What is it that you want from me?" The stark question just slipped from her because she did not want games.

"I already told you. Thought I'd been very clear on that point. I want everything. Now scoot over."

What? "You think you're sleeping here with me?"

"Yeah, that's what I think. If I go back to my room, I'll just fantasize about you for the rest of the night. If I stay here, it won't be a fantasy. I'll have the real deal next to me." A roll of one powerful shoulder. "I want the real deal. I want far more than one time with you."

So did she. Her body seemed to be starving for him. Already, she could feel a surge of longing build for him once more. She squeezed her legs together, trying to get some control of her traitorous self.

"You know what? Hold the thought." He let her go. Turned away. As he exited the room, she grabbed for the covers and pulled them up over her body. "Holden?"

But he'd slipped from the room. She wasn't in the mood to hold any thought, so—hauling the covers around her body—Claudia went after him, just as she'd done before. She didn't run into him in the bedroom doorway. Not this time, instead, she found him just as she neared the guest room. Holden came out, carrying not just one condom, but a whole box.

His brows lifted when he saw her. "Couldn't stand the thought of staying away, huh?"

He would never know how true that was. "You think you need a whole box?"

"I think it's a good start."

Her grasp on the covers tightened. "You said you hadn't been with anyone since me."

"You said the same thing. Made me want to rip apart the French guy a little less."

Her body gave a slight jerk. "You wanted to rip him apart?"

"Turns out I have more than a small bit of a jealousy issue where you're concerned. Any guy that I think gets to see you naked? Gets to fuck you? Oh, yes, sweetheart, I want to rip them apart. Because like it or not, I think of you as mine."

"But I'm not."

"No?" Another shrug of those insanely powerful shoulders. "I'm yours, you know."

She knew no such thing.

"Have been from the moment I asked you to marry me. Maybe we didn't go through with the ceremony, but that doesn't mean I ever thought of you as any less *mine*."

The covers tried to dip and slide down her body. She'd just been completely naked with him, so she shouldn't be having this weird flash of modesty. But his words were upending her whole world, and everything around her felt unbalanced. No, *she* felt unbalanced. "You always were possessive."

"Only when it came to you. You mattered. But, yes, with you, I'm possessive. Jealous. A bastard who wants you all for himself. As I'm standing here right now, all I want to do is rip away that covering and devour every single inch of you. I want you raking your nails all over me and crying out for me when you come."

She licked her lips. "That's...a lot."

He stared back at her. "If I'd been with someone else while we were apart, how would it make you feel?"

Like clawing someone's eyes out. "All you have is my word that I *haven't* been with anyone else. Just like all I have is your word."

"Um, yep, it's called trust. And I trust you more than I trust anyone else in the world."

That simple?

"But do you trust me?" he pushed. "Do you believe what I've told you? And I'm not just talking about lovers because I swear, there haven't been any since you. There is *only you*. I'm talking about the FBI. The kidnapping. Everything. I haven't shown you proof, but you've seemed to take me at my word." He put down the condoms, setting the box on the nearby dresser. "Is it for real? Do you believe what I've told you?"

Her chin rose. "When I came to your office and told you about my *accidents*, you immediately took my case. You believed me from the start."

"Of course, I did. It's *you*."

Her chest ached. Warmed. "And you saved me. From the mugger. At the winery. You've been there for me. So..." *Do it. All in.* "Yes, I believe you, and that scares me. It scares me because the things you've told me mean that my father was murdered. That other people I trusted betrayed me. I'm not sure who all I can actually trust but..." She stared straight at him. "I trust you. If I didn't, you can be assured I would not have just had sex with you."

Sex and trust went hand-in-hand for her.

"I trust you with my life," she told him. Wasn't that exactly what she'd been doing? Trusting him to protect her?

"Good." His left hand reached out and curled under her chin. His fingers slid over her skin.

"Because believe me when I say, I would kill to keep you safe."

A shiver slid over her. "Really hope it doesn't come to that."

"You never know..."

CHAPTER ELEVEN

Step Eleven: When you get close to her again, don't blow it. Don't look too desperate. Too eager. Stay in control and—fuck, those covers around her body have got to go.

She stood in the doorway, with the covers from her bed wrapped around her body like a shield. The problem with her shield? It was already falling, dipping to reveal one smooth shoulder. A gentle tug would have the whole thing at her feet.

Then he could have *her* again.

His dick was already hard and aching once more, fully stretched and saluting her. He'd just been buried balls deep in her. Her cries of pleasure had filled his head, and her sweet scent had intoxicated him. *More. More. More.* Yes, he'd gone back for the box of condoms because he wanted to fuck her endlessly.

Five years was one hell of a long time. A whole lot of fucking would be needed to make up for those years of doing without her.

"I haven't been with anyone else. I just had a doctor's checkup. Everything is good with me, and I'm on birth control."

It took a hot minute for Claudia's words to fully register. *She's telling me we don't need the box of condoms. That I can have her, skin to skin.* His muscles locked down, and it took all of Holden's strength not to pounce on her. "I'm clear, too. You have nothing to fear from me." Before her, he'd always used condoms. The first time he'd gone bare had been with her—talk about nearly losing your mind with pleasure. To have her that way again...

We are not making it back to her bedroom. I am going to fuck her right here.

Claudia pulled in a quick breath, and then she let the bulky covers fall. They hit the floor with a rustle of sound.

For a moment, he just held her gaze. That blue that pierced him. "Tell me if I get too rough."

"You won't."

"Tell me," he urged her. "Tell me if I do anything to hurt you because, baby, I am fucking you here." And he looked down her body. Drank her in. His dream. His fantasy. Right there. He locked his hands around her waist and lifted her up. He pinned her against the nearby wall and kept her caged there with one hand around her waist even as his other hand guided his dick to her core. She was still slick. So soft. Her legs curled around him, and her hips arched toward him as he slid into her.

His gaze found hers once more. He wanted to watch her as he filled her. Every single inch. She was so insanely tight around him. Her inner muscles clamped fiercely around him, and he *loved* it. When he was locked in all the way, he savored her for one precious moment. *Skin to skin. Nothing between us. I'm part of her.*

Then he let go.

Frantic. Wild. Racing. He pounded into her and took and took and took, but she was there with him every moment. Those nails that he loved bit into his shoulders and raked down his back as she urged him to give her more and more. Nothing could have stopped him from giving her everything that he had. So intense. So powerful. He wanted to imprint himself on her because she had branded him long ago.

Faster. Deeper. *Mine*.

She screamed his name on a startled, high-pitched cry as her release surged through her. He saw the pleasure fill her eyes and make them seemingly go blind for a moment.

He didn't stop. The delicate contractions around the thick length of his cock just urged him on. *Again and again*. He drove in, pulled out. She gasped and moaned, and he was pretty sure he'd just made her come another time. Her sex squeezed him, and it was too good. He couldn't hold back any longer.

He poured into her on a wave of release that obliterated him.

***

"You want me to tell him everything about your father?" Dawn was coming. Holden could see the streaks of light spilling through the curtain in Claudia's bedroom. He'd had her over and over again during the night. Sometimes, he'd reached for her. Other times, she'd woken him from a light slumber with her hands and mouth on his body.

Paradise.

But the night was ending. Something he hated because that meant it was time to face the light. All of their enemies that were out there. Everyone waiting to close in.

"He might not believe you," Claudia said as she turned toward him in bed.

He reached out and tucked a lock of hair behind her ear. "My work with the FBI is classified, so it's not like I can show him a lot of proof. But I can get an agent to vouch for me, a friend I still have at the Bureau."

"That who you called last night?"

He'd made lots of phone calls during the night. "One of the people, yes."

"Cooper won't have an easy time believing that our father was murdered."

"Isn't that better than believing that he chose to leave you and Cooper because Caldwell was having an affair?" His hand lingered against her soft cheek.

"You're going to tell him that our father was a criminal. That he was involved in jobs with the mob. I don't think Cooper is going to jump on that train."

"He needs to know. At first, I wanted to keep him out of this as much as possible."

Her long lashes flickered. "Because you don't trust him."

"When it comes to your safety, no, I don't trust him. I don't trust anyone else." Her safety was too important. But the situation had changed. "I need to know more about the PI that he hired. Your brother is quite possibly the key to learning more about what happened five years ago and about what is happening to you now." And he *hated* to say this next part but... "We can't overlook the fact that your brother...might be involved."

As expected, the news jarred her. Claudia immediately surged up in bed, bringing the sheet up to cover her pert breasts. *Such a shame.*

"Involved?" Her voice cracked on the word. "He wouldn't hurt me!"

"No, but we don't know if he picked up your father's, ah, business model or not." And this was going to be another problem for her. "You understand that if your brother is still using the Fairmont Winery in some sort of shady partnership...Baby, do you get that your family's business could be in jeopardy?" If Cooper had decided to play with fire—just like his father had before him—then the whole place could potentially go up in flames.

"Cooper isn't involved in anything illegal." She climbed from the bed. The sheets whispered as they slid away with her.

Holden couldn't let Claudia bury her head in the sand. "Cooper isn't involved." He sat up. "Just like your father wasn't?"

Her back was to him. "I'm not convinced he was. Maybe...maybe my father just found out about something that Edward was doing. Maybe that's why he went to your mom." She peered over her shoulder at him. "My dad doesn't have to be the villain, you know."

Sweetheart, all signs point to your father definitely being a villain. But for now, he let that one go. Later, he'd reveal more. Not now when they had just established such a fragile peace. "Do I tell all to your brother or not? Your call."

"Tell him. He needs to know what we're facing." She swung toward him. "The problem though, is that Cooper and Seth are best friends."

Seth Wellington. Yes, he knew they were.

"Seth probably has no idea what his father did."

He stared back at her.

She blinked and said again, "Seth probably has no idea what his father did?" Only this time, she'd made the words a question.

"That's one of the things I intend to find out today." It was time for a chat with Seth. But first...

He'd deal with her brother. And Holden already knew, the guy was gonna be a pain in the ass about things.

***

"He's a damn liar," Cooper charged as he paced the closed confines of the library. A grandfather clock tick, tick, ticked from the corner. Sunlight streamed through the window, and Cooper strode back and forth like a caged lion. "*A liar.*" Cooper whirled and pointed at Holden. "And, seriously, Claudia, I can't believe you would buy his BS story for even a minute. I mean, really? He couldn't come to the wedding because he was kidnapped? I was *at* the bachelor party. Grudgingly so, but there. He was fine. I saw him walk out. The guy left with two friends."

"Those friends had vanished by the time I was attacked." And he had never remembered seeing Cooper leave the club. Something that had nagged at him. He could recall the others all leaving, but not Cooper. *I had waited out there because I wanted to tell the bastard off.* But...Cooper hadn't come out. "I was alone on the corner, waiting for my ride share driver." *And waiting for you.* He'd had too much to drink, another reason those jerks had gotten the drop on him. *Never will make that mistake again.*

"A gang of men kidnapped Holden." Cooper began to pace again. "They put a gun to his head. *A gun?* Because what? This is some action movie? And they *made* him call you to say he wasn't coming to the wedding? This is crazy." He turned on his heel and strode toward Claudia. "You are smarter than this. Are you seriously so desperate to get him back that you're buying his BS?"

Holden rose from his position in one of the— rather comfy—sitting chairs. "Watch the tone with Claudia. The way I figure it, we're all in this mess because of your fool ass."

"*Mine?*" His gaze jumped between Claudia and Holden. "How the hell is this *my* fault?"

Cooper had been fairly quiet while Holden had revealed all the big details from the past to him, but Holden had known an eruption was imminent. *Hello, eruption.*

"This could not possibly be *my* fault," Cooper blustered.

Sure, it could be. "You hired the PI that turned my information over to the target I was after."

"Right." Cooper's hands went to his hips. "The mysterious crime boss who—if what you say is true—was connected to our father's murder. Only you haven't said his name yet. Want to fill me in? Why wait longer for the big reveal? Just tell me who he—"

"Edward Wellington," Claudia said.

Cooper's mouth dropped open, only to immediately snap closed. He shook his head.

Claudia hadn't been sitting. She'd stood the whole time near a collection of leather-bound classics, but now she stepped closer to her brother. "I know you think Edward was a good man—"

"He was our godfather! Yours and mine! He was in our lives forever." A hard, negative shake of Cooper's head. "Edward helped me keep the business going after Dad died. Without him, I would have lost it all. He told me how to make investments. How to meet with the suppliers. How to get the best deals and he..." Cooper stopped. "No. You're just wrong."

But Holden smelled blood in the water. "What were you going to say he did? Don't leave me in suspense. You had a good list going, then you stopped."

Cooper cut him a glare. "You wanted her back so badly that you concocted this crazy story? Can't believe she bought it."

"The attacks on your sister are real. And the story we're telling you is real, too. I've got members of my team looking into the PI you hired. I'm already betting we'll find proof that he was really Eddie's man all along—"

"Eddie?" Cooper broke in as a line appeared between his brows.

"Eddie Wells was one of his aliases before your godfather decided to get a brand-new image and become Edward Wellington. See, you never really knew him. Betting he never once told you that when he was eighteen, he was suspected in the murders of two men."

Cooper blinked, but rallied. "Suspected doesn't mean convicted."

"No, he wasn't convicted, because the witnesses conveniently died in a car accident."

Cooper flinched.

"That's happened a lot with people who went against Eddie. *Accidents*." And now accidents were plaguing Claudia. Cooper had to connect those dots.

Cooper's hand raked through his hair. "You're saying...you're saying that you were working with the Feds, but when I hired that PI, Edward got tipped off. He kidnapped you—*why* kidnap you? Why not just—"

"Kill me?" Cooper finished helpfully.

Claudia cut him a glare.

He shrugged. "That was the plan. My death. I was told the boss wanted to handle the job personally for some reason. Only the cavalry arrived in time to save my ass. By the way, I didn't exactly *know* Edward was the one gunning for me at the time. In fact, the Feds only recently got enough evidence to close in on him. But word reached Edward before they could, and then he was found with a bullet in his brain."

"He had cancer," Cooper snapped. "He'd told me about it. He was struggling. He wasn't some kingpin! He helped me!"

"Did he help you? Or did he take over your books long enough to erase the evidence of his crimes? Did he turn things back over to you when he couldn't be incriminated any longer?"

Cooper's stare darted to Claudia. "You believe this about Edward?"

"I believe that I want Holden and his friends to dig into Edward's life and investigate. I believe someone is after me, and I don't know why."

Cooper's brow furrowed even more. "You think—you think what is happening to you is tied to Dad and Edward?"

"The accidents that I've been having started six months ago. Right after Edward died." She rocked forward. "I didn't think anything about the timing until Holden told me what he knew about Edward. Now, with the PI possibly being mixed up in this, too, how can I think anything else?"

"And don't overlook the fact that the PI died right after Edward. Damn convenient, don't you think?" Holden didn't like it when things were convenient.

"I've got a different scenario for you." Cooper nodded abruptly as his expression hardened. "One that came to me last night. A dead man can't be the bad guy in this. Edward is cold in the ground, not like he can be pulling the strings and directing all the attacks on Claudia. And that's *if* I buy the story about him being some super villain."

Holden turned his head toward Claudia. "Knew he'd be a dick about this."

"It's Holden," Cooper announced. "He's the bad guy."

Holden's head swiveled right back toward him. "Say that again." A dare.

Cooper strode toward him. "It's. Holden." Clear. Angry. He pointed his index finger at Holden. "He's the one behind the accidents. He wanted a way back into your life, so he set up all this shit. He's causing the accidents to scare you, Claudia. He knew you'd come running to him for protection. After all, he's the big, bad Wilde agent now, isn't he? So he just needed to set the scene. He needed to figure out a way to get you to come back to him because that sure wasn't going to happen on its own." A nod as his hand fell back to his side. "And he did. He set it all up. And you went running. Did you know he has a partner working with him while he's here? Found out last night about her. *After* he kicked me out of the guest house. Her name is Harley Adaire, and she just happened to be near the security room right before the footage went down." His nostrils flared. "He trapped you. A careful, long-planned trap, Claudia, and you fell right into his hands again."

CHAPTER TWELVE

Step Twelve: Lie, trick, fight. Do all of these things to get her back. Do anything necessary.

Cooper delivered his bit of news like it was a bombshell that would blow up her world. With a hard, satisfied expression on his face, he glared at Holden. "You can see your own self *out* of her life. Claudia is done with you."

Frowning, Claudia decided it was time to take charge. The men were just mucking things up. "Uh, no, I'm not done."

Both men swung toward her. Surprise was clear on Cooper's face. But it was Holden's face that was so much harder to read. His expression was tight. Closed down. Yet for a moment, she could have sworn that she saw a flicker of fear in his eyes.

"He's *tricking* you," Cooper charged.

"No, he's protecting me. Saving me. Being there for me when I need someone to be." She wanted her allegiance clear, so she stepped right to Holden's side and took his hand.

He gave a little start of surprise.

Why should he be surprised? His hand swallowed hers, but she still managed to give him somewhat of a squeeze as she added, "Holden believed me from day one."

"Uh, yeah." Cooper cleared his throat. "Because he was behind the accidents. And now he's spinning some elaborate lie about a dead man to cover his own ass. Edward didn't have him kidnapped. Edward didn't kill Dad. I won't believe it."

Her eyes narrowed. She'd warned Holden that her brother would fight the idea that their father had been involved in anything illegal. "You'd rather believe Dad just left us. He fell in love with another woman, and he left willingly. That's easier for you. Easier than thinking that he was a criminal. That he hadn't gotten involved in illegal activities and that everything we've always known was a lie." She nodded. "I understand that because, at first, I didn't want to believe the truth, either."

"You're still infatuated with him." Cooper glared at Holden. He seemed to love doing that.

Her brother was wrong, though. "No." She had never been infatuated. "But I happen to believe him. His team is gathering intel right now. The PI you hired is a connection that is going to turn things around for us. Holden's already contacted the FBI—"

"*What?*" Cooper's eyes widened.

"And they are going to check out the PI, too. Cooper, this is big. And it's real. And we don't get to just bury our heads in the sand because we don't like where things are going." She hadn't liked anything about the last six months. "Someone has been stalking me. Maybe the stalker is tied to Edward and the PI. Maybe not. But we have to dig in order to find the truth."

"You don't think," Cooper rasped, "that Holden is lying to you? That he's doing all of this? That he is pulling strings to do everything?"

She glanced at Holden. "What would be the end game in that?"

"To get you back!" Her brother's fiery response. "Because he knew he couldn't get close to you any other way. He had to scare you into coming back to him. Think about it—I sure as hell did last night when I was talking with Seth. The attacks have all been *near* hits. Even the chandelier—it didn't actually hit you. And who had the idea of going in the VIP room? You or him?"

Going in had been Holden's idea, but—

"Nothing too dangerous has happened. You've been able to escape every single time. Because Holden doesn't want you hurt. Seth thinks that he just wants you scared. He wants you to turn to him—"

"You talked to Seth about this?" Horror filled her as her head swung back toward her brother. He could not be serious right now. "We're standing here, telling you that Edward was involved, and you talked to his son?"

"He's my best friend!" Cooper's hands flew into the air. "And I didn't know this crazy story last night. Seth came by because he wanted to tell me that he'd seen that Harley woman acting suspicious at the gala. He was worried about you. Because he cares about you!"

Shock had her taking a step back and pulling her hand from Holden's. "Seth wasn't at the gala last night." He hadn't been on the invitation list because the man was supposed to be out of the country on business. "I didn't see him there." Granted, she'd been more than a little distracted at the end of the night, but still...

"Yes, well, you didn't see him because he just dropped by for a little while." Cooper squared his shoulders. "He was there right before the whole scene in the tasting room. Like I said, he noticed that Harley lady, and he wanted me to know what she'd been doing. He was worried. He actually wanted to see you last night, but when he found out that Holden was in the guest house with you, Seth decided to talk to you at another time."

Her stomach twisted. She'd always gotten along well with Seth. He'd treated her like a kid sister forever. She'd never felt scared or threatened with him...

Until now. Now she was looking at him through a veil of suspicion and not liking anything she saw. "Harley isn't a threat. She's someone who is helping me." But what about Seth?

"*You're telling me that Seth Wellington was here last night?*" Low. Ice cold. That was Holden's voice.

Cooper's chin stayed in the air. "My best friend was here, yes."

"Fuck."

Claudia could have echoed that sentiment.

Cooper's brow wrinkled. "Seth has an open pass to get on the property. The guards at the gate know to always let him in."

"Not anymore," Holden vowed. "That standing order is changing. As of now, *no one* gets on the property without my okay."

"Oh, right, because you're in charge of *our* property?" Cooper shot back.

Holden nodded. "Glad you understand." A pause. "I am now. I am completely in charge of the security here."

Cooper opened his mouth to argue.

"Someone is after me," Claudia said fiercely.

Cooper's lips clamped closed.

Good. Because he needed to listen. "Either Holden is in charge of security and you follow his orders here, or I am leaving."

There was no missing the shock on Cooper's face. "You don't mean that."

"I said it. I meant it." It was Claudia's turn to straighten her shoulders. "I love you, but when it comes to Holden, you've always had tunnel vision."

"My vision is crystal clear," he threw right back. "You're the one who is still infatuated. *He is going to hurt you all over again.*"

That word again. Infatuated. "I'm a grown woman." A reminder he should not need. "I know the difference between love and infatuation. I loved Holden. I believe what he has said about the past. I believe—"

"You want to believe him! You're desperate to believe him because you can't get over him!" Cooper surged forward and curled his hands around her shoulders as he pulled her away from Holden. "You think I don't know? You hardly date. Definitely don't get serious about anyone. You've been hung up on him, and you need to move the hell on. He is not good for you."

"Get your hands off Claudia or lose them." Holden's voice was flat and even colder, and it was that very coldness that was so alarming.

Both Claudia and Cooper glanced at him.

Faint lines bracketed his mouth. "She just got the stitches out," he said. "Plus, I don't care if you are her brother, I don't like it when anyone gets grabby with her." His eyes narrowed. "Hands off, or they will—"

"*Jesus.*" Cooper yanked his hands back. "He's freaking savage, you get that? No sense of self-control at all."

"Not where she's concerned, there isn't any control," Holden agreed. "Now are you following the rules or am I taking Claudia away from here?" He sawed a hand over the stubble on his jaw. "Got to admit, I do like that idea." He zeroed in on just her. "We can disappear. I'll have my team ferret out the bastard after you. You'll be safe. Completely secure. And you don't have to worry about—"

"Living in a prison?" Claudia supplied for him. Because she understood what he meant by "safe" and "secure"—she might as well be locked up. "No, thank you. I'm not going to let this guy send me into hiding." And who knew how long she'd have to hide? Claudia just wanted the nightmare to *end*. But... "I'm not giving up my life." Though she would give up the guest house. She had money to get a rental. She and Holden could go somewhere else. Maybe that would be for the best.

"Fine. I'll be your shadow, we'll move into a new place together, and we'll wreck the bastard

ASAP." Holden seemed pleased with the plan. "Let's go get your bags, right now." He reached for her.

"Slow the hell down!" Cooper snapped. "I'll follow the rules. Shit." He blew out a long breath. "Claudia, don't leave. *Don't.*"

She needed his assurance first. "Holden will be in charge of security for the property?"

"Yes, fine. Dammit, if that's what it takes! Until these attacks stop, you need to stay close!"

"I'll be taking over security at the winery, too," Holden announced, voice all smooth. "My team will be moving to make certain that there are no more incidents when the cameras just magically fail."

"Fine," Cooper bit off.

She looked between the two men and caught the wide smile that spread on Holden's face.

Holden smiled, and Cooper glared.

Her temples throbbed.

Before she could tell them to both stop acting like assholes, Holden's phone beeped. He pulled it from his pocket and scanned the text. "Well, well."

Well, well...what? Her left foot tapped against the floor.

His stare shifted to her. "Turns out that the asshole PI your brother hired had a second office, one that he kept hidden. Just got the address. Want to go search it with me?"

"Absolutely." Hell, yes, she did. Claudia whirled for the door.

"How is taking her to his office going to keep Claudia safe?"

Her brother's angry snarl had her steps faltering. She looked back.

Holden said, "Simple. Where I go, she goes. I'll be her fucking human shield. So *no one* will get to her. And I'm also not about to sideline her on an investigation about *her* life. Good, bad, everything in between—Claudia deserves to know what's happening. I won't be keeping secrets from her this time."

Was it her imagination or had her brother's eyelids just flickered? She sure thought they had but before she could push too far, her phone started vibrating, too. Claudia hauled the phone from the bag on her shoulder. Looking down at the screen, she saw that the call was from Mercedes. Crap. She hadn't talked to her friend since the attack.

"Give me just a second," she told Holden. "I need to take this." She hurried toward the door and the privacy of the foyer that waited outside. Her finger swiped across the scene. "Mercedes, look, I promise, I—"

"I have been going crazy!" Her friend's frantic shout had her ear aching. "The cops wouldn't let me talk to you last night. Are you okay? What in the hell? A chandelier fell on you? What is going on?"

A stalker may be trying to kill me. "I'm okay," she said. She wanted to tell her friend everything. But...

This time, looked like she was the one keeping secrets.

***

"Bet you're thrilled, aren't you?"

Holden watched the door close quietly behind Claudia. Thrilled wasn't quite the word he'd use. Claudia was in danger. He was feeling more *violently protective* and *severely pissed off*. Not so much thrilled.

"She chose you." Disgusted. "You finally got what you always wanted."

Time to set an asshole straight. Holden turned toward her brother. "This isn't what I want. There is no scenario where I want her scared or threatened or in danger. So get that shit through your head right now." He stalked toward Cooper. He just could not like the guy. "And my goal is not to make Claudia choose between me and her family."

"No?"

"No." He crossed his arms over his chest. "If I wanted to do that, I would have told her that you offered to buy me off years ago. At the bachelor party, remember? Didn't get why you attended at first, then you pulled me aside and offered me five hundred thousand to walk away from her."

Cooper swallowed. His Adam's apple bobbed as his gaze darted to the closed door. "Lower your voice."

"Well, if you hadn't tried to bribe me, there would be no need to lower anything." He also did not, in fact, lower his voice. "I told you to go fuck yourself, and the next thing I knew, I was being attacked and waking up tied to a chair in some shit-smelling cabin."

Again, Cooper's Adam's apple bobbed.

"First, I've got to say, I did wonder if you'd used your money to get me out of her life. Thought you might have hired those jerks, and I started immediately plotting ways to destroy you."

"I didn't hire them!"

"Figured that out." Those goons had been on a different payroll. "But I'm still thinking you might have seen something that night. You know, when I was jumped and you just happened to be on the scene." He'd been waiting for this moment.

"I wasn't *on* the scene! I was in the bar!" Cooper took a step back. "You think I stood there while you were attacked? That I just watched it happen?"

"Did you?"

"You have a fucking low opinion of me. No, no, dammit, I didn't do that! I would have helped you!"

Holden cocked his head to the side.

"I wouldn't have let my sister's fiancé get hauled away like that!"

"Interesting, isn't it? When you think someone should believe you, but they still seem skeptical? Weird-ass feeling."

Cooper glared at him. "You're going to tell Claudia about the money I offered you."

"I don't want to keep any secrets from her. I also don't want her to lose the guy who raised her and made sure she felt loved and cherished as a teen." *That* was the reason he hadn't obliterated Cooper already. "Her hating you? That just *hurts* her. It's the reason I didn't tell Claudia before. But like I said, I don't want to keep any secrets from her." He paused. "So you're going to tell her."

"What?" Cooper blanched.

"You tell her. Because if you don't, the truth will come out in a way you don't like."

"I don't like anything about this mess." His hand flew through his already disheveled hair.

"Join the club," Holden invited him.

Cooper's hand froze. "That bullshit about my father—"

"The truth?" Holden corrected. "What about it?"

His hand fell. "My dad wasn't involved in anything illegal, and Edward wasn't some...some criminal."

Holden stared back at him. He could see and hear the doubt already slipping through for Cooper. Suspicion had taken root. Maybe the jerk would actually see the light. "Be real careful what you tell your best buddy Seth. Sometimes, you don't know people nearly as well as you think. One minute, you believe you can trust them. That they have your back. The next, you find out they've been lying to you for years. Coming to have dinner at your house. Laughing and smiling even though they have blood all over their hands."

Pain cracked through the mask on Cooper's face. "Seth might not even know about his father. *If*—and that is *if*—you are telling me the truth."

"I would do just about anything to get Claudia back." He could admit that. Easy. "But put her in situations where she was threatened? Where she could be hurt? No fucking way." Never. "I think, deep down, you know it."

Cooper's gaze darted from him.

You do know it, you bastard.

"If it's not you," Cooper pushed out, voice gruff, "then who the hell is it?"

"Got a few people on my suspect list. At the top would be your bestie Seth."

Cooper's stare jumped back to him. "Why would he do that?"

He had some suspicions on that count, too. But he wasn't ready to share them with Cooper. Mostly because he didn't completely trust Claudia's brother. "I'll have more info once Wilde is finished tearing into the financials of your clusterfuck of a dead PI."

Alarm flashed on Cooper's face. "What do you mean, tearing into the financials?"

He'd meant exactly what he'd just said, but it was Cooper's reaction that intrigued him. "More secrets, Coop?"

Cooper's lips thinned.

Holden had his answer. "The Wilde team is good." Elias was a genius when it came to untangling numbers and following his leads. Forensic accounting was his specialty. "So if you've got something you need to get off your chest, better do it now."

"Don't know what you mean."

"Right." He turned away. "Not sure if anyone ever told you this before, but when you lie, your left eye twitches."

"What?"

Holden opened the door, locked his eyes on Claudia, and walked into the foyer.

"I swear, I'm fine," she was saying into her phone. Claudia turned at his approach. "Yes, he's here with me. Holden is staying with me." She grimaced. "Uh, no, he's not looking at me that way right this second."

Looking at her what way?

"He actually looks kinda pissed." Her brow crinkled. "No, not with me. Probably with Coop."

Definitely with Coop.

"Don't worry about me. And, yes, I will call if I need you. Thanks." She hung up the phone, but clutched it tightly in her grip.

Conscious of Cooper watching them from the doorway, Holden took his time walking toward her. With every step, he drank her in. *Nothing can happen to her. I will protect her.*

Her eyes looked over his shoulder at her brother. "You two managed to not tear each other apart."

For the moment. "Ready to go?" He lifted his hand toward her.

Without hesitation, she placed her hand in his. "Absolutely."

His fingers closed around hers. *She chose you. You finally got what you always wanted.* Cooper's words rang in his head. But the other man was wrong. Holden didn't have what he'd always wanted. Not yet.

Maybe when he'd brought down the bad guy. Destroyed the jackass and made sure that no other threats to Claudia remained. Maybe when she was safe. Maybe when the danger had passed.

Maybe then...he could get her to fall in love with him again.

Holden and Claudia headed for the elaborate doors in the house's entranceway.

"You protect her!" Cooper called out, voice strangled, as if those words had been pulled from him. "Don't let anything happen to my sister. Guard her like—like—"

Holden looked back. "Like she's the most important thing in my world? Don't worry. I think I got that covered." He held Cooper's gaze. "I protect what's mine." This message needed to be fully understood. "And I will do anything necessary to eliminate the threats out there. What can I say? I'm savage like that. Sometimes, savage is exactly what you need."

Because some jerk who played by the rules and never got his hands covered in blood and dirt? He wouldn't get shit done. Holden would. He would fight and fight until the battle was over. No threat to Claudia would be allowed to stand.

Savage?

He would fucking burn the world down on her enemies.

CHAPTER THIRTEEN

Step Thirteen: Everyone is a suspect. Family.
Friends. Sometimes, the danger is right there,
and it's the intimate connection that lets the
enemy slide so easily into a person's life.

Trust no one. And make sure she only trusts
you. An easy task, right? Just get her to forget
the past.

If only.

"I've never broken into an office before."
Claudia bit her lip as she watched Holden bend
over the lock. "Technically, I've never broken into
any place before." But, clearly, he had. He'd
pulled a little lock-picking set out of his pocket
like it was the most natural thing in the world. Did
he just go around with that set on him all the
time?

"If it makes you feel better, the owner is dead
and the place has been locked up for months, so
you're not exactly committing the crime of the
century." He straightened and turned to send her
a quick grin. That devilish grin that made her
insides warm.

With his hand, he pushed open the now
unlocked door.

That had been *fast*. Curiosity tugged at her. "Just how often do you employ your lock-picking skills?" And where had he even gotten those skills?

Holden's shoulders rolled in a shrug. "Probably more often than you'd suspect." He tucked the set back into his pocket. "Elias found this location when he was doing his deep dive on the PI. The lease was paid through the year, but it was under the name of a dummy corporation. Our not-so-good PI was trying to keep this location hidden. Seen it before with guys like him. They like to have separate locations to store back up files. Typically, the stuff they want to use as leverage against people."

She read between the lines. "You think he was blackmailing clients and he kept the info he had against them—you think he kept it here?" Claudia took another look around. An unassuming building on the outskirts of town. Quiet, tucked away. It was still early, and the area seemed deserted. The exterior of the building had just shown one business name, that of a cleaning service. But when they'd parked and gotten closer, she'd realized there was actually space for three businesses. The cleaning service, a bail bondsman, and...the unmarked office that had belonged to Danny Crenshaw.

"One way to find out." He pulled out a gun and prepared to enter the PI's office.

She grabbed his arm. "*Do we need that weapon?*" Claudia whispered. Her frantic gaze jumped around again. But no one else was close by.

"Better safe than sorry. With you, I don't intend to be sorry."

"Where did you get it? When?" She hadn't seen him take the gun from the guest house.

"From my car. When you were getting out. Sweetheart, someone is going to come along sooner or later. How about we go inside and shut the door behind us so we can search like the professionals that we are?"

She wasn't a professional.

But she followed him inside and hurriedly shut the door. Locked it, too.

He kept the gun at the ready as he made a sweep of the place. Not that there was much to sweep. A small waiting room with a slumping couch led to an even smaller office. The desk inside was completely empty, but a large filing cabinet perched to the side. Blinds had been pulled over the lone window in the office. A tiny bathroom snaked to the left.

Satisfied that no one was waiting in there to attack, Holden tucked his gun into the rear waistband of his jeans. His shirt slid over the jeans, and he pulled something small and black out of his front pocket. "Here." He tossed the items to her.

She caught them.

"Gloves. Don't want to leave fingerprints when we're not sure what kind of hell we're stepping into here. Gonna want to wipe down the locks and the doorknob before we leave, too."

Since they were committing a B&E, she figured not leaving prints was an excellent idea. The gloves were big on her, but Claudia didn't care. He'd already put on his pair, and she could only shake her head. "You are definitely prepared for your break-in."

Holden's shoulders stiffened. He'd been leaning over the filing cabinet, but his head turned toward her. "That bother you?"

"That you know how to break into a place so easily? That you can pick a lock in less than five seconds?"

"I think it took ten."

She wet her lips. "It makes me feel like I don't know you very well." The truth was...she didn't. Five years had passed. A person could do a whole lot of changing in five years.

"You know me better than anyone else ever has or ever will."

A shiver slid over her. "I think you have secrets that I can't possibly know."

The filing cabinet let out a loud screech as he hauled open the top drawer. The keening cry had Claudia flinching.

"Empty," he announced. He quickly hauled open and searched the next two drawers. More screeches. But all empty drawers.

Her gloved fingers trailed over the desk. "Think someone beat us to the B&E?"

"If this was where Danny kept his backup files, then, hell, yes." He marched toward the desk. "It would explain how you're getting those pics. Someone took them from Danny's stash and has been leaving them for you to find."

Claudia winced. "Just how many of those do you think are out there?"

"Depends on how long your brother had that asshole trailing us." He opened the top desk drawer. Empty. No, a few paper clips were inside. Nothing else.

He made quick work of searching the other drawers. Every single one just opened to reveal a cavernous interior. "Fuck."

She crept away from him. Poked her head inside the small bathroom. They hadn't turned on any lights. Danny Crenshaw had paid the lease, but had he paid the electricity? She didn't know, and there was enough illumination spilling through the old blinds on the window for her to see easily enough. And what she saw? "There's nothing here." Disappointment had her shoulders sagging. She'd really hoped they'd burst inside, find evidence, and boom, have the bad guy.

"Appearances can be deceiving." His cool reply.

She whirled around and saw that he'd actually hauled out the top desk drawer and flipped it over so that the drawer was upside down. And...

Something was taped to the bottom of that drawer.

"Someone was just not very thorough." His gloved hands reached for the big, brown envelope taped to the bottom of the drawer even as she rushed back toward him.

"How did you know to look there?" Color her impressed.

"I felt the drawer snag on something when I tried to shove it closed again." Carefully, he opened the envelope. "Someone emptied his files, took every damn thing, but Danny had this hidden away from the other stuff. Probably as insurance and—*sonofabitch*."

Her head and body craned as she peeked around him to see the picture, and when she did get a glimpse of the one on top of the little pile in his hand, the breath left her body in a rush. "That's Seth." She would recognize Seth Wellington anywhere. Judging by Holden's reaction, she knew he'd recognized Seth, too. Seth, and the other man in the picture.

Because Seth wasn't alone. He stood in a room that she knew and knew well. After all, she'd been in that room plenty of times in her life. It was the study at Edward Wellington's home. And Edward Wellington was *in* the picture, too. Edward sat while Seth stood a few feet away.

In the photo, Seth gripped a gun in his hand. A gun that he'd pointed straight at Edward.

"Oh, God." Her knees shook.

Holden thumbed through the pictures. Several pics—all of the scene in Edward's study. Rage clearly appeared on Seth's face.

Fear showed on Edward's.

In the images, Seth got closer and closer to his father.

But...

There was no picture of the gun being fired.

But the men were *in* Edward's study. In the room where his body had been found. The scene of the suicide. Except...

Holden turned toward her. She was so close their bodies bumped. Her throat had gone absolutely dry.

"I think we need to revisit the possibility," Holden said softly, "that Edward Wellington killed himself."

***

He gripped the brown envelope in one hand and held tightly to Claudia's fingers with the other. Holden had dragged out all of the drawers from the desk and the filing cabinet, just to be sure there weren't any other hidden photos or files waiting to be discovered. But he'd turned up nothing else.

Danny Crenshaw had only taken time to hide one stash of photos.

The photos that had cost the man his life?

Is that what the intruder broke into your house searching for? The pictures of Seth Wellington holding a gun on his father? But instead of finding the photos at Danny's house, the intruder had wound up killing the dirty PI.

Sunlight blared down on him as he hurried toward his rental, a light gray SUV that waited and...

Movement. To the right.

A flash of movement that shouldn't have been there. Because the gray SUV was the only vehicle in the lot, but someone else was clearly there. Hiding. *Ambush.* Holden staggered to a stop, and using his grip on Claudia, he pushed her back. "Go," Holden began. "Get back to—"

But it was too late. A swarm of men rushed from every direction. One came in swinging a bat.

Another had a knife in his hand. Five? Six men? They surged for Holden all at once.

And Holden was the only thing standing between them and Claudia.

Fuck this.

He let go of her wrist, but only long enough to yank out his gun. "Stop or you're dead." The men rushing at him didn't stop. Because, apparently, they were dumbasses. So Holden took aim, focusing on the fucker with the bat first and—

"Drop the gun or *she's* dead." A rasping voice that came from behind him.

No, no, no. Holden whirled, not caring about the bastard with the bat or the man with the knife or any of the others who'd been lunging for him.

Claudia stood a few feet away. A man had grabbed her. Unlike the others, his face was covered. Some kind of stupid monster mask, like part of a Halloween costume, had been pulled over his features. He wore all black. Big, bulky clothes. And that stupid mask that looked like a twisted demon grinning.

"Not fucking Halloween," Holden snarled.

The man had one arm around Claudia's stomach, and he had put a gun to her temple.

"Trick or treat," the bastard sneered back. "Drop the gun now, or I put a bullet in your girlfriend."

Fucking fucker. "Do you want to die slowly and painfully? That the end goal for you?" Holden lowered his gun to the concrete.

"Kick it toward me."

He kicked it as hard as he could. It flew past the bastard.

"Beat the shit out of him," the freak in the mask ordered. His voice was still muffled. Distorted. From the mask?

And at his order, Holden felt a bat slam into his back.

"No!" Claudia screamed.

That was when they all closed in.

"Get the envelope!" the freak yelled. "*And make sure he doesn't leave.*"

Then he started dragging Claudia back.

"No!" She fought in his grip. "Holden!"

He heard the *whoosh* as the bat swung again. Holden whirled, and, this time, he swung, too.

CHAPTER FOURTEEN

Step Fourteen: They want savage? Show them just how savage you can be.

"Told you that he couldn't protect you," the masked man whispered into Claudia's ear.

At least six men were attacking Holden, and some jerk had a gun shoved to her head. Fear blasted through every cell in her body as Claudia screamed, "Holden!"

A bat came right at his head. But he caught the bat and wrenched it out of his attacker's hand. Then Holden swung. The sound of that bat thudding into flesh filled the air. Once, twice.

The attacker went down. He didn't get up. The others jumped on Holden all at one time. A massive pile on as they tried to take him down.

Except Holden didn't go down. The envelope slid beneath his booted feet as he took brutal swing after swing at his attackers. When one jerk tried to stab him, Holden dodged and elbowed the man in the face.

"Get the envelope!" A shouted order from the guy still holding Claudia.

No one moved to follow his command.

Swearing, he let her go and leapt forward. He shoved his own men out of the way and grabbed for the envelope, then the creep in the mask lifted his gun and took aim at Holden as he fought the other men.

She didn't waste time screaming. Another scream from her might just have Holden whirling toward her. If he whirled, the bastard with the gun would be taking dead aim at Holden's chest.

And from this angle, he'll still shoot Holden in the spine. Not happening. Claudia flew forward, and she slammed her body into the man holding the gun. They fell together, a tangle of limbs, and the gun exploded. The sharp blast made her ears ring.

"Bitch," he muttered.

She went for his eyes. Or, wherever his eyes would be behind that stupid mask that he wore. Her nails raked straight at him and dug, but he jerked up his forearm and shoved her away.

When she rolled back, the ringing in her ears cleared, just a little, and she heard a man screaming in agony. She looked up, and at first, she just saw the blood.

Holden!

But, no, he wasn't the one who'd been shot. A younger guy, with ruddy skin and thin blond hair, was howling as he clutched his bleeding shoulder.

"Claudia!" Holden jumped toward her.

The man in the mask swore once more and scrambled for his gun. But when they'd hit the concrete, it had slid out of his grip. The gun waited several feet away.

Claudia glared at her attacker even as she realized—*You won't get the gun in time.*

Holden was too close.

The man in the mask must have realized that fact because he jumped to his feet and ran toward the parking lot. "End the bastard!" he bellowed. "*End him.*"

But the men he was leaving behind were already looking bruised and beaten. One of them was seriously bloody. Hardly looked like they were going to *end* anyone.

Holden reached for Claudia. He pulled her to her feet. "Baby? You okay?"

She gave a jerky nod, then tried to lunge away from him. She wanted that jerk who was fleeing.

The men who'd fought Holden formed a line—a somewhat shaky, human wall—blocking her and Holden from going after their boss. Ragged and worn, they were a rough crew. But fury blazed in their eyes.

Holden caught Claudia and tugged her behind his body. "Don't want to get blood on you, princess," he told her, voice soft. "Just give me a minute, would you?"

"I—"

He sprang forward with fists swinging in a blur. He jabbed at a man with a shaved head, Holden's fist striking with the force of a battering ram as he pummeled his opponent. Blood spilled down the other man's face, and his body went slack before he hit the concrete. When another attacker yelled and ran at him, Holden's round kick sent the guy flying. A third bastard was caught in Holden's quick grip. Holden yanked the man's head forward, and the guy's face connected with Holden's rising knee. When that would-be attacker hit the ground, he was moaning. And crying.

The other men looked at Holden—the few men left standing—and shook their heads.

"Screw this," one mumbled. He turned to run. He'd taken all of four steps when—

"*Freeze*." A cold, clear, and very female voice. A woman stepped forward, moving from the side of the building, and she had a gun gripped in her hand. The light hit her dark hair, making the red in its depths shine. "Take another step, and my itchy finger will squeeze the trigger."

The fleeing men turned as still as statues.

"You should call the cops, Claudia," the woman directed as her grip remained steady on the gun. "They need to come in and clean up the scene." Her gaze drifted over the fallen men. "And some here will certainly need an ambulance ride." She sighed. "Just had to play rough, didn't you, Holden?"

"Was wondering when you'd join the party, Harley," he tossed back as he flexed his hands into fists. "Nearly missed all the fun."

"Well, someone had *fun* with my car, and smoke and flames exploded from my engine on my way over here to watch your ass." Crisp. "Took longer than I expected to arrive."

Claudia pulled her phone out and called nine-one-one with shaking fingers.

"Where the fuck did the masked prick go?" Holden demanded.

The woman—Harley—shook her head. "Don't think I saw him." She still kept her gun aimed at the men.

Holden's hands flexed and released. He retrieved the gun he'd been forced to drop earlier. He looked toward the parking lot. Claudia followed his gaze. No sign of the freak in the mask.

Holden looked back at her. His eyes glittered. She knew he wanted to give chase. She also knew he wasn't leaving her.

It's too late. The jerk in the mask is long gone. And he'd taken the photos with him.

Holden's jaw hardened as Claudia began speaking with the nine-one-one operator.

"Did I say move?" Harley asked suddenly.

One of the men stiffened and went back to his frozen position.

"Good life choice," she applauded.

"We were attacked," Claudia said into her phone as she spoke with the operator. "Five, no, six men," she counted quickly as she looked at them. Wait, was that a seventh sprawled to the side?

"Do you need medical assistance?" the operator asked.

"I don't. They do." She rattled off the address—or, the main street location, anyway. She didn't know the exact building number, and she gave the best description that she could. "Send the cops and ambulances."

The operator said something else, but Holden had moved in front of Claudia, so she barely heard the other woman's words because her heart thudded so hard and her whole focus shifted to him.

"Hurry," Claudia whispered. She lowered her phone, but kept it on, just in case the operator was tracking her location via the signal—or however that worked on TV. She knew people were always told...*stay on the line*.

Her breath heaved in and out as she stared up at Holden. A cut bled along his right eyebrow, the red streaking over his skin. A faint tremble slid over her at the sight, but Claudia just stiffened her spine. The fight had been brutal, and there was blood *everywhere*. She wouldn't think about it. Or about the way her knees wanted to shake.

Holden. He was what mattered. He was big and solid, and she could feel the tension pouring from his body as his gaze swept over her.

"I'm okay," she told him softly.

He gave a jerky nod before swinging around to aim his gun at the men who'd jumped them. He and Harley had trapped the attackers. Harley stood on one side with her gun, Holden on the other.

At least three of the men appeared to be unconscious. The others were still in statue form.

Holden aimed his gun at the nearest statue. He closed in on the man. "Tell me who hired you," he ordered flatly. "Or I shoot you now."

"Holden." Alarm flared in Harley's voice.

"I didn't hear a name." Holden stayed focused on his prey. "How about we try that again?"

"OhGodohGod," the man whimpered. He squeezed his eyes shut. "If I talk, I'm dead."

"Yeah, I have a gun, and I'm right in front of you. You don't talk, and I'll get trigger happy."

"Holden." Harley stepped forward. "This isn't us. This isn't Wilde."

His head turned toward her. "This is me."

Claudia rushed toward him. She curled her hand around his arm. "Holden."

He didn't look her way. He glowered at the man before him. "You won't ever be safe from me, not unless you talk," Holden warned him. "Because you came after something of mine. Your boss had a gun to her head, and I won't ever forget that. Now I'm dealing with a whole lot of rage right now. I can either take that rage out on you...or on the prick in the mask. So *tell me* who hired you and I won't break every single bone that you—"

One of the other statues cried out, "You don't turn on Big Eddie! You do, and you're dead."

Big Eddie? Claudia's already frantic heartbeat increased even more because she knew he...he meant—

"Big Eddie?" Holden laughed. The sound was cold and twisted even as a siren screamed somewhere in the distance. "Eddie Wells is dead. Why the hell would you fear a ghost?"

"But...but..." The man before Holden shook his head even as blood dripped onto his shirt. "We were told this was a gig for Big Eddie! We wanted to get in good with him and...I mean...he's not dead. Is he?"

"Yeah, he fucking is." The sirens were louder, and the disgust in Holden's voice was even stronger. "You're damn idiots. Let me guess, you all took the job without actually *seeing* who hired you?"

Silence.

"Got to tell you, the last guy who did that wound up dying."

Claudia flinched. What? *Dying?* Was he talking about the man who'd tried to mug her in Atlanta? Holden had said that attacker vanished after making bond. There had been no talk of him dying.

"Better hope you have better luck than he did," Holden added as the sirens shrieked even louder.

Her head whipped to the left. She could make out the swirl of flashing lights heading their way. Moments later, a group of cops stormed to the scene with their guns drawn.

"Drop the weapons," one of them blasted.

Holden and Harley both put down their weapons. "We're not the bad guys," Holden told them. "I'm a victim."

A familiar figure in uniform stepped away from the other cops. A low whistle escaped him. "Oh, yes, the fact that you're standing and so many men are on the ground unconscious screams victim." Officer Gains cocked his head and studied Holden, then Claudia. "Guessing there was another incident?"

"You could say that," Holden allowed. "If by 'incident' you mean some prick putting a gun to Claudia's head and then running away while I had to deal with his gang wannabes. Then, sure, yes, there was an *incident*."

"He fucked me up, man," one of the guys on the ground groaned. "I lost a tooth."

Blood was, indeed, pouring from his mouth.

Claudia quickly looked away from him and tried to breathe evenly. *Do not pass out right here. Get your shit together, woman.*

EMTs hurried forward.

Holden stepped to Claudia's side. His arm brushed against her as he pointed at the man who'd lost his tooth. "You don't cooperate fully with the cops, you'll be losing a whole lot more than just a tooth."

Gains winced. "You're not supposed to threaten people like that. Especially not with cops present."

"Yeah, these bastards were not supposed to jump me like they did, either. Guess we're all learning new shit today, huh?"

***

"You sure you don't need an ambulance ride?"

"I'm fine, Officer Gains. The EMTs checked me out. I took far worse hits than this in my time." The bruises already forming were bullshit to Holden. They didn't matter. The only thing that mattered? Catching the SOB who'd put a gun to Claudia's head.

"This the mask he was wearing?" Gains held up the demon mask with its black hood. "Officer found it tossed in a dumpster at the hotel down the road."

"Yeah, that was it." Rage poured through Holden's veins. "Tell me that hotel has some security cameras up and running." He needed just one bit of good news. Was that so much to ask?

"Wish I could. The place barely has electricity and sure as hell not an operational security system." Gains bagged the mask. "Want to tell me again why you were here in the first place?"

"Following a lead." A true response. "Got word that a dead PI named Danny Crenshaw had a second office here. I learned that he'd tailed Claudia years ago." His gaze sought her as she stood with Harley. Harley had made sure to stick close to Claudia while the cops went through their questioning routine. "Thought we'd check it out." She was pale. Too pale for his liking, her skin nearly matching the white of her blouse.

"And did you? Check it out, I mean."

Holden shrugged. "Door might have been open so we slipped in. Drawers were all empty." The gloves they'd used in the search were shoved deep in his pocket.

"You think those guys followed you here?"

Only way to be sure would be to interrogate the hell out of them. Some of those jackasses had been taken away in ambulances. Others had been driven off in the back of cop cars. "I think they were hired to attack us. The bastard in the mask grabbed Claudia."

Gains rubbed his chin. "You think he wanted to kidnap her?"

I think he wanted to take the evidence we had. And, yes, dammit, I think he also wanted her, too. But first, he'd wanted Holden out of the way. "He could have shot me dead. Instead, he wanted those goons to beat the hell out of me."

"Only you beat the hell out of them instead."

Holden rolled his shoulders. "Had to defend myself."

"Uh, huh." Gains rocked back. "When he realized you weren't going down easy, the leader decided to run?"

"No." Claudia's voice. She'd been close enough to hear their conversation, and she advanced with her chin rising. "At that point, the man in the demon mask decided to shoot Holden in the back."

Shock rolled through Holden. "What?"

"So I hit him. Gave him my best football tackle." A faint tremble slid through her words. "Because I wasn't going to stand there and just let him *shoot* Holden right in front of me. We both hit the concrete." She looked down. "The gun flew from his fingers. He was going for it when Holden came at us."

Holden's breath shuddered out. *She saved my life.*

And risked her own in the process.

"Holden stopped to make sure I was all right."

Because I saw you on the ground fighting that bastard, and I lost ten years of my life.

"If he hadn't stopped to be with me, Holden could have caught the man in the mask. Even with the guy's goons closing in, Holden could have taken him down."

Holden had to swallow the lump in his throat. "Appreciate the confidence in my skills."

Her gaze didn't waver as she stared straight at him. "I have confidence in you."

Tension stretched between them. Utterly helpless, Holden took a step toward her. He needed her in his arms.

Gains cleared his throat. "Yeah, um, I'm still here."

Obviously.

"There anything specific you can tell me about the man in the mask? Because the fellows we loaded into the patrol car just knew they were supposed to follow his orders. Or at least, that's all they are saying right now. Maybe the unconscious ones will prove to be more talkative."

Her head moved in a jerky nod. "I do know something very specific."

Gains perked up.

"The man in the mask is the person who has been stalking me. The one behind the accidents or incidents or attacks—whatever you want to call them. *He* is the one who did everything."

The guy pulling the strings? And not just another flunky hired to do the dirty work? Sure, Holden had realized the guy was the leader of the goons who'd swarmed. He'd clearly been shouting orders at them. But that bastard had been the one behind everything?

And I let him get away. Sonofabitch.

"How do you know that?" Gains asked.

"Because he told me."

What. The. Hell?

Gains raised his eyebrows. "He admitted to being behind the incidents?"

"I got a text when I came back to town." Her words were low, strained. "The text said, 'He can't protect you from me.'" She wet her lips. "When that man in the mask held me tonight, he-he said, '*I told you he couldn't protect you.*' Same thing from the text. Deliberate." Her stare held Holden's. "It was him."

The bastard.

***

The scene was chaos. Claudia wanted to run away as far and as fast as she could. Instead, she kept her spine stiff and her chin up. Holden was alive. He was safe.

But the leader of the bad guys had escaped.

"Did you recognize his voice?" Gains pushed her. "Was anything about him familiar? I need something to go on."

"He had on black gloves, so I didn't see his hands. Thick, heavy clothes covered him. And that stupid mask." She darted a glance at the evidence bag. Another piece to add to her nightmares. "I didn't recognize his voice. It sounded funny, like it was muffled."

Gains and Holden shared a look.

"They think you might know the guy," Harley told her, as the other woman came to her side. "And are you beyond the point of wanting to pass out? Because you were scaring me a moment ago."

The lightheadedness had finally passed. "I don't do so well with blood."

Gains grunted. "Yep. Plenty of that was here. Courtesy of your boyfriend."

"He saved me." He'd taken on all of those men with no fear.

But Holden shook his head. "Wrong." He crossed to her side. His hand lifted and tenderly stroked her cheek. "You saved my life. I won't ever forget that."

Her head turned into his touch, and she wanted to just sink into him and escape. But escape wasn't an option. Harley's words were jabbing at her. *They think you might know the guy.* "Do you think I know him?" she asked Holden.

He wouldn't lie. Wasn't that their deal? No secrets? No lies?

He nodded grimly. "Why else wear the mask? Why muffle his voice? He did it in case his crew didn't succeed in taking me out. If he had to run—"

"Which he did," Harley inserted crisply. "Ran like the coward he was."

"Then he wanted to make sure you couldn't identify him," Holden concluded. His fingers caressed her cheek once more. "Baby, he's close to you. Someone in your life. Someone you know very, very well."

She thought of those pictures. Seth had been in those pictures. "He was about Holden's height." So was Seth. "When we fell together, I could feel his body beneath the clothes. He was fit. Lean." *Seth.*

"I get the feeling there is something else you want to tell me," Gains drawled.

She hadn't mentioned the pictures. Because Holden had whispered for her not to talk about them, right before the cops had started to question them.

"If you've got more to say, do it." Gains waited.

Holden dropped his hand. She immediately missed his touch.

"Your team should check the mask for DNA," Holden advised him. "Maybe you'll get lucky and find a hit in the system."

"We'll be sure to do that. But you know that kind of thing takes time. Weeks, maybe months. These attacks are getting one hell of a lot more intense. You think your lady has that much time?"

The lines near Holden's mouth deepened. "I think she's got all the time in the world. It's the bastard after her who doesn't." His fingers twined with hers. "Let's go, sweetheart."

But Gains stepped into their path. "If you know who it is, tell me. Don't go after him on your own."

"No worries," Harley piped up to say. "He's not on his own."

"That is *not* what I meant," Gains groused. "You can't take the law into your own hands."

"Understood." Holden's voice was as cool as you please. "Good luck interrogating those suspects. Maybe they'll turn on their boss and tell you everything you want to know." He tugged Claudia forward.

They didn't speak again, not until they were inside the shelter of the gray SUV. He pushed a button to start the ignition, and the motor flared to life.

Claudia stared through the windshield at the scene of chaos in front of her. "There a reason we didn't tell Officer Gains about Seth? Do you not trust him?"

"Every bit of intel I have says that Gains is a good guy, but I think this is over his head."

Gains was still questioning Harley.

"I'm calling in the Feds. They need to know about Seth. But before they take him out, I'm gonna make sure I have a run at him *because he fucking hurt you.*"

She sucked in a breath. "Without the photos, we don't have any proof that it is Seth." Even the photos hadn't shown him actually killing Edward. *Just holding the gun.*

"Would he do that?" she whispered. "Would he kill his father?"

"One way to find out. Let's go ask the bastard. Buckle up, sweetheart. The ride might get rough."

CHAPTER FIFTEEN

Step Fifteen: Go in on your target like a missile.
Forget being subtle. Detonate.

"And by 'ask' him," Holden added grimly as he locked his hands around the wheel and got them the hell out of that lot. "I obviously mean kick his ass."

"You didn't tell me that the mugger was dead."

Hell.

"I thought you weren't going to keep secrets from me."

His breath blew out as he navigated through traffic. He knew where Seth's house was located. Basic intel he'd picked up earlier. "Found out when I was making my calls last night. His body was discovered behind a club in Atlanta. Just...didn't get the chance to tell you all the details."

"You mean that you didn't want to tell me the details." A careful correction in a guarded tone. "So you delayed passing the info along to me."

He braked at a red light and glanced her way. The details weren't pretty, so, no, he hadn't wanted to dump them on her. But if she wanted the full, gory truth, he'd give it to her. "He'd been stabbed seventeen times."

Her breath sucked in on a sharp gasp.

"The cops are saying he picked the wrong person to rob. They have zero leads."

"They...don't think it's related to my case?"

"They don't." Holden disagreed with them. "I can't overlook the possibility it was. Maybe that mugger couldn't be trusted to keep his mouth shut for long. So he was eliminated. If that's the case, it tells me someone with power and reach was after him." The light changed, and he drove forward. "The men today thought they were working for Big Eddie."

"Only Edward is *dead*."

Yes, but... "The public doesn't know that Edward Wellington *was* Big Eddie." An important point to note. "Those guys? They didn't know jack. They were lackeys, following orders. They were low-level, looking to cut in with someone in charge. They were used, and they'll be discarded." He stared straight ahead. "When Eddie died, there was a power vacuum. I heard a few rumors that someone was stepping up to take power. Can't help but suspect the person going for the power play? It's the same bastard who has been terrorizing you."

A tense moment, then, "You think it's Seth."

She'd just said the not-so-quiet part out loud.

"Damn straight, I do." His gaze slid to the rear-view mirror, and Holden caught sight of Harley two cars back. She was watching his six.

He was glad to have her at his back. Time to see if the son was really as much of a bastard as the father had been.

"Why would Seth have killed his own father?" Claudia asked.

Simple. Power. If Edward Wellington hadn't been willing to step down, then Holden figured Seth had just taken the older man out of the way. But before Holden could reply, Claudia's phone rang.

"It's Cooper." Fumbling, she pulled out her phone. "Coop, this really isn't the best—" She stopped. "What do you mean Seth wants a meeting?"

What the hell?

"He's at the winery? Now?"

Holden pulled the SUV off the road and into the parking lot of a strip mall.

"Cooper, I want you to be very careful with him," she rushed to say. "I was just attacked and—"

Holden heard the explosion of words from her brother.

Wincing, Claudia removed the phone from her ear and held it a few inches away.

"May I?" Holden asked quietly.

She shoved the phone at him. "By all means."

Holden put the phone close to his own ear and heard Cooper's frantic barrage of, "*Attacked? Who the hell attacked you? Where is that dumbass Holden who is supposed to be watching—*"

"I'm right here," Holden answered. His voice cut right over Cooper's raging words. "And your sister is safe. She actually saved my ass, and that's just one of the many reasons why I'm so fucking in love with her." His stare didn't waver from

Claudia's even as her eyes widened at his casual comment. "The bastard was gonna shoot me, and Claudia tackled him." *She risked herself for me. No hesitation.* "You think I can ever live without her in my life? Not gonna happen."

Her lips parted.

Silence. In the SUV and on the phone.

Cooper cleared his throat. When he spoke again, his voice was a lot less frantic and a whole lot more considering. "I'm guessing you stopped the man who attacked her—and you?"

"He got away, but the cops have all his goons in custody."

"He got away? Well, that's great. Now he'll just make another attempt. How many more attempts until Claudia is seriously hurt?"

"No more." His grip tightened on the phone. "Seth Wellington is there with you right now?"

"Yes, at the winery. He came in a few moments ago and demanded that I call Claudia. Says that he has something urgent to tell us both." Cooper's voice lowered. "He's in my office right now, and I'm in the lobby. He's—he's acting strange."

Because he could be afraid that Claudia recognized him at the PI's place. "Do not let him leave. We're on our way."

Another car braked beside the SUV. Harley climbed out. Sashayed toward the driver's side. Her knuckles rapped on the window.

"*Do not let him leave,*" Holden ordered again. "And don't let down your guard."

"He wouldn't hurt me," Cooper said. But...

He hadn't quite sounded confident.

"Get someone else in the room with you guys," Holden advised. If something happened to Cooper, Claudia would be wrecked. "Someone you trust. A security guard. Someone who can handle a dangerous situation."

"*I* can handle—"

Nope, he couldn't. "Get someone else in there, understand? Now I need to call the FBI, so I have to let you go. Stay alive, would you?"

"What the—"

Holden hung up. Claudia's beautiful eyes were still huge. "Totally fine," he reassured her. "Your brother told me he can handle a dangerous situation."

"He can't," she stated very definitely.

Right. Holden's thoughts, too.

Harley rapped on the window again. Holden hit the button to lower the window.

"Why are we stopping? There some great sale going on at the mall that I need to know about?" A faint smile tilted her lips.

"Seth Wellington is at the winery. Seth told Cooper that he wanted to meet with him and Claudia. I'm going to call and brief the FBI, then we're storming the place." He had to pass along all that had happened to his Fed contacts. Shit was hitting the fan, and he might need a clean-up crew to sweep in, fast.

Her eyelids flickered. "How about I go ahead and get there while you brief the Feds? Better chance that our guy doesn't cut and run or, you know...create any other *incidents,* as I believe they have been called."

"Get there," Claudia urged her before Holden could speak. "Please protect my brother."

Harley didn't say another word. She headed back to her car.

"Call your FBI friends. Call them and *drive* at the same time," Claudia ordered. "Because my brother is many things, but he is definitely not someone who can handle danger well."

***

Cooper shoved his phone into the pocket of his pants. His sister had been attacked? And Seth had shown up at his winery's front door, demanding an audience with her. What was happening? Determined, he took a lunging step back toward his office.

"Sorry I'm late!" Reese's breathless voice as he bustled inside the winery's main entrance. "My damn alarm chose today of all days to stop working, then I had to haul ass across town and—boss?"

Cooper whirled toward him. Before being promoted to the director of operations position, Reese had been the chief of security. Reese was a former Marine, and a guy who always busted ass to get the job done.

"You okay?" Reese frowned at him. "Look, I know I said I'd be here first thing because the cops are supposed to be coming back with the crime scene team, but I'm just a little late. They aren't gonna be here until noon, so there is still plenty of time."

"Come with me."

"Uh, come where? If you want me to look at the chandelier mount in the tasting room, I really think we should wait for the cops. That's a crime scene, and they aren't gonna want us in there without them present."

Cooper grabbed Reese's arm and herded him toward the office.

"You okay?" Reese asked one more time. "You seem...stressed."

He felt damn stressed. Cooper shoved open his office door. It was a Saturday, so no one else was there. Like Reese, he'd gone in early because the cops were supposed to be coming back.

Instead, Seth had appeared, unannounced. Normally, that wouldn't be such a big deal. Seth was his best friend, after all. He often made surprise visits, both to Cooper's house and to the winery.

But...

But...

But when the office door flew open, Cooper saw that Seth was behind his desk, tapping at his computer. Seth jolted in surprise.

"What the hell are you doing...*buddy*?" Cooper asked flatly.

Seth flashed a quick smile. "Sorry. Just realized I needed to check some stocks. Figured you wouldn't care." His attention shifted over Cooper's shoulder. "Reese."

"Hey, Seth. How's it going?"

Cooper ignored the small talk between the two men. He edged around his desk just as Seth's finger tapped on the keyboard.

The screen went dark.

Seth's smile dimmed a little. "Everything okay?"

"I keep asking him the same thing," Reese rumbled. "Think he's still shaken up because of what happened to his sister last night. Close call, you know?"

"Yes, I know." Seth moved away from the desk. "That's why I'm here."

Cooper's gut twisted. "You've got intel on what happened to Claudia?"

"I do." His stare darted to Reese, then back to Cooper. "That's why I wanted to talk to you and her together."

"She's on the way." And he tapped on the keyboard. Why had Seth sent the computer into sleep mode?

"I should probably get to my office..." Reese began.

"No," Cooper said, voice abrupt.

Reese tensed.

The computer screen flickered back to life. It just took a moment and then...

My email. His email was open. Seth hadn't been checking his stocks. He'd been accessing Cooper's email. Cooper's head whipped toward his best friend.

"I can explain," Seth told him with a grimace. "It's—it's not what you think."

Cooper's hands flattened on his desk. He stared at the man who had been his best friend since they had been six years old, and he wondered if Holden had been right. Did he really know this guy at all? "You have no idea what I think."

"I really need to be going." Reese inched toward the door. "This feels like a personal chat. I don't think I should be here for it. There was something I wanted to check out regarding our security system and—"

"Do *not* leave this room," Cooper ordered him.

Seth turned for the door.

"I meant that order for both of you."

Seth whirled back around. Surprise flashed in his eyes.

"You wanted a meeting? A talk with me and my sister?" Cooper nodded. "I think it's time we had that talk. You know what? How about we go ahead and get things started?" He slowly lowered into his desk chair. "Here. I'll ask the first question."

"Coop..." Seth swallowed. His Adam's apple bounced.

"Did you know that your father killed mine?"

When Seth flinched—*dammit!* With that flinch, Cooper had his answer. "Sonofabitch." Pain knifed through him. Pain. Betrayal. Anger. And... "That bastard Holden was right, and he'll never let me forget that."

***

Holden braked the SUV in front of the winery. He saw Harley's rental to the right and knew that she was already inside. Before he could say anything, Claudia threw open the passenger side door and leapt from the vehicle.

"Dammit, baby, *wait!*" He raced after her and caught Claudia just as she was reaching for the entrance door. "Can you not run straight into danger?"

"*Can you not risk your life for me?*" Claudia tossed back, voice shaking. "Because I saw your body when the EMTs were checking you out. Your back is black and blue already. They thought you might have broken ribs—"

"I don't." He'd had them before. No way did he have them now. Bruises? Plenty of battering? Double check. "I'm fine."

"What if he'd shot you?" Rage flared in her eyes. "I am *done* with whatever game he's playing! You won't get hurt protecting me again."

She tried to break from his hold.

He wrapped her in his arms and lifted her away from the door.

"Holden!" Claudia yelled.

"You don't understand some things." This really wasn't the time to go over them all. Not with Seth waiting inside. On the drive over, he'd talked to an FBI confidant. His contact had seemingly been frothing at the mouth with the news Holden had dropped on him. Holden took Claudia a few feet from the winery's entrance and put her down.

She whirled to face him. "I understand plenty! I understand that I brought this danger to your door. Literally. I understand that we've had trouble chasing us for years, and I am over it. I understand that—"

"I love you?"

Her breath shuddered. "Don't say things you don't mean."

"I mean it. I realized you didn't believe it when you didn't say a word in response before."

"You didn't tell me. You told my brother. Didn't know I was supposed to respond." Her gaze snapped to the doors. "We need to get inside."

"I love you," he told her again. Making very, very sure to tell *her*. "And I can't have you at risk. Don't rush into danger. Stay with me. Fuck, stay *behind* me. That way, if bullets fly, they have to go through me before they can get to you."

Blue eyes blazed at him as her stare whipped back to pin Holden. "That's not funny."

"It wasn't supposed to be." He reached for her hand. Brought it to his lips. Kissed her knuckles. "It was supposed to be dead serious. Let me stand between you and danger. That's why you came to Wilde, remember?"

"I came to Wilde—" Claudia stopped, her lips clamping together.

He lifted his eyebrows. "Because you wanted my help?"

"Because you always made me feel safe. Didn't matter what happened between us personally, I knew you'd still keep me safe." Her lips thinned. "Now let's get inside and make sure my brother is protected, okay?"

"Right. The brother. On it. But how about you let me do the human-shield bit with you?"

"Why? I wasn't the one who nearly took a bullet to the back." She pulled her hand from his grip.

"He had the gun at your head." A memory that would haunt Holden until he died.

"If he'd wanted me dead, I would be dead right now. He had the opportunity to shoot me. He didn't."

And she was right. Something that terrified him the most. In those horrible moments when Holden had been forced to drop his gun, the bastard *could* have shot her. But he hadn't.

"I don't think he wants me dead." She bit her bottom lip, then added, voice catching, "I think he's trying to kill you. And I'm scared—very, very scared—that I was part of some terrible setup to bring you to him." As he watched, her eyes filled with tears. "I think that maybe I was never really the target. I think it was you. I think *I* put the bull's eye on you, and you're here, risking yourself because—because you still love me."

Absolutely. "Never stopped," he rasped. "Never will. I will love you until I die."

Her hands slammed into his chest. "Do not say that!"

His heart ached. "Why? Because you don't want to hear that I love—"

"Because I don't want to think about you dying! Not now. Not ever!" Claudia sent him a glare hot enough to burn. "Don't you get that? You matter. You always have. Stop being a human shield. Stop risking yourself. Dammit! You know what? *You're fired.*" She spun away, rushed forward, and grabbed for the door handle.

His mouth hung open. "Claudia?"

She was going in the winery without him. Hell, no. Holden bounded after her and curled his fingers around her shoulder. She'd yanked open the door and the cold air from the winery drifted out to him. "Baby, you can't fire—"

"*You can't force me to stay here!*" A raised, male voice. Angry. Scared?

Holden slid past Claudia to enter the winery's elaborate lobby. He caught sight of Seth Wellington marching furiously toward him, with Cooper, Harley, and Reese following on his heels. When Seth caught sight of Holden, he staggered to a stop.

The line behind him didn't. They barreled forward. Well, Harley and Cooper barreled forward. Reese stood back, looking a bit uncertain.

"Claudia." Seth's neck craned as he tried to see her as she stood behind Holden. "We need to talk."

She stepped to Holden's side. "That's why I'm here. But you seem to be running away."

Cooper caught up to Seth. He slapped a hand on his best friend's shoulder. "We aren't done, damn you."

The wild fury in Cooper's voice caught Holden off guard. "Did I miss something?"

"He *knew*," Cooper raged. "He knew what his father had done! He knew Edward murdered our dad!"

Holden heard Claudia's gasp of surprise. "Is that why you did it?" she asked, voice cracking.

"I need to explain—" Seth broke off, frowning. "Wait. Did what?"

"Killed your own father!"

Seth's mouth dropped open.

But Claudia wasn't done. She lunged toward him. *"Is that why you killed your own father? Because you knew what he'd done to mine?"*

CHAPTER SIXTEEN

Step Sixteen: Screw it. I don't care how long it takes. I don't care what I have to do.

I won't give up. Some people are just worth fighting for.

Seth gaped at her. "Kill my own father? What the hell are you talking about?"

Holden curled his hands around Claudia's waist and eased her back. For a moment there, he'd thought she was about to slam her fist into Seth's jaw. Satisfied that she was out of attacking distance, he sized up his enemy. "You heard her just fine." She'd been perfectly clear. And loud. "We saw the photos."

Seth swallowed. "What photos?"

"The photos of you pointing a gun at your father!" Claudia snapped.

He shook his head. "Don't know what you're talking about." Another click as he swallowed. "This is obviously not the time for a chat. My mistake. I'll just come back again some other day. I was worried about you, but, ah, again, not the time. I see that." He moved to step around Holden so he could get to the exit.

Holden just slid into his path. Seth wasn't getting away so easily. "I really think we should have that chat, now."

Reese cleared his throat.

Everyone looked at him.

Reese sent them an awkward wave. "This feels...like a lot. Should I be calling the authorities right now?"

"No!" Seth bellowed.

Uh, huh. Like that cry didn't make the man seem guilty.

Seth's shoulders heaved. "I can...explain."

But Cooper was already shaking his head. "Explain how your dad killed mine? How you knew about it for years and kept it secret?" His hands clenched into fists. "How you pretended to be my friend, my sister's friend, when all along—"

"I *am* your friend." Seth's eyes glittered. "I wouldn't be here if I wasn't. I'm trying to *help* you. Dammit, someone has put a hit on your sister. On her and that asshat next to her." He gestured to Holden. *"I am trying to help you all."*

Holden's blood iced. "How would you know about a hit?" Not something an average, ordinary citizen would know. But someone high in criminal circles? *That person would know.*

Seth whirled, his attention shooting over everyone who'd gathered in the lobby. After a tense moment, his attention seemed to center on one individual. "I don't know her." He pointed at Harley. "Just saw her being suspicious as hell at the gala."

"You saw me being awesome, not suspicious." She sent him a cold smile. "Harley Adaire. And it's not a pleasure."

"Right. I'm sure it's not. I'm also sure I'm not talking in front of you."

"Harley's with me," Holden rumbled. "As in, she's a Wilde agent."

"Wonderful. I don't care." Seth moved his hand to point at Reese. "He needs to go, too. What I have to say is on a need-to-know basis. Harley and Reese don't need to know." He spun back toward Holden. "You want me to talk? Then you get them out of here."

His gaze slid to Harley. She gave a slight nod. Holden knew she'd act like she was leaving, but Harley would stay close. A Wilde agent didn't leave a partner behind. As for Reese...

"I don't want to be here anyway," Reese muttered. "Couple of things I need to check, you know, *before the cops get here.*"

Seth stiffened.

"Coming back with a crime scene team," Reese hurried to add as he backed away. "Just so we are all clear. Let me say one more time...*The cops are coming.* I don't need to call them since they already have a visit scheduled. That's what they said last night. So maybe you guys sort out whatever is happening here pretty fast? Because I am hearing a lot of talk about people being killed. That is *not* the kind of talk that cops like."

Cooper gestured to his open office door. "Let's talk inside."

Holden had the feeling that what he really meant was...*Let's beat the crap out of this bastard inside*. And, normally, Holden would be game-on for some ass kicking. As it was, his world felt ready to implode.

A hit on Claudia?

He was holding onto his self-control, barely. He intended to get answers. *Now*. Answers, then the ass kicking.

Seth stormed back into Cooper's office. Cooper followed him, while Holden and Claudia were the last to enter. Holden made sure he shut the door. Then he took up a position in front of it, crossing his arms. Seth wouldn't be running out, not until Holden was good and ready to let him go. "Talk," Holden ordered.

Seth's cheeks puffed up, then he blew out a hard breath. "I got word very early this morning that an attack on Claudia—and you—was imminent. Someone had been looking to hire a crew, and they were doing it under the name of-of someone I used to know."

Looking to hire a crew, huh? "Save us the mysterious-air BS. We know that your father was Big Eddie. That he was involved in the underworld up to his eyeballs. If the bullet to the brain hadn't killed him, the Feds would have tossed him in jail and thrown away the key."

Seth seemed to pale. "I see." His shoulders sagged a bit. "What else do you know?"

"We know the *crew* that was hired to come after me and Claudia? Half of that crew is currently at the hospital, and the other half is being booked and getting thrown in jail."

"They already attacked?" Seth's voice rose. His frantic gaze ran over Claudia. What could have been worry filled his eyes.

"I'm fine," she said.

Holden shook his head. "She's not fine. The lead fucker put a gun to her head." That would never, ever be fine in his book.

Seth took a step back, only to find that Cooper had taken up a position right behind him. Seth's elbow collided with Cooper, and Seth jolted in shock. He spun to face his friend.

"You knew they were going after my sister?" Cooper's voice was low, but rough with fury. "You knew, and you did nothing?"

"No! Dammit, I came here as soon as I could! It took a bit for the intel to reach me. I came here to talk to Claudia, to warn her." His head shook. "The last thing I want is for her to get hurt. She's family to me."

"No, she's family to *me*," Cooper corrected grimly. "The only family I have. Our mom has been gone for years, and she won't ever be coming back. My dad is in a grave, one that...your father put him in?"

"I'm sorry." Brittle. Seth moved to the right so he could face them all. "I didn't know...not until...Jesus, he wanted me to be like him. Can you believe that? My father was proud, at the end. Telling me everything. Showing me everything. Saying I had to take over because there wasn't time left for him. I thought I knew my father. I *loved* him, and I thought I knew everything about him but he..." Seth swallowed. "He admitted to killing Caldwell Fairmont. Told me that it was the only way to handle someone who betrayed you. You didn't accept betrayal. You punished the betrayer."

Holden's stare shifted to Claudia. He hated the pain he saw on her face. Both Claudia and Cooper looked like the gates of hell had just opened before them.

But it wasn't just Claudia and Cooper who felt pain. The beast tore Holden's insides apart. Shredded him. "Caldwell Fairmont wasn't the only one in the fucking car. My mother was there, too."

Claudia grabbed his hand. Her fingers squeezed his. Sympathy. Support.

"I'm sorry." Seth's choked apology. "I'm sorry for everything he did. That last night, I-I told him I was going to the cops." Seth's voice dropped more. "And he told me not to be a disappointment. He called in one of his guards. The bastard—he pulled a gun on *me*."

That hadn't been in the photos. The only people in the photos they'd seen had been Seth and Edward Wellington.

"That's not what I saw in the pictures," Claudia said, her words seeming to echo Holden's thoughts. "When Holden and I were at the PI's office today—"

"What PI?" Seth cut in to ask.

She ignored his question. "We found photos of you. You and your father were in the study, and you had a gun pointed right at him."

He gaped at them. "You..." His stare jumped from one to the other. Then came back to rest on Claudia. "You seriously think I killed my father?"

"Did you?" A fast retort from her.

Cooper moved closer to his sister. His shoulder brushed hers. "Did you?" he repeated her question, his tone just as angry.

"No. I swear, I didn't! I took that gun from his guard. Made the bastard get out so I could talk to my father alone." A ragged exhale. "And, yes, I pointed the gun at my father. I told him that he had to stop. That we were going to the cops. That he had to confess. He just...laughed. Said he was dying anyway, that nothing would be done to him, and I had to take over the family business." He blinked. Narrowed his eyes. "What was the family business? Because I thought we worked in investments. Start-ups. That we had an interest in your winery. I thought he was a good man who loved his family. Loved his friends. But he *killed* his best friend, and kept calling him a betrayer. You know why?"

Holden had a pretty damn good idea. "Because Caldwell was turning on him. Caldwell went to my mother for a deal." *And she died, trying to just do her job.*

A grim nod from Seth. "Yes, it was because Caldwell was going to testify against my dad. He killed Caldwell." His gaze flickered to Holden. "He killed your mother."

He destroyed two families.

"How many more people had he killed?" Seth choked out. "I stared at him, and I saw a monster."

"So you shot him," Cooper growled.

"No. No! I put the gun down. *I didn't want to be anything like him!* But he was smiling at me and saying I had the killer instinct and I wanted him to be *wrong*. I walked the hell away. I went back into the hallway. Told that sonofabitch guard to get the hell out of my sight...and that's when I heard the gunshot."

Silence.

"I left the gun in there. I told him he was a worthless bastard. That I was turning him in to the cops. That he'd have to kill me in order to keep me quiet. And I *left the gun*. Except he didn't kill me. He turned that gun on himself." Seth's lips twisted. "But maybe it's the same—the same as me killing him. I put the gun there. I walked out. *I walked away*. And he blew his brains out."

Holden slid his attention to Claudia. To Cooper. They both stared at Seth in shock.

But Seth wasn't finished.

"I could have told the world what he'd done when he was dead, but it just wasn't that fucking easy." A muscle flexed along his jaw. "He'd set it all up—everything was in my name, and when I dug and dug...it looked like I was as guilty as he was. I started trying to clear everything up. I wanted to get a fresh start. I wanted to make things right. There were good people who worked for the company. Hundreds and hundreds of people. If the corporation had gone down, they would have lost their livelihoods."

"You mean that you would have lost your fancy life," Holden corrected.

"*No*. It wasn't about me. I was trying to make things right. But the people he was connected to— the criminals—they thought I was like him. They still damn well do. I am working my best, doing as much as I can and I—" His lips clamped together. "There are some things I can't tell you."

"Can't or won't?" Cooper wanted to know.

"It's bigger than me. Bigger than your family, too. I'm sorry. I am doing my *best*."

Holden thought his best was jackshit. "Your best almost had Claudia being kidnapped and me getting a bullet in my back."

Strain marked Seth's face. "I am going to find out who put out the hit! I will, I swear."

But Cooper didn't seem convinced. "Maybe we're looking at the guy who did it."

"No." A fast shake of Seth's head.

"Seth." Claudia's soft voice. "Why didn't you tell us the truth? Coop and me? Why not us at least?"

Pain flashed on his face. "Tell you that your dad was as much a criminal as mine? That he just decided to try and make a deal so he could get a new life? You'd buried him. You'd grieved. Understand that I didn't learn the real truth until six months ago. Then when I did, I thought it might be better for you to remember a father who was a cheating spouse and not a man who was as twisted and cold as my dad turned out to be. *I thought I was protecting you both.*"

"Not your call." Fury spilled from Cooper. "You don't get to make the call about deciding what's best for someone else's life. You don't get to—" But his gaze jerked to Holden. Then to Claudia. Realization seemed to dawn on him. "Fuck me."

Right, buddy. Fuck you. Because you tried to play with our lives, too.

Cooper squeezed his eyes shut a moment. "Fuck me," he said again. "Claudia, there is something you need to know."

Oh, great. *Now* was the moment he wanted to make his big confession? Like they didn't have enough shit hitting the fan right then?

"Did you know the PI took the pictures?" Claudia asked Seth as she stepped forward. "Was he blackmailing you with them?"

Seth's expression tensed. "You keep mentioning a PI..."

"Danny Crenshaw." It was Cooper who supplied the name. "Recommended by your father. Turns out the bastard might have been stalking my sister years ago and taking pics of her and Holden while they were—you know what? Screw what they were doing. Your father told me I could count on the PI. I hired him, and it looks like he was nothing but some two-bit con who liked to take compromising pictures of people."

Seth blinked. "Like...a picture of me holding a gun on my father?"

Holden exhaled. "Danny Crenshaw was killed days after your father was buried. Someone broke into Danny's house and killed the PI with his own gun. Cops thought it was a robbery gone wrong because the place was trashed, but I'm thinking his attacker was just searching for something. Probably a certain set of photos." *Photos of you aiming a gun at your father.*

"Despite everything I just told you, you still think it was me?" Seth's hand slapped against Cooper's shoulder. "You *all* think it was me?"

What Holden thought... "I think Reese was right when he said the cops would be arriving soon. But I also know the Feds will be closing in, too. See, they happen to have a long-standing interest in your father's business. Not-so-funny story...your dad had me kidnapped years ago, and he made me miss my own wedding."

Seth's gaze flickered to Holden.

Rage pulsed inside of Holden. Rage and pain were a deadly combination. "But you knew that, didn't you, you bastard?"

"No, no, I *didn't!* I'm still just discovering all the terrible things that he did. Trying to make it right. To untangle things and pay for his sins—"

"Oh, you will pay," Holden assured him. "If you've been behind the attacks on Claudia, you will pay dearly."

Seth sidled to the right. "I haven't tried to hurt Claudia. She's like a sister to me."

"She's *my* sister," Cooper snarled. "Not yours. And I don't trust you a bit around her."

Pain hardened Seth's face. "You're my best friend."

"She's my family. Someone has been after her, and I thought I was helping, but, dammit, now I think I've just been trusting the wrong people and *you* are one of those wrong people."

A sharp knock sounded at the door. "Uh, boss?" Reese called out.

"Not now." Cooper's curt reply.

"You...you really need to hear this, though."

There was something about Reese's voice. Following his gut, Holden hurried and opened the door.

Reese stepped inside. Winced as he looked around. But then his attention focused on Seth, and his eyes hardened. "Why were you in the VIP tasting room last night?"

"Excuse me?" A negative shake of Seth's head. "I have no idea what you're talking about."

"I just did a fast rewind through the footage that we *still* had. Everything vanished right before Holden and Claudia went inside, so I decided to go back more. No one should have been in the VIP room last night. It was off-limits to regular guests."

"It was locked," Holden added as all his muscles tensed. "I snagged Claudia's key to get access."

Seth wet his lips. He also edged a little more to the right. "Look, we all need to calm down. I came here today in order to try and help."

"I'm calm." So easy to say. Holden shrugged. "Do I not look calm?"

"You look calm to me." Cooper's instant reply. "I think I'm pretty calm, too."

No, he wasn't. Cooper was cracking at the seams.

"I had the idea to look back at the earlier footage." Reese's words seemed to tumble over each other. "I mean, I know the cops will do it, too. Probably review everything, so I just started going back myself and..." He kept looking straight at Seth. "You were coming out of the tasting room. About thirty minutes before Holden and Claudia went in, you came out."

A shrug. That was Seth's answer? Just a shrug?

"Why were you in there?" Claudia asked.

"I wasn't," Seth denied. "Must have been someone else."

But Reese took a quick step forward. "Someone who looked exactly like you? You got a twin brother running around this place that I don't know about?"

"I don't have any family." Bitten off. "My mom died when I was seven, and as we all are clearly aware, a bullet tore into my father's brain. Now, this chat hasn't quite gone the way I hoped, so I will be leaving." He strode for the door.

Holden didn't have to block his path this time. Cooper did. "Why were you in the tasting room last night?"

"I *wasn't.*"

"I thought..." Reese's quiet voice filled the room. "When I originally heard about what happened, it seemed like someone must have been in there *with* Claudia and Holden. That the attacker made the chandelier fall right then. But maybe...maybe you went in earlier and did something to the chandelier's control panel. Sabotaged the lifting and descending mechanism. Because I swear, my crew would not have made an installation mistake. I called them last night. Talked to the two men who installed the chandelier. They swear it was secure. And maybe it was, until you went in and messed around with it."

Cooper and Seth stared at each other.

Claudia put her hand on Seth's shoulder. His head jerked toward her.

"Why would you do that?" she asked quietly.

"I *didn't*."

"Swear it to me, Seth." A fast order. "Swear you had nothing to do with any of this. Swear that you are not—"

"I am *not* my father. I would not hurt you or Cooper. I'm trying to protect you both, can't you see that? Why the hell would I sabotage the chandelier when you weren't even in there? How would I know that you *would* go in there at some point? I'm not psychic!"

No, not psychic. But Holden had a suspicion of his own. "Maybe you just wanted to cause some chaos. Maybe you didn't care when the chandelier fell, you just wanted it to plummet." Maybe Holden and Claudia being inside had just been a coincidence.

But I don't like those...

"You all think I'm guilty, don't you?"

Claudia was the first to respond. "I don't know what to think."

Seth looked at his best friend. "Coop?"

"If you've tried to hurt my sister, I will destroy you."

Holden blinked. Well, well. Cooper was starting to sound...*hell, a bit too much like me.*

"I have the video footage," Reese chimed in. "And I'm going to show it to the cops. You can explain to them why you—"

Seth shoved Cooper out of his way and rushed for the open door. Cooper went down, hard, his body slamming into the floor.

Shit.

Claudia cried out and reached for her brother.

Dammit, Cooper had always been a lightweight. As soon as possible, Holden would be training that dumbass so things like this would not happen again. For the moment, though, he just jumped over Cooper's prone body and gave chase after his prey.

Innocent men don't run. And Seth wasn't just running. The guy seemed to be hauling ass in a truly Olympic contender-type sprint. Seth's hands slammed into the glass doors at the front of the winery, and he surged outside. Holden flew forward, just steps behind him and—

"*Ahh!*" Seth's body jolted. As if he'd been hit by electricity.

Because he had.

Harley stood with her legs braced apart and her taser still in her hand. "Looked like he was trying to make a getaway."

Holden heard the clatter of footsteps rushing up behind him. He grabbed Seth and slammed him to the ground.

"Figured I should stop him," she added.

Seth groaned and turned his head. He glared up at her. "What. The. Hell?"

She sent him an angelic smile. "Betting you'll never forget me, huh?" Then her gaze darted to Holden. Winking, she asked, "Am I the best partner ever?"

"Definitely in the top five."

CHAPTER SEVENTEEN

*Step Seventeen: When the case ends, you won't
have a reason to stay close to her any longer.
The pretense will end.*

*So go for the real deal. Do not give up. Never
give up on her.*

"Questioning?" It sounded like her brother
was strangling as he talked to Officer Gains.
"That's it? He's just being brought in for
questioning? Do you *know* how many lawyers
that Seth will get to stonewall you? He's not going
to answer any of your questions."

Gains winced. "Look, he was just tased on
your property—"

"Uh, because he was making a run for it,"
Harley interjected as she threw her hands into the
air. "We've got a pile of suspicious evidence
against him. Seth attacked Cooper and ran."

Claudia slanted the other woman a quick
look. She was ninety-nine-point-nine percent
sure Harley hadn't known that Seth had thrown
Cooper to the floor before he'd tried to make his
getaway. She didn't mention that fact at the
moment, though. Her mind was still reeling from
everything that had happened. Holden had kept a
tight grip on Seth until the cops had arrived. She'd

been the one to call Gains since he'd been the cop to work her case so much. He'd arrived just before the other patrol cars had roared onto the scene.

"Circumstantial evidence." A careful correction from Gains. "I don't see any smoking gun."

If you'd seen the pics, you might have. But she didn't say that part. Because the pictures were long gone. Unless...maybe Seth hadn't been able to destroy them? Not yet?

Was Seth really the man who put the gun to my head? He was the right height. And he could have gone from the PI office over to the winery but...

But this was Seth. The kid who used to let her trail after him when he and Cooper went to ball games and movies. The guy who'd wiped away her tears at thirteen when Bobby Westing had dumped her before the Middle School prom.

Would he have really done that to her? Put a gun to her head?

"You should go home."

She blinked and realized that Gains was talking to her.

"The crime scene team is going to work here for a while as they finish up the investigation they started last night in the tasting room. If they find anything useful, I will make sure you know. But you've had one hell of a morning, and you need some time to decompress."

Decompress? She felt more like she was about to shake apart. Everywhere she looked, Claudia swore she saw more secrets and lies, and she was so done with them.

"Is there anything you haven't told me?" Gains put his hands on his hips. "Anything else I need to know?"

They still hadn't told him about the photos. She didn't even look at Holden as she blurted, "Ask Seth about his father's death."

"His father?" Gains raised his bushy brows. "The suicide?"

"We found photos...at the PI's second office." She sucked in a breath and could feel the weight of Holden's stare on her. Silent, strong, he was right at her side. "They were pictures of Seth holding a gun on his father."

"*What?*" The cop's mouth dropped open. He hurriedly snapped it closed. "Where are those photos? I need them!"

"They were taken from us by the guy in the stupid demon mask." A shiver slid over her. Why the shiver? It wasn't cold out there. Not even a little chilly. In fact, her skin felt too heated. "The evidence is gone, but we saw the pictures. Holden and I both could swear to that."

Gains crept closer. "You saw a photo of Seth Wellington killing his father?"

"No." A quick denial as her brow scrunched. "We just—we saw him holding the gun."

Gains whistled. "This is one hell of a tangled mess."

Tell me about it.

"You should have told me about the pictures before," he groused.

They were in the winery's parking lot. Several patrol cars had pulled to haphazard stops. As they stood there, a big, black SUV rolled up.

Claudia didn't know where her brother had gone. Seth had already been loaded into the back of a patrol car. Harley kept pacing nearby as she listened to their conversation, and Holden? He'd stayed by Claudia's side every moment.

He had to be hurting. He'd taken hit after hit from that stupid bat when he'd been attacked. But he stood there, strong and steady, waiting with her. Just being with her.

Because he loves me? His words had wrecked her, but she'd tried not to show her response. With everything else happening, she just—she *couldn't* stop to think about what was happening between them. And what they meant to each other. And she could not analyze the hope that tried to blossom inside of her.

Someone wanted to kill her. And Holden. Hoping seemed dangerous.

But...

Maybe we have the bad guy. Maybe it's all over.

"Who the hell are they?" Gains demanded.

Two men and one woman had just climbed out of the SUV. They all wore suits. The woman was in a fashionable, gray suit with black flats. One of the men wore a drab, brown suit, while the other was dressed in a light blue one that fit his body as if it had been individually tailored for him.

"Thought the winery was closed today." Gains motioned toward a nearby cop. "Get the customers out of here."

"Not customers." Holden finally spoke, his voice growling a little. "FBI."

"What?" Gains did a doubletake.

"The black SUV didn't give them away? Always warning them to be less obvious assholes, but they just don't listen."

The three FBI agents closed in.

"Didn't tell you about the pics because we had to tell them first," Holden explained to Gains. "They have an ongoing investigation into the Wellington family, so, yeah...I think this is the part where the cops and the Feds engage in a pissing match. Got to tell you, man, they don't like losing competitions." He rolled back his shoulders and inclined his head to the newcomers.

"Is one of them your main contact?" Claudia watched the three approaching carefully. They'd certainly gotten to the scene fast. She'd had no idea that Holden's contact had been in the area already.

"No. Never seen them before in my life." His tone had become guarded. "I just know the look of the agents by now. All have that same swagger, and there will always be one with a really crappy suit." A long sigh. "Have to say, though, I am highly suspicious."

The agents were almost upon them. The woman flashed her ID.

"How *did* they get here so quickly?" Holden murmured. "Even with my contact reaching out to the local office, this is fast." Beneath his breath, she was pretty sure he muttered, "Too fast."

But Claudia didn't get to question him more because the agents were right there. Offering smiles that didn't reach their eyes and scoping out the scene.

The woman spoke first. "I'm FBI Special Agent Francesca Garcia. These are my associates, Special Agent Brent Marchello and Special Agent Angelo Tate." The men dipped their heads forward. "And we are here to take charge of—"

"Do *not* say my investigation," Gains groused. "Because I don't know you agents from jack, and I have just taken a suspect into custody."

Unerringly, Francesca's dark gaze lit on the car that held Seth. "You mean you took *our* suspect. And don't worry, we will be sure to keep you in the loop on every step of this investigation." Her stare slid to Holden. "I've been briefed on you," she revealed. "Your cooperation is appreciated."

He grunted. "I am sure it is."

"Appreciated, but no longer needed." A delicate clarification delivered in ice. "We'll be taking over now."

That certainly sounded like a dismissal to Claudia. "That's it? No other explanations? Just—basically you want us to get out of your way?"

Francesca shared a look with the other agents. Then she sent a smile to Claudia. A sympathetic one. "I understand you've been under a great deal of stress."

"I'd call it more than stress." Multiple attacks. A near kidnapping. All of that equaled a whole lot more than just stress.

"Agent Marchello will be following you home. He'll keep an eye on you for the next few days."

What? "Why?" She gestured toward the police car. Seth stared at her from the backseat. "The suspect is in custody. Are you planning to let him go so he can have another run at me?"

The sympathetic smile dimmed. "You should really go home now. You're overwrought."

Over— Claudia surged forward.

Holden's arms wrapped around her stomach. "Sweetheart," he breathed in her ear. "Let's get the hell out of here."

Francesca's hands went to her hips, pushing back her coat to reveal the holster on her right side. "You've been through an ordeal. You should rest. After I've had a chance to question the suspect, I will be following up with you."

No. No way. This was not good enough.

Francesca's lips tightened. Her head turned toward Gains. "Give us a moment alone, would you?"

"Oh, sure. You just send me away from talking to a witness at *my* crime scene."

"*Officer* Gains, I know the chain of command. And I know there are plenty of people who rank above you. This is not your scene. Stand down."

His face darkened.

"Besides, Agent Tate has some questions for you." She motioned with her hand. "Your cooperation is appreciated."

Was that a standard FBI line? If so, Claudia sure didn't like it.

Tate walked away with a still-glaring Gains.

As soon as they were gone, Francesca peered back at Holden and Claudia. "Holden, I know you're aware of the investigation into the

Wellington family." Her voice was soft as she edged closer. "I was briefed about your involvement several days ago, and my team has been monitoring your progress with the recent, uh, unfortunate turn of events here."

Unfortunate? "You're calling what happened to us unfortunate?"

Francesca winced. "There is a lot I can't say now. I'm not big on the cloak and dagger bit, but my hands are tied. Rest assured that I am taking everything in this investigation seriously. When I can tell you more, I will. Right now, Claudia, I was advised to get you away from the crime scene, and to keep eyes on you for your safety."

"Is this because of the hit?" Holden asked bluntly. "Did other bastards take up the offer? Will more people be gunning for us?"

"I can't say yet. Though, that is certainly a possibility. So, please, go with Marchello. Stay safe and out of sight until I contact you again." She inhaled and straightened her shoulders. Her voice rose as she said, "Thank you for your cooperation. The FBI appreciates all you have done."

All they have—

Holden began to lead her away. Claudia dug in her heels because she had a whole lot of other questions to voice.

"Save them," Holden advised, as if reading her mind. "Because something isn't right."

Oh, he thought that now? Things hadn't been right for a while in her world.

But Cooper suddenly appeared. Breathless, eyes a bit crazed, hair askew, he popped in front of her. "We have to talk," he told Claudia.

"Fuck it." Holden's irritation was clear. "Should have known he'd get in my way. Cooper, *save it*."

"No, no, I won't. She needs to know." His jaw hardened. "I'm not like them. I *won't* be like them. Not like our dad. Sure as hell not like Seth's. I'm sorry."

What did he have to be sorry for?

"I've been keeping secrets from you, Claudia. Dammit, I am *sorry*."

"He gets a conscience, now of all times. Fantastic." Holden wasn't just irritated. She heard disgust in his tone, too. He also kept leading her toward the waiting vehicle. A light rain began to fall on them as Cooper dodged her steps. Growling, Holden ordered, "Move it, Cooper."

Cooper backed up, just a bit.

Holden opened the passenger side door and gently pushed her inside.

"I offered him five hundred grand!" Cooper blurted.

Holden attempted to shut the passenger door. The rain picked up, pelting lightly against him.

Her hand flew out to keep the door open. "What?"

She saw Harley skulking behind Cooper. Listening. Watching.

"Five hundred grand." His shoulders dropped. "At the bachelor party, I told him that I'd pay five hundred grand to him if Holden would just walk away from you."

Her hand moved away from the door and balled into a fist.

"Your timing is total shit," Holden barked at Cooper, then he slammed the passenger door shut. Lightning snaked across the sky. A quick flash. When had the sky darkened so much? It was so early in the day. She hadn't even been aware of the growing storm.

Not until it surrounded her.

Cooper stared at Claudia through the glass. Behind him, she saw Holden move to whisper something to Harley. Harley nodded and hurried off.

Cooper didn't move. His hand lifted to the glass. "I'm sorry." Did she hear the words? Hard to say because her heart pounded so hard and seemed to echo in Claudia's ears. But she saw the movement of his mouth, and she knew what he'd meant.

Holden jerked open the driver's side door. "Coop, get the hell away from the vehicle before I run over your damn foot." He jumped inside and gunned the engine.

Cooper stepped back.

She looked down at her hands. Both had balled into fists.

Holden got them away from the winery. Away from the cops and the questions and the pain. And...

"Aren't you going to ask me what I told your brother when he offered me the cash?"

She swallowed. "No." The rain fell harder. The windshield wipers flew across the glass.

"Why not?"

"Because I already know." Her gaze stayed on the wipers. Faster, faster, they flew.

He turned at the light. "You do?"

Her nails bit into her palms. "It's what I would have said if someone offered me cash to leave you."

Silence. He drove straight ahead. She tried to relax her fists, but the fury inside of her was too great. Fury. Pain. Betrayal. Heartbreak.

The miles passed in a blur. They were close to the Fairmont mansion and guest house when Holden finally asked, "What would you say? If someone offered you half a million to leave me?"

She saw that his knuckles had whitened because he had such a strong grip on the wheel. "Fuck you," Claudia enunciated clearly. "There's no amount of money that can make me leave the person I love."

"Pretty close to what I said." Ragged. He braked in front of the big gates that led to the property. His head turned, and his eyes locked on her. No, saw straight *in* to her. "Fuck you," he said, just as clearly as she had. "There is no amount of money worth giving her up. Claudia is *everything* to me. I would die before I hurt her."

And he almost had. Damn him. He *almost* had. On their wedding day, a gun had been put to his head...

And a gun was put to mine today.

They'd been torn apart. Too long. Too much pain.

Too much.

The security guard saw them. Recognized her and Holden, and he opened the gate. They didn't speak again. Not as he followed the drive to the guest house. Not when they exited the vehicle. Not as they dashed through the pelting rain. Not as they started to climb up the steps that led to the guest house—

Claudia spun around. She grabbed his shoulders. Shoved onto her tiptoes. And dragged him down to her so that her lips could crash into his as the rain poured onto them.

CHAPTER EIGHTEEN

Step Eighteen: Sooner or later, you have to let the past go. You want a future with her. So bury the past as deep as you can. Shove that bitch into the ground.

The rain hit him. Thunder rumbled across the sky. He wanted to stand there and keep kissing her forever—screw the rain—but he had to get her inside. It was safer inside. Holden tore his mouth from hers. "Inside, baby. *Now.*" He could taste the rain and her, and he wanted so much more of her. All of her.

He hurried up the steps and shoved the key into the lock. She moved behind him, and her hands curled over him. They'd reached the shelter of the small porch, so the rain didn't hit him. He stood there, just feeling her behind him. The rain fell in a heavy, hard blur. He turned back to her, helpless.

Her shirt was soaked. So was his. But he could see through her shirt. See the tight nipples that he wanted in his mouth. The rain had wet his face. Rain drops slid down his body, just as they slid down hers. Her perfect, tempting body.

She was wet and sexy, and he wanted her to be *his.*

Her hands went to the front of his shirt. Jerking, shaking, she unfastened the buttons, and his shirt gaped open. She pulled away the wet fabric, and her fingers touched his skin.

Holden sucked in a sharp breath. Immediately, her gaze flew up to his. "Did I hurt you?"

He caught one of her hands. Held it in place. "You would only hurt me if you left me." *Don't leave me. Not ever again. I can't go back to living without you.*

He wanted to fuck her right there. No, to move back into the rain and take her as the water pounded down on them. The rain could wash away the past and his regrets. It could wash it all away, and they could start new.

I want to start over with her.

But it wasn't safe out there. Even with the guard at the gate and the Fed tailing them, he didn't feel safe. He also didn't intend to give anyone else a show. What happened between him and Claudia was just for them. He was already infuriated enough that her stalker had pics of them.

She is just for me.

Using his grip on her hand, he tugged her over the threshold and into the house. A shiver slid over her as she stared up at him. Water dripped from them onto the floor. The rain had been hard and brutal. They should strip. Get rid of the wet clothes.

I just want in her.

His hands curled around her hips, and Holden started to lift her up against him—

"No!" Claudia pulled back. Stumbled back. Eyes wide, she shook her head. "No, you've got bruises all over you!"

Like that was something new.

"They attacked you in front of me. *With a bat*. One of them had a knife. And that man in the mask came at you with a gun." She shook her head, and water from her hair slung lightly in the air. "Seth. It could have been Seth who tried to shoot you."

Wait, was that just rain water on her cheeks? Or was that...more? Holden narrowed his eyes on her.

Oh, no. Oh, hell, no. Were those tears in her eyes?

They *were* because she was angrily swiping them away with the back of her hand. "Money didn't make you stay away from me all this time. You didn't stay away because my brother offered you cash."

No, he hadn't. Holden truly had told Cooper to fuck himself when he got that offer. Holden shed his wet shirt. Let it hit the floor. Kicked away his boots and socks. The wet jeans clung to him. "There is no amount of money in the world that would keep me from you."

"You stayed away to protect me." She didn't strip. Just stood there in the white shirt that let him see her nipples. Made him want to taste and take.

But her words were true. He had stayed away to protect her. So Holden nodded.

"Damn you!" Claudia cried out. "You should have told me! I am sick to death of being kept in the dark."

He *had* told her this, well, okay, fine, the reveal had been fairly recent, and he could get that she was pissed and he—

"The night you came to me. On my porch. Five years ago. When that stupid car revved outside, you thought it was one of the bad guys, didn't you?" More drops of water fell onto the floor. She was wet and beautiful. *And mine. I want her to be mine.*

"I knew I was being watched. I knew you were a weakness that would be used against me." *I couldn't let that happen. I couldn't let anyone hurt you.*

Another swipe of her hand over her cheek. "So I make you weak?"

He advanced toward her. His hand lifted as he saw a tear slide over her silken skin. That tear hurt him more than any swing of a bat. Tenderly, carefully, he wiped away the tear. The rain. "If something happened to you, I would be lost. You make the world worth living in for me, sweetheart. Even when we weren't together, knowing you were *out there,* happy, alive. That's the shit that kept me going." Did she understand? "Whether you're with me or not, I need to know that you're safe and happy." He also needed her out of her clothes. So she'd be dry. She couldn't stay—

"You should have told me everything years ago."

"You were in France. And then you seemed to hate me." They'd been over this. "And I—"

"Can be really clueless because I never hated you," she snapped, finishing his words in a way he hadn't intended and shocking him. "I *never* hated you. Not ever. How could I? I never stopped loving you."

He blinked, absolutely certain that he had misheard.

Another tear fell down her cheek. "What? You think you're the only one who gets to say 'I love you' in this relationship?"

He couldn't speak.

"I love you." Flat. She yanked against her wet shirt, pulling it away from her skin. "I have loved you for years. Loved you when it hurt so much I could barely breathe, but I still loved you. And I love you even more now, though I don't know how that is possible because I was already pretty crazy for you before—"

He kissed her. Hard. Desperate. Almost begging. And he never, ever begged.

I would beg for her. I would kill, lie, steal. I would do anything it took for her.

She didn't pull away this time. She kissed him with a frantic desire and need that rivaled his own. Love and lust tangled within him. He didn't care about the aches in his body. The pain from the attack. Screw that. He held the only thing that mattered. Claudia would always come first.

Her hands flew between their bodies. She grabbed his belt. Unhooked it and shoved down the top of his wet jeans.

"Baby..." He moved to press frantic kisses to her cheek. Once more, he tasted her tears and the rain. *I don't want her ever crying again.* "Baby, give me a second. I'll take off my jeans and get rid of yours."

At his words, she eased back. Her shoulders shook as she sucked in deep breaths. Her eyes were on his bare chest. Slowly, her gaze dipped to his abs. "Holden." Soft. Sad. Her trembling fingers touched his skin. "They hurt you so much."

He looked down. In the light, yeah, the bruises that had already formed looked pretty bad. But they didn't matter. "The only thing that would have hurt was losing you."

Her head lifted. Those incredible eyes of hers locked on his.

"I can't lose you again. It would rip me apart." Nothing would hurt him more.

"You won't lose me." Then, she lowered to her knees.

"No, baby, no." He should be the one on his knees. Fucking begging her to forgive him for all the lost years. *I cannot lose her again. I won't.*

"You're hurt." Her breath feathered over his skin as she leaned toward him. "So we have to use extra care with you."

What? "Claudia?" What they needed to do was get rid of her wet clothes. They needed—

Her fingers curled around his eager dick. A portion of his anatomy that certainly wasn't hurt. In fact, his dick was at full attention and more than game for any action she wanted to throw his way. And she was...

Pumping him. Stroking him. Leaning forward even more and parting her lips and taking the head of his cock inside her mouth.

"*Fuck.*" His hands curled over her shoulders. Dug into the damp material. He should pull her away. Lift her up. Get them to a bedroom. His bedroom was close-ish.

But she took him in deeper. He watched her. Nothing was sexier than seeing her mouth open wider as she took more of him. Helpless, his hips surged against her, and she moaned around his dick.

His eyes wanted to roll back into his head because this felt so incredibly good. Her hot, wet mouth. The way she licked and sucked was driving him to the absolute edge, and he'd be going over soon. He'd erupt into her mouth. Fuck her mouth. Fuck her. And he would— "*Enough.*" Because he wanted her coming around him. This wasn't just about him.

Claudia first. Wasn't that his life motto? *Claudia comes first.* And not just in sex. She came before everything for him. Every damn thing.

Did she realize it?

One day, she would.

"I wasn't done," she groused.

He looked down at her. Pouty lips. Flushed cheeks. Gleaming eyes. His whole world.

Holden scooped her into his arms.

"No, Holden! You're hurt!"

"The only thing that would hurt me is losing you." How many times did he have to tell her? Did she have any idea how truly gutted he'd been five years before? Now wasn't the time to explain it to her. He was doing good to be able to talk at all, and that sure wasn't gonna continue for long. Holding her tightly in his arms, he carried her to his room and went straight to the bed.

He lowered her onto the mattress. Stripped her with fingers that trembled. The wet clothing clung to her, but he got the stuff off with rough force. Normally, he would have caressed her. Savored her.

This wasn't a normal time.

A gun to her head. He put a gun to her head.

Holden took a step back.

She pushed up on her elbows. Naked now, she sprawled in the middle of the bed and peered at him. Her damp hair slid over her shoulder. "Why are you stopping?"

"I'm afraid..." His voice was too grating and rough.

"Afraid of what? Because I was pretty sure you feared no one and nothing."

Not true. "Afraid I'll hurt you." Because her mouth had felt like paradise around him, and his control was *gone*. He was trying his best not to jump on her in a frenzy.

"That's cute. You won't. You'll just give me pleasure." Her legs parted a little more. "Don't make me wait."

That was it. He did jump on her. He was in a frenzy. Holden pounced. Leapt on the bed. Took her mouth even as he pushed her legs apart even more. His fingers went straight to her core. Slid inside. Withdrew. Slid in again. *Have to make sure she's wet.* She was. Wet and ready.

"Going down on you turned me on," she confessed against his lips.

Hell, yes. Hell, *yes*.

His cock lodged at her entrance. Her sensual heat soaked the head of his dick. Then he slammed deep. No hesitation. No restraint. He was too far gone for that.

Faster and deeper and harder, he drove into her.

Thrust. Withdraw. Thrust. With—

Her nails raked him. Her body arched as her hips surged toward him.

Deeper. Stronger. He never wanted to be apart from her. He wanted her always. Needed her. Loved her.

"Holden!"

Her climax sent him into oblivion with her. The orgasm slammed through him, and all Holden heard was the distant thud of his heartbeat as pleasure consumed him. That heartbeat drummed and drummed as the waves of release pulsed through him.

Drummed and drummed...

And then he heard, over that pounding...

"I love you," Claudia whispered. "I always have. Always will. I love you." Fast, quick pants of breath. Rushed words.

His head lifted.

She stared straight into his eyes. "I love you."

The rain kept falling outside.

Washing away the past.

***

"Do you think you'd ever...want to marry me?"

Claudia almost dropped the wine glass she'd just filled. The day had passed in a blur of sex and sleep. Lots of sex. A few random naps. Too many orgasms to count. The guest house felt safe. Holden's arms felt safe. She'd wanted to stay with him and let the nightmare end.

The sun had just set. He'd made dinner, and she'd gotten the wine ready. But as she turned toward him and he asked that low, rough question...

She had to make a frantic and very ungraceful grab so that her glass didn't shatter. "Uh, say again?" She steadied the glass just in time.

He crossed his arms over his chest and leaned his hips back against the counter. He didn't have on a shirt, just jeans that clung low on his hips. The bruises darkening his skin made her angry, but he didn't seem to care about them.

And he was still sexy as hell.

"Do you think you'd ever want to marry me? Because I want to marry you." His penetrating gaze never wavered. "It's what I've wanted for years. When the danger is over, when we're both free from the past, would you consider marrying me?"

She put the glass onto the table. It was either put it down or her trembling fingers would be dropping it. "Is this a proposal? Because it doesn't really feel like a proposal. Last time, there was a guy playing a violin and a fancy restaurant and a ring." At the mention of the ring, she swallowed.

She'd tried to give him back the engagement ring five years ago. He hadn't taken it. The ring had fallen and been left on her doorstep.

"I can give you all of that again. I can give you anything you want." His nostrils flared. "I just want to know if you'll have me."

"If I'll have you?" She could feel the flush in her cheeks. "I'm pretty sure I've *had* you in every room here."

He shoved away from the counter. Stalked toward her. Slow, certain steps.

Her hip bumped the table.

Holden stopped in front of her. Towered over her. All big and hot and predatory. Then he dropped to one knee.

"What are you doing?" The words came out like a squeak. So embarrassing.

His head tipped back as he looked up at her. "At least I can get this part right." He sucked in a deep breath and reached for her hand. "Claudia Fairmont, will you marry me?"

"I—"

His phone rang. It had been doing that a lot during the day. Interrupting at the wrong times. Over and over again. The Feds had called. Harley had called. Elias. Cooper. Officer Gains. So many people had kept calling.

But this time, he made no move to answer this call.

"Holden?"

"Let it ring."

"It could be important." Probably was very important considering the mess they faced.

"This is important. You're important." His fingers held hers so carefully. "We can be engaged as long as you want. And we don't have to do the big wedding routine."

"Oh, God, no, let's not do that." She shuddered at the thought of a big wedding. All those people, gawking at her.

Pain spasmed on his face. "I am so sorry, sweetheart. I wish that I could change the past. I would in a minute if I could. I would be in that church with you because all I want is to love you. To be with you, forever. But I can't fix what happened. I can just promise that I will give you the future you want. I will do *anything* to make you happy."

Anything...

Like fight off six—had it been seven?—men to protect her. Like believe her when no one else seemed to take her seriously. Like jumping between her and danger. And she *knew* it wasn't because of some Wilde job. "You haven't sent me a bill."

His brow furrowed. The phone kept ringing.

"To be my bodyguard. You never even told me how much it would cost for your services."

His head tilted to the left. "You know what it costs."

Nothing. The phone stopped ringing.

"I will always protect you. Always. And that goes for whether you marry me or not." He stayed on one knee. "You can tell me no, you can tell me it really was some revenge fuck business, and things won't change for me. You will always be protected. You will always be safe. You will always be loved—"

"Yes."

He didn't move.

"Yes," Claudia said again because maybe he hadn't heard her. The damn phone had started to ring again. His phone. Hers was somewhere in her bedroom. Maybe. Honestly, she'd lost track of the thing. "I will marry you. But how about we just elope this time?"

He lunged up. Locked his arms around her in a grip that took her breath away right before his mouth crushed onto hers. She felt the tremble that shook him. Or maybe it was her own tremble. Did it matter?

His head lifted. "I love you."

She knew he did. Just as Claudia knew she loved him. And this time, things would work. "You really should get the phone." Her breathless order. "Because I think it's important."

"Nothing is more important than you."

"It's probably about the guy who has been terrorizing us. Maybe the Feds are locking Seth away." Her stomach twisted at the thought because she still had trouble accepting that Seth had put a gun to her temple. *He was family.* As close as family could be.

Sometimes, family could break your heart.

Holden kept an arm around her waist, but he also reached for his phone.

"No, I-I need to get something." Claudia pulled from him and hurried from the kitchen. As she left, she heard—

"What the hell, Harley? Please be shitting me."

Hesitating a moment, she glanced back.

A dark cloud covered Holden's face.

I take that to mean Harley is not shitting him.

"Dammit, stay on him, got me? No, no, I'm fine here. You keep your eyes on Seth Wellington at all times."

Claudia rushed for her bedroom. With quick steps, she went to the closet and pulled out her old jewelry box. After searching inside, she grasped her prize and curled her fingers into a fist as she spun and made her way back to Holden.

But he was already waiting in the bedroom. He'd come in on silent steps. "The Feds are letting Seth go." Grim. "Harley is watching him be released right now. She said the Feds seemed way too chummy with him. I told her to stick with him. Not to let the guy out of her sight for a moment. If necessary, she can tase his ass again." His gaze dropped to her left hand. "What are you holding?"

Her fist tightened even more. "If they're letting him go, that means someone else is guilty. We were wrong about Seth."

"Guilty people are let go every day. Right now, it just means the authorities don't have enough evidence to hold him." He eliminated the distance between them. When he stood in front of her, his hand reached out and took her fist in his. Slowly, he uncurled her fingers.

The engagement ring glinted when the light hit the diamond.

"You kept it."

"I tried to get you to take it back."

His fingers traced lightly over her palm, not touching the ring. "It was yours. I couldn't take what was yours." He kept tracing lightly with his callused fingertips. "Figured you'd sold it. Or just thrown it away."

She shook her head. "No. Just boxed it up. Like I tried to box up all the memories I had of us." Box everything up and forget. Only forgetting Holden had been an impossible task.

"Will you wear it again?" Rasped. "Please?"

"You have to put it on."

His fingers stopped tracing. Time and tension stretched. He picked up the ring, and then slid it into place on her finger. Holden lifted her hand and pressed a kiss to her ring finger.

And the phone on the nightstand gave a hard chime. It vibrated against the wood as a text came through—her phone, not his.

"I should look at that," she murmured.

"Yes."

But she kept looking at him.

Another chime. Another vibration. "It could be a text from Officer Gains."

"Could be." Another kiss from Holden. "Go check, baby. I'm not going anywhere. Never again, got it? Nothing is going to take me from you."

Pressing her lips together, she eased away from him and grabbed for her phone. "It's from Cooper." Her finger swiped over the screen. "He says—" Claudia stopped because she could not say more.

The picture had appeared first. A picture of her brother sprawled on the floor with red liquid around his head. *Blood? Was that blood?* Her breath choked out as her grip tightened on the phone.

Then she read the message beneath the image.

Come to the winery. Come alone. Tell no one or your brother dies.

Was he already dead? Cooper's eyes were closed in the picture, and that sure looked like blood all around his head. She'd spent the day having sex with Holden, relishing every moment with him, while her brother had been—what? Being attacked? Possibly dying?

"Claudia."

Her head whipped up.

Holden frowned at her. "What does Cooper have to say?"

"Nothing." *He can't say anything. He's unconscious.* Unconscious, not dead. He could not be dead.

"Just checking in, huh?" Holden nodded.

Her heart slammed into her chest.

Tell no one or your brother dies.

But if she went alone to the winery...

We'll both die. She knew it. This was a trap. One designed to drag her under and separate her from Holden. Her body shook. The person who'd sent the text wanted to separate her from Holden. *Because he's afraid of Holden.*

He should be. He should be afraid of her *and* of Holden.

A furrow appeared between his brows as Holden edged forward. "What is it?"

She loved her brother. Always would. And she was not going to let him die.

CHAPTER NINETEEN

Step Nineteen: Forget everything else. The only priority? Her.

The winery was dark. Claudia sat in her car and stared up at the business she'd loved for so long. Not a single light glowed from inside, and the lot was empty.

Appearances could be deceiving. She killed the ignition and slowly exited the vehicle. Claudia could feel eyes on her as she advanced toward the building. With an effort, she kept her spine straight and her chin up. It took her three tries to get her key in the lock, and she shoved the door open with a bit too much force.

The security system didn't beep when she walked inside. But, then, she'd already suspected that it had been taken offline. More darkness waited for her, but, screw that. She wasn't about to stumble around in the dark. Her hand flew out and hit the light switch on the right.

Illumination immediately flooded from the recessed lights overhead—and she saw the body slumped on the floor. But it wasn't her brother. It was Reese. She rushed toward him, her tennis shoes flying over the marble flooring and crunching the broken glass of a wine bottle that waited next to him. Red wine pooled on the floor, and when she fell to her knees beside him, the wine wet her legs. She'd gone straight to the winery, only pausing long enough to grab tennis shoes, so she still wore her shorts and t-shirt.

"Reese!" Frantic, her hand went to his throat. She thought she could see the slight rise and fall of his chest, but she wanted to make sure and check his pulse.

But her fingers didn't make contact. Because *his* hand flew out and curled around hers. His eyes opened, completely aware, and he smiled at her. "I always knew you cared."

She tried to jerk back, but he just tightened his hold with bruising force.

"I mean, I was right the fuck here all along," he added, voice snarling, "and you had to care. You just needed to stop focusing on the past and see what waited for you."

Her breath choked out. "*You* texted me from Cooper's phone."

A shrug. "Had to get you here, didn't I? So glad you joined me."

He held her right wrist tightly, squeezing the bones, and her left hand flew back, only to touch the cold wine on the floor. "Where is my brother?"

"Come on. I'll show you." He heaved upward, dragging her with him.

But her left hand caught the broken wine bottle, and when she rose, she swung it at him. The sharp edges sliced down his arm.

"Bitch!" His yell seemed to echo around them, but he'd let go of her wrist. She sprang forward, her sneakers sliding in the wine, and Claudia almost went hard, but she caught herself. She dropped the broken bottle and rushed straight for her brother's office, running as fast as she could.

But Reese caught her right before she reached the door. His arms locked around her stomach, and he started to haul her back.

The door to the right swung open—a door that led toward the stockroom and the back of the winery. While she'd come in the front door, Holden had gained entrance through the back.

Now Holden stood in the doorway. Angry, no, *enraged* Holden who held a gun in his hand. The gun that he'd taken before they'd left the guest house. Because no way had she been planning to leave without him.

Walk into a trap alone? No, thank you.

"Let her go, or I will shoot you between the eyes right now."

But instead of letting her go, Reese laughed. "You fire a shot, and my partner will immediately kill her brother. What do you think about that, hero? Think she'll love you forever when you're responsible for the death of her brother? Think she'll want you touching her when you've got blood all over your hands?"

A partner? Her eyes widened in horror. Was Reese lying or telling the truth? And could they take the gamble? "Holden..."

"Trust me, baby."

Her heart thundered faster.

"Oh, sure," Reese breathed in her ear. "Trust him. Trust him like you trusted him to show at the wedding, but he left you all alone. Trust him to save your brother when he has always *hated* Cooper. This is his chance to get rid of the man he despises. He can eliminate your brother from his life—"

"We called the cops!" Claudia cried out. "Gains is on his way here. You're not going to get away with anything!"

He spun her to face him. Her hand flew into the pocket of her shorts.

"The boyfriend won't shoot," Reese said as he brought his face right next to hers. "Because he's afraid he'll hit you. So he's gonna stand there with the gun, and I'm going to—"

She yanked up her hand and shoved the small taser against him. His body jolted, hard, over and over, and Claudia could have sworn that she heard his teeth clattering together.

He let her go, and when she surged to the side, Holden leapt into action. He yanked out handcuffs and had Reese secure in moments. Once the cuffs were in place, Holden hauled Reese so the jerk was sitting up, with his back inches from the wall.

Reese's body still twitched with aftershocks.

Her breath rushed in and out as she stared at him, and she kept clutching the taser. Holden hadn't just taken his gun at the guest house. He'd given her a weapon, too. And she'd waited for the moment to use it. When she'd been on her knees next to the broken wine bottle, Claudia hadn't thought that she could get her taser out—it had been in her opposite pocket, and Reese had been holding her right hand too tightly. So she'd grabbed the wine bottle.

This time, the taser had been easy to access.

"You okay?" Holden asked. He'd closed in on her. His fingers slid over her cheek. "Baby?"

Her head bobbed in a nod. "I need to find my brother."

Jaw locking, Holden eased away from her and put his gun in Reese's face.

Reese tried to back up but just hit the wall.

"Not fun, is it?" Holden asked. "When you've got a gun in your face. See, it's happened to me, and I fucking hated it. But I hated it even more when some sonofabitch shoved a gun against *her* face."

The door to the VIP tasting room was open. Ajar just a little. Claudia crept toward it.

"You were the one in the damn demon mask, weren't you?" Holden demanded.

"*Her brother is dead! Dead!*" A shout from Reese. "*Do you hear me?*"

"Oh, I fucking hear you," Holden shouted right back. "I just don't—"

"*Shoot him!*" Reese screamed.

And she realized that he hadn't been talking to Holden at all. He'd been shouting orders for his partner.

Holden realized it, too. She saw him slam the butt of his gun into the side of Reese's head.

Then she heard the blast of gunfire. A boom that came from the VIP tasting room. Claudia stopped creeping toward that door and ran full-out for it.

"*Claudia!*" Holden roared after her.

But she'd already shoved open the door fully. She rushed inside. And...

Officer Gains.

Officer Gains was waiting inside the tasting room. She'd called him on the way to the winery, asking for backup. How had he beat them there? How had—

Gains stepped to the side. She saw her brother sprawled on the floor behind him. Not moving. Not...breathing?

"One down," Gains said. He pointed his gun at her. "Another to go."

Her eyes widened in horror. The taser wasn't going to do her any good. He was about to shoot and—

Holden slammed into her. The bullet thundered and hit its target.

Holden, not her.

Holden.

She slammed into the floor and rolled over, screaming, *"Holden!"* Her hands grabbed for him, but when she touched his chest, she touched blood. Wet and sticky and warm.

No, no, no, no. Claudia let go of the taser and put both hands over his wound and ignored the tremor that pulsed through her body. Her cheeks felt numb, her head was spinning, but her hands stayed over the wound. He was bleeding too much. She had to stop the blood flow. She had to save him.

"He's already gone," Gains told her. "You just don't know it yet."

She could feel tears on her cheeks. The wound seemed so close to Holden's heart. He'd dropped his gun when he was hit. Holden had taken that shot to protect her.

This wasn't the way they ended. "I love you," she told him. "Holden, *I love you.*"

"Yeah, that's just really gonna piss off Reese. Guy's got quite the crush on you." Something poked into her back. She was pretty sure that it was the muzzle of a gun. "Thought you might have noticed considering the way he's been stalking you like mad for the last six months. Started once he found those sexy photos of you. He was *supposed* to be looking for the photos that dumbass PI had taken of Wellington's death. Instead, he found videos and pics of you. Guy always had a crush, but that took things to a whole other level."

Holden hadn't opened his eyes.

"Gonna need you to step away from Holden. Unless, of course, you want to die right here with him."

"*No!*" That shout came from the open door. Her head jerked in that direction.

Reese stood there, weaving, with blood trickling from his temple. His hands were still cuffed behind his back. "She's not supposed to die! I told you how we needed to play this scene. Holden is the fall guy, and she comes away with *me.*"

Holden's blood soaked her fingers. Nausea rose in her throat. Holden's eyes wouldn't open. "Holden?" She leaned closer to him. "Holden?"

"Get her up and let's get going!" Reese blasted. "We need this place to burn, and we need to be the hell away from here before that happens."

A strong hand gripped her shoulder. "Stand up." An order from Gains. "Told you, Holden is already dead."

The hell he was. She stared at her hands, red with his blood, and hate filled her. "I trusted you."

"Yeah. Your mistake."

"Gains was working with Edward Wellington long before I came along," Reese admitted. "Wellington had his people everywhere. There was not a move made in this area that he didn't know about."

So Gains had been a cop in Wellington's pocket.

"Gains, get these freaking cuffs off me! I know you have a cuff key on you, and a handcuff key is supposed to work on most of the damn handcuff locks, right? Be nearly universal? Isn't that how the shit goes?"

Gains let her go.

She kept crouching next to Holden.

"I can get you out," Gains told him. He closed the distance between them. "But I won't." He fired his gun. Straight at Reese.

The blast sent Reese flying through the air. His body slammed into the floor even as blood sprayed. Claudia didn't scream. She didn't have the breath for it.

Gains squinted down at him, then looked over at Claudia. "You gonna faint?"

She didn't speak.

"Because I know blood upsets you. Reese made a point of knowing everything about you. Man was seriously obsessed. You should probably thank me for shooting him." From the corner of her eye, she saw him kick Reese's leg. "He wanted to kidnap you. Wanted to take you away and keep you like you were some weird pet. He's been stalking you for months. It was him that night you had the flat tire. And he set the fire at your place. Think it was an accident, though. He told me once he liked to sneak into your house and watch you sleep."

A sob tore from her. She still had her hands on Holden's chest. So. Much. Blood.

"He found some crap of Holden's and burned it, but the fire got out of control. Next thing he knew, you were back with Holden. Got to say, that really pissed him off. He set that chandelier to fall. Told me he'd loosened the screws a few days before the gala. All he had to do was hit the button to descend on the control panel, and the loose screws would make the whole thing crash. He was just intending to scare you, but when Reese watched you in the tasting room with Holden, the guy lost his mind."

And I nearly lost my life. She looked up at him.

Gains lifted the gun he held. "You'll notice I'm wearing gloves. Not gonna leave any of my prints here."

"Who's the fall guy?" Claudia forced out the question as she tried to buy time. "Holden or Reese?"

"They both are. Reese is the crazy stalker. Holden tried to stop him from attacking you. Unfortunately, in the fight, they both died." He looked beyond her. "So did your brother. Terrible, terrible tragedy."

"*Why?* Why did you do all of this?" And how could she stop him?

"Because of the fucking PI. He knew I worked with Wellington. Kept telling me that he had pics of Wellington's death that he thought I would find...*interesting*. I tried to find the damn photos. Broke into Danny's house, but they weren't there."

"And you killed him."

A shrug. "You eventually led me to the photos. Didn't know you'd do that, but you went to the PI's second office and found them when I couldn't. Reese understood the value of the envelope you had so he got it. He was in the stupid mask. I wouldn't wear something like that. But when he showed the pics he'd recovered to me..." A rough laugh. "It was just Seth. Such a waste of my time."

"You thought you'd be in the photos." It was the only thing that made sense. The only reason he'd kill to possess them.

"Seeing as how I was the one to put a bullet in Edward Wellington's brain? Yeah, I did. But after looking at them, I realized the PI took those photos before I entered the room. Guess he left and followed Seth when that asshole stormed out. I thought Danny had seen me slip into the study. But he didn't."

"You killed Edward Wellington."

"I was tired of taking orders. Told Wellington that, right before I pulled the trigger." He smiled at her. "I'm really good at setting scenes. You'll see exactly what I mean soon." His neck craned as he looked around her. "Bet all this alcohol will go up quickly. But you really don't need to be aware for that part. Want me to shoot you first?"

Shoot me first? Before what? But she suspected. *Before I burn.* "We didn't come here alone."

"I know. Reese was such a dumbass. He actually thought you would." He scooped up Holden's discarded gun and tucked it into his waistband. "You called me. Because I am so trustworthy."

She held his gaze. "We also called Holden's partner. Surely you remember Harley? The one who tased Seth? Not sure what cover story she gave you, but she's a Wilde agent, and she is in town working with Holden."

Frowning, Gains stepped closer to her.

"I've been talking to you this whole time in order to keep you distracted. She needed time to get in the building, you see. Harley's behind you right now."

He stiffened.

"And Harley has her gun pointed right at your back." It was her turn to smile. "Either you drop your weapon, or she will fire."

"You're lying."

"Harley?" Claudia called out. *"Fire."*

Cursing, he spun around to face the threat.

Only no threat was there. Because Harley wasn't there. At least, not yet she wasn't. They *had* called her, and Claudia was sure the woman would be rushing to the scene, soon, but Claudia couldn't wait any longer. Not if the asshole was getting ready to shoot again.

When Gains turned, Claudia leapt up and at him. Her blood-stained hands reached for his back. She'd tackled one bastard with a gun before. She would do it again. She would—

"Nice try." The gun was right between her eyes. "But I heard what you did to Reese. He was pretty upset that you caught him from behind when he was getting ready to shoot Holden." Once more, he kicked at Reese. Reese didn't move. "Not that it matters now."

Her hands were still up, her fingers curled like claws.

"Step out of the tasting room, Claudia. You're going to come with me."

"Thought you were going to shoot me. Then let everything burn."

"Oh, I am...*after* I deal with Harley. Because she is coming, isn't she? That part was true."

Her lips tightened.

"Right. Thanks for the tip-off."

"Go fuck yourself."

"Let's go meet her, shall we? When she sees us together, I'm sure Harley will understand the value in dropping any weapon she may have."

He hauled her forward. Her gaze darted back. Fell to Holden.

Holden.

His eyes opened.

CHAPTER TWENTY

Step Fucking Twenty: Pain for pain. Blood for blood. Make her enemies beg for mercy. Give none.

Not what a real hero would do? Oh, well. Like I give a shit.

Holden assessed the situation and decided he was fucked. He had a bullet in his chest that hurt like a mother, he didn't see his gun, and, from what he could tell, Cooper might be dying a few feet away from him.

Oh, yeah, and the love of his life had just been taken away at gun point.

Fucking *fuck*.

Cooper let out a long groan.

Holden rolled over. Pain blasted through him as blood soaked his shirt. It was embarrassing as hell to admit, but he'd passed out. He was back now and about to figure out how to end Gains in the bloodiest way possible.

Cooper groaned again.

"You're alive," Holden rumbled. "Good." He managed to sit up. Gritting his teeth against the pain, he looked for a weapon.

Lots of wine bottles. Lots and lots of them. He could grab one from the racks along the walls and use it like a club to slam into Gains.

"G-gonna...burn us..." Cooper's slurred words. "H-heard him..."

Holden staggered to his feet. He turned for the door. The bottles of wine were *behind* him. The door that led to the lobby was now in front, just a short distance away. Claudia was beyond that door, somewhere out there with Gains. He peered down and saw that Reese was on the floor, just outside of the tasting room.

Oh, yeah, he was dead.

"B-burn..." Cooper muttered again.

Holden wasn't in the mood to get burned, thanks. Standing up was hard enough and...

His gaze slid to the side of the door. To the beautiful, red fire extinguisher that waited right there.

He could stagger his way back across the room, get a wine bottle from one of the shelves, then give lumbering chase or...

His hands grabbed the fire extinguisher.

Or he could just make do with the weapon that was right there. *I'll take the extinguisher*. He pulled out the pin, yanked down the nozzle, and he went after the woman he loved. One slow and painful step at a time.

He tried not to make a sound, and Holden was highly conscious of the blood dripping down his body. One step. One slow step. Then another.

Thunder rumbled outside. Another storm was coming. Holden saw Gains. The guy had his back to Holden as he peered out the windows near the front of the winery. Claudia was to the right of Gains, with his gun jabbing into her side. Her head turned, and her eyes locked on Holden.

He saw fear in her gaze. Fear for him. And love. So much love.

That gun needed to get the hell away from her body. *Now.* "Hey, asshole!" Holden called out.

Gains swung around. He lifted the gun away from Claudia and tried to bring it around on Holden. Holden squeezed the trigger on his fire extinguisher. Carbon dioxide blasted from the extinguisher, and Holden sprayed it at Gains.

Claudia leapt away, and the cold spray slammed into Gains.

Gains shouted and batted at the white blast as it came at him, an instinctive response. Holden gathered his strength and jumped toward his enemy. He brought up the extinguisher, aware of the carbon dioxide drifting around him like smoke, and with all of his strength, he slammed the bottom of the extinguisher into Gains's chest. Gains stumbled back and hit the glass door. Holden drove the extinguisher into him again.

He lifted it, aimed once more, but Holden missed Gains this time and hit the glass door. The glass shattered. So Holden drove the fire extinguisher at Gains *again*. The extinguisher caught Gains in the shoulder, and he fell through the broken glass of the door. Holden stumbled after him, vaguely aware of the glass cutting into him. Gains was on the cement, no weapon, and Holden raised the extinguisher, ready to drive it straight into the bastard's head.

"Holden! I've got him!" Harley's cry.

Holden froze.

He looked down. Light from the lobby spilled onto his prey. Gains had raised a forearm as if to ward off a killing blow.

And it would have been killing. Holden could feel the fury still coursing through his blood.

Harley rushed forward. She had a gun out, and she pointed it at Gains. "Show me your hands! Both of them!"

Gains brought up his hands.

"He's the cop." Harley's feverish words. "Tell me that we have a whole lot of evidence here..."

Holden swayed.

And Claudia grabbed him. He heard glass crunch as her feet flew over the wreckage he'd made.

"We have plenty of evidence!" Claudia spoke feverishly. "And I think we need to call the—"

The FBI burst onto the scene. Or, at least, their black SUV came in hot, bouncing a bit as it took a curve and flew into the parking lot.

"They followed me," Harley admitted in a rush. "I might have been busted tailing them and Seth Wellington, and then when I got the message from Holden about meeting here, they realized we were on the scent of something. Of course, they'd fly in to try and take credit for, well—whatever is happening here." A pause. "What *is* happening here?"

"Gains was on the take. Reese was obsessed. Both are bastards." Speaking in full sentences was getting too hard for Holden. His head turned so he could see Claudia. "Safe?"

"I'm safe." Her voice shook. "You're the one bleeding all over the place."

"Brother is...alive. Needs ambulance." Yep, his strength was fading. Fast. He might be about to pass out again. Sonofabitch. "Used...extinguisher." Was he still holding it? Maybe. Hard to say. "Know you...like them."

"What in the hell are you talking about?" Claudia demanded as her words broke with what could have been a sob.

"Once you said..." Fuck, he *was* passing out. Everything was spinning. Including her beautiful face. "Wouldn't come back...even if...only man with..."

"Holden?"

The fire extinguisher fell from his fingers. Then he plummeted forward, dragging Claudia down with him.

***

"We're roommates."

Holden opened an eye and saw Cooper Fairmont in the bed across from him. Immediately, Holden squeezed his eye shut again.

"I'm telling you because the last four times you've woken up, you've asked me why the hell I'm in your room. It's because we're roommates. Claudia arranged it. She didn't want to be running back and forth between rooms, so she had the hospital staff put us together. I'm really fine, though, just a concussion because that dick Reese hit me in the head with a wine bottle, and I got a bullet wound in my side, courtesy of Gains.

Luckily, nothing major was hit. You're the one who had to have a super long surgery."

The sound of Cooper's voice made Holden's head hurt. And the man was just talking. A whole lot of talking.

"And you bled one whole hell of a lot, but you're going to be fine. Claudia, though, she was seriously impressive. You know I heard she only fainted *after* they took you into surgery. According to Harley, Claudia looked down, saw all of the blood that covered her—your blood, by the way—and she hit the floor."

"Cooper." Oh, damn, he sounded hoarse.

"Yeah?"

"Stop talking." Because he needed a minute of silence so he could figure out what the hell was happening.

I'm in a hospital. I was shot. Claudia had my blood all over her.

Yeah, that checked because he vaguely remembered falling on her after the Feds had rushed the winery. He opened his eyes. Both of them this time. His head was angled to the side, so, yes, he was staring at Cooper.

"Hi, there," Cooper said.

Holden's eyes narrowed. His head turned, *away* from Cooper, and his gaze swept the room. No Claudia.

"She was here about five minutes ago. You were dead to the world then. She kissed your brow. Held your hand. Ignored me when I asked for ice chips, then she went out to talk to some of the Feds again. Apparently, this case is a big deal to them."

Holden reluctantly returned his gaze to Cooper. "Where is Gains?"

"Jail. The Feds told Claudia that he'd been working with Edward for years. Get this—Claudia said Gains admitted to killing Edward. Can you believe that?"

Considering that Gains had shot him? "Yes, yes, I can."

"Gains thought the PI had videos and pics of *him* shooting Edward, but he didn't. Gains and Reese were working together. See, Gains knew that Edward had used the winery before, and he was trying to take over and start up Edward's old business channels again. To do that, he needed an inside man at the winery. So he approached Reese. Dammit, I *trusted* that guy."

"He was obsessed with Claudia."

"Super obsessed. Like probably wanted to wear-her-skin obsessed."

"Jesus, Cooper."

"The Feds found pics of her all over his place. Videos of her and bondage stuff and—the guy was *crazy*."

"He's dead." His voice was stronger.

"Oh, definitely. Gains killed him." After that admission, Cooper fell silent.

Finally. Blissful silence.

That didn't last long.

"Seth was innocent." Quiet. "Gonna have to add him to my long list of people that I have to make amends to." Cooper stared at him. "You're on that list."

"I don't want to be." He just wanted Claudia.

"Too bad. You are. You're on it. So is he. A man can do a whole lot of thinking when he faces death—"

"You don't say." Holden sat up. Machines beeped like wild somewhere near him.

"I don't think you're supposed to be moving around like that."

"Probably not. I don't care. I need to see Claudia." Because he had a giant ache in his chest, one that had not come from a bullet wound. That ache had come from the sheer terror that consumed him when he'd been afraid that she would die.

Need her. Want her. Love her.

Before he could swing off the bed, the door to the hospital room opened. His eyes widened when he saw Claudia standing there. His beautiful Claudia. She glared at him.

The ache in his chest eased. Claudia was safe.

"Don't even think of getting out of that bed, Holden Blackwell."

Safe.

All was right in his world. Well, mostly right. Once he had her wed to him, *then* the world would be right.

For the moment... "If you don't want me getting up, you'd better come over here and kiss me."

She ran to him. And kissed him as if nothing else mattered.

"Jeez," Cooper muttered. "I am right here. But no, carry on."

They would.

"Hope you're planning to marry her," Cooper added.

Claudia lifted her head.

Holden held her stare. "I am. As soon as possible."

Her fingers fluttered over his face. "You scared me."

"You terrified me."

"Let's not ever do that to each other again."

"Baby, all I want to do is love you."

Tears gleamed in her eyes. "Let's do that always."

Damn straight. Always. He kissed her again.

EPILOGUE

Final step: Love her with everything you've got. Then wake up, and do that shit again. And again. And again.

"Holden looks nervous."

Claudia's head turned at her brother's announcement. "Why?"

"I don't know. I mean, there are like five people here for the ceremony. Seth, Harley, Mercedes, and us." He motioned between his body and hers. "The man is flipping out. Seriously sweating. He asked me seven times to come in here and make sure you were ready."

She was more than ready. She wore a simple white dress that skimmed her knees. Her right hand clutched a bouquet of red roses. And she was about to walk out onto the beach and marry the man she loved. A quiet beach along the North Carolina coast. Far away from prying eyes and reporters. Because there had been *plenty* of reporters in her life once the details about Gains and the attacks on Claudia had been leaked.

The truth about Edward Wellington had shocked everyone who knew him. Well, the people who *hadn't* been involved with his criminal enterprises. Seth was trying to put out fires left and right regarding that big revelation.

As for the hit that had been put out on her and Holden? It had come from Gains. He'd used the Big Eddie name to hire the goons who had jumped them at the PI's office. He'd wanted any information they retrieved from the place, and he'd wanted Holden out of the picture.

Reese had...wanted her. When she'd seen the photos that he had of her at his place...

She'd been sick. *But he's dead. He can't hurt me. He can't hurt anyone ever again.*

Gains had hired the goons, but Reese had been the one in the mask. He'd been the one to try and take her from Holden. He'd also been the one to hire the mugger. *He wanted access to my phone. Twenty-four seven access to me.*

But Gains had admitted to getting rid of the mugger. Or using his contacts to get the guy killed. Gains was looking to make a deal. A cop didn't want to wind up in general population when he went to prison. But so far, she'd been assured no deals were on the table for him.

No one would ever take her from Holden again. And *no one* would take him from her. When his blood had pulsed between her fingers, she'd been terrified to her core. She hadn't cared about her own life. Just his.

Just keeping him *alive.*

"Claudia?" Her brother's brows rose. "You okay?"

Claudia nodded. Sometimes, fear would still sneak up on her. She would look over her shoulder for a threat that wasn't there. Maybe she'd be doing that for a while but...

But the threat is gone. I'm safe.

She opened her mouth, preparing to say it was time to get the show on the road, but someone rapped on her door.

"Claudia?" Holden's worried voice. "You good?"

"See?" Cooper muttered. "The man is *losing it.*"

She crossed the room. Opened the door. And saw her life waiting for her. Saw that life in the warm smile Holden sent to her. In the gleam of his green eyes. Eyes that she hoped her kids would have.

It had been four weeks since the attack at the winery. Gains was in jail. Seth had been officially cleared. Life had returned to normal.

Or as normal as it could get.

She'd mourned for her father. Mourned with Holden for his mother. They'd finally gotten justice. Their parents hadn't been runaway lovers. Holden's mom had been a woman dedicated to justice, just trying to do her job. A woman who loved her son. A heroine who had been hurt so badly by everything.

But finally the real truth about Holden's mother had been shared to the world.

No more secrets.

Just as there were no more stalkers. No more danger. No more regrets. Just hope. Hope was better than fear any day of the week. "I'm better than good." She took Holden's hand in hers. Her fear had melted when she saw his face. "I'm happy."

Her left hand twined with Holden's, and with her right, she held her bouquet. She, Holden, and

Cooper walked out together. The sun was setting as they approached the beach, and the waves crashed in a gentle roar.

The scene stole her breath. And, a little while later, when Claudia was told that she and Holden could kiss...

Joy seemed to pour through her body. They kissed and laughed, and as Holden swept her into his arms and spun her around, Claudia wildly threw her bouquet into the air. She didn't bother to see where it landed. She was too busy holding tight to Holden with both hands.

This was love. This was joy. This was the kind of life worth fighting for.

He kissed her again.

No fear. Just hope.

***

Harley wasn't sure what to do with the bouquet. The thing had come hurtling toward her, so she'd just lifted her hand instinctively. And she'd caught it.

Now she had a bouquet and a really ominous feeling in the pit of her stomach.

"At least it's not a taser."

Seth Wellington. He smirked at her. "Can't hurt me with that." He motioned toward the bouquet.

Harley was sure she *could* find a way to make the bouquet into a weapon. Her dad had taught her that pretty much anything could be a weapon, under the right circumstances. But, she was trying to be on her best behavior. For Claudia and

Holden. "I suppose I should officially apologize for tasing you." Something she'd been avoiding.

"An apology would be nice." His gaze slid from hers. Went to the happy couple.

How long did Holden intend to keep kissing Claudia?

"In my defense," she cleared her throat and went in for the kill, "how was I supposed to know you were working undercover with the Feds?"

His stare snapped right back to her.

Didn't think I realized that? Seriously? "The Feds went out of their way to protect you. It was crazy obvious. They really need to work on being a little more subtle, or whatever con you guys are trying to run is just going to fail in a colossal manner."

"A con?"

His innocent act was adorable. "Con, undercover mission, whatever. If I were you, I'd be really careful. Maybe you should talk to Holden. He worked with them before, and got very, very badly burned."

Seth swallowed. "What do you suggest I do? Get my own security?"

She shrugged. "Your call. Just handing out some friendly advice." The bouquet was actually quite pretty. Smiling, she looked down at it and turned away. She'd taken three steps when—

"You're hired," Seth told her.

She almost dropped the bouquet. "I wasn't looking for a job."

"No? Because you've got one...but only if you promise not to tase me again."

Harley glanced over shoulder at him, trying not to notice just how sexy his grin was. "I can't make you any promises..." But she just *might* be interested in him. Or, rather, in the job. *I'm interested in the job. Not the man. The job.* "Just what is it that you want me to do?"

THE END

A NOTE FROM THE AUTHOR

Thank you so much for reading this book!! And I hope you enjoyed HOW TO HEAL A HEARTBREAK. I love second chance romances (both writing them and reading them). Pair a second chance romance with a protective, alpha hero, and I am set!

I really appreciate you exploring the "Wilde" world with me. It has been such an absolute pleasure to write these stories. Thank you for your support and encouragement.

If you'd like to stay updated on my releases and sales, please join my newsletter list.

https://cynthiaeden.com/newsletter/

Again, thank you for reading HOW TO HEAL A HEARTBREAK.

Best,
Cynthia Eden
cynthiaeden.com

ABOUT THE AUTHOR

Cynthia Eden is a *New York Times*, *USA Today*, *Digital Book World*, and *IndieReader* best-seller.

Cynthia writes sexy tales of contemporary romance, romantic suspense, and paranormal romance. Since she began writing full-time in 2005, Cynthia has written over one hundred novels and novellas.

Cynthia lives along the Alabama Gulf Coast. She loves romance novels, horror movies, and chocolate.

For More Information

- *cynthiaeden.com*
- *facebook.com/cynthiaedenfanpage*

HER OTHER WORKS

Wilde Ways: Gone Rogue

- How To Protect A Princess (Book 1)
- How To Heal A Heartbreak (Book 2)

Ice Breaker Cold Case Romance

- Frozen In Ice (Book 1)
- Falling For The Ice Queen (Book 2)
- Ice Cold Saint (Book 3)
- Touched By Ice (Book 4)
- Trapped In Ice (Book 5)

Phoenix Fury

- Hot Enough To Burn (Book 1)
- Slow Burn (Book 2)
- Burn It Down (Book 3)

Trouble For Hire

- No Escape From War (Book 1)
- Don't Play With Odin (Book 2)
- Jinx, You're It (Book 3)
- Remember Ramsey (Book 4)

Death and Moonlight Mystery

- Step Into My Web (Book 1)
- Save Me From The Dark (Book 2)

Wilde Ways

- Protecting Piper (Book 1)

- Guarding Gwen (Book 2)
- Before Ben (Book 3)
- The Heart You Break (Book 4)
- Fighting For Her (Book 5)
- Ghost Of A Chance (Book 6)
- Crossing The Line (Book 7)
- Counting On Cole (Book 8)
- Chase After Me (Book 9)
- Say I Do (Book 10)
- Roman Will Fall (Book 11)
- The One Who Got Away (Book 12)
- Pretend You Want Me (Book 13)
- Cross My Heart (Book 14)
- The Bodyguard Next Door (Book 15)
- Ex Marks The Perfect Spot (Book 16)
- The Thief Who Loved Me (Book 17)

Dark Sins

- Don't Trust A Killer (Book 1)
- Don't Love A Liar (Book 2)

Lazarus Rising

- Never Let Go (Book One)
- Keep Me Close (Book Two)
- Stay With Me (Book Three)
- Run To Me (Book Four)
- Lie Close To Me (Book Five)
- Hold On Tight (Book Six)

Dark Obsession Series

- Watch Me (Book 1)
- Want Me (Book 2)
- Need Me (Book 3)
- Beware Of Me (Book 4)

- Only For Me (Books 1 to 4)

Mine Series

- Mine To Take (Book 1)
- Mine To Keep (Book 2)
- Mine To Hold (Book 3)
- Mine To Crave (Book 4)
- Mine To Have (Book 5)
- Mine To Protect (Book 6)
- Mine Box Set Volume 1 (Books 1-3)
- Mine Box Set Volume 2 (Books 4-6)

Bad Things

- The Devil In Disguise (Book 1)
- On The Prowl (Book 2)
- Undead Or Alive (Book 3)
- Broken Angel (Book 4)
- Heart Of Stone (Book 5)
- Tempted By Fate (Book 6)
- Wicked And Wild (Book 7)
- Saint Or Sinner (Book 8)
- Bad Things Volume One (Books 1 to 3)
- Bad Things Volume Two (Books 4 to 6)
- Bad Things Deluxe Box Set (Books 1 to 6)

Bite Series

- Forbidden Bite (Bite Book 1)
- Mating Bite (Bite Book 2)

Blood and Moonlight Series

- Bite The Dust (Book 1)
- Better Off Undead (Book 2)
- Bitter Blood (Book 3)

- Blood and Moonlight (The Complete Series)

Purgatory Series

- The Wolf Within (Book 1)
- Marked By The Vampire (Book 2)
- Charming The Beast (Book 3)
- Deal with the Devil (Book 4)
- The Beasts Inside (Books 1 to 4)

Bound Series

- Bound By Blood (Book 1)
- Bound In Darkness (Book 2)
- Bound In Sin (Book 3)
- Bound By The Night (Book 4)
- Bound in Death (Book 5)
- Forever Bound (Books 1 to 4)

Stand-Alone Romantic Suspense

- It's A Wonderful Werewolf
- Never Cry Werewolf
- Immortal Danger
- Deck The Halls
- Come Back To Me
- Put A Spell On Me
- Never Gonna Happen
- One Hot Holiday
- Slay All Day
- Midnight Bite
- Secret Admirer
- Christmas With A Spy
- Femme Fatale
- Until Death
- Sinful Secrets

- First Taste of Darkness
- A Vampire's Christmas Carol